Caroline had hardly ~~~~~~~~~~~~~~~~~~~~~~
with its enormous fe ~~~~~~~~~~~~~~~~~~~~~
tress, clutching his sh ~~~~~~~~~~~~~~~~~
*a knock on the communicating door and Edmund
came in.*

*She retreated on her pillows. "What are you doing
here?" she asked. He came towards the very side
of the bed and reached out and pulled something
towards him. "A pillow, if you don't mind."*

*How tiny she looked in his big bed! How young!
He stopped at the foot of the four-poster and
looked at her. An immense tenderness arose in
him. How could they think of marrying this infant
to Robert de Lisle Devonshire—that handsome,
spoiled, bullying lout! She put a brave face on it,
but she did need taking care of. A self-truth suddenly came uppermost in his mind. It was a need
with him to make her safe. That was it! He wanted
to be the one to make her safe. "My little feminist!" he murmured.*

*"I'm not a feminist particularly. I just want to be
free," she said.*

*For the life of him he couldn't help but laugh. He
reached forward to where Caroline's small feet
stuck up in the coverlet of the bed, and squeezed
her toes with his hand. "Sleep tight!" he said with
a boyish smile. And he was gone.*

WERE THIS WILD THING WEDDED

Anna Wibberley

A FAWCETT CREST BOOK

Fawcett Books, Greenwich, Connecticut

WERE THIS WILD THING WEDDED

THIS BOOK CONTAINS THE COMPLETE TEXT OF THE ORIGINAL HARDCOVER EDITION.

A Fawcett Crest Book reprinted by arrangement with St. Martin's Press, Inc.

ISBN: 0-449-23377-4

Printed in the United States of America

10 9 8 7 6 5 4 3 2 1

WERE THIS WILD THING WEDDED

Chapter 1

Caroline Hamilton stood at the top of the stairs, that beautifully curving stairway, with its centre rail of intricately wrought iron, and looked down the long, turning, shallow but wide steps, close-carpeted in silken, gold carpet, with, woven into it, deeper gold flowers and pale green leaves.

Looking down at the young people who thronged the stairway steps, it seemed to her that they were all sparkling in gold and silver. Her own ball gown was gold lace over champagne satin. It had been made at home by the family dressmaker, and Caroline was conscious that it did not quite compare with the lovely gowns from London and Paris which all the girls around her wore as a matter of course. Overhead gleamed chandeliers in crystal with gilt leaves, holding the light of many candles. Below her, where the silky carpet aproned out as the bottom stairs belled to shape themselves gracefully into the great hall, she could see other chandeliers, hung with glittering lights. Beyond that hall was the ballroom, from where she could hear violins. She saw the ballroom in her mind's eye, with the duennas sitting gossiping against the panelling and the mirrors, and the young couples turning, turning, turning in the waltz. The waltz still shocked Aunt Millie a little, as she was more used to the *schottische* or the *galop,* where hand might touch hand but no closer contact was expected.

The richness of the house was not what Caroline was used to. And she felt herself bemused almost by the opulence, the feeling of flowers, silks, perfume, jewels, champagne, the endless invitation of the violins. It was a world of utmost wealth. Touching the rented pearls at her neck, she thought, "I don't belong to this world. I don't belong at all!" She should have been feeling carefree and happy. The little dance programme hanging by a ribbon from her long-gloved wrist was full of young men's names: young men who did belong to this golden world, and who had chosen to partner her. Why, she had hardly missed a dance!

She was alone now only because Aunt Millie had one of her sudden sick headaches, and Caroline had accompanied her to a bedroom so Aunt Millie could lie down, a handkerchief soaked in vinegar over her poor brow. Only on the promise that Caroline would find Mrs. Smythe-Taylor straight away had poor Aunt Millie consented to get rest, her red cherry silk ball gown, bustle and all, upon a chair, her stiff whaleboned corsets unloosed, herself in one of her hostess' wrappers. It was an elaborate wrapper, all contrived charm—like its owner, their hostess, Lady de Lisle Devonshire.

Caroline was dutifully on her way to find Mrs. Smythe-Taylor, who would take over the chaperonage of Aunt Millie's niece. For Aunt Millie and Mrs. Smythe-Taylor were distant cousins, so Caroline had some relationship to that formidable lady, a woman who wore peacock feathers in her hair, and whose dress and manner bespoke an earlier century.

But now Caroline had paused at the top of the stairs for just a moment, upon her face that false smile she had been taught to wear in deportment class for public view. Caroline thought of the smile as like the smile of a china doll, lips parted, pearly teeth showing, eyes alive but vacant. But the eyes in Caroline's face looked sombre. She could not stop thinking. And her thoughts were not only of the falsity of her present position but also of its humiliation.

Her claim to belong to this world was as false in her own mind as the "rats" Aunt Millie had insisted on pinning into the upsweeps of Caroline's curly black hair to make its fine locks as thickly luxuriant as fashion demanded. Caroline felt a cheat. Some of these people must already know it, or would presently find out. She was the daughter of a tradesman, a builder of homes for profit. And here she was, masquerading as a blue blood, coming "out" in Society. A society to which she had not been bred. And something in her rebelled at the thought. She disliked pretence.

Uncle Hamilton, with whom she had grown up, was himself a builder and had made a fortune out of building London's homes. Even though he was a very successful builder and had made so much money that he had easily retired, that still left the source of his money "in trade". And this was no world, this world of Society, for tradesmen.

Caroline had been five years old when she had lost both parents in a train accident and the Hamiltons had taken her into their home. Her Uncle Hamilton had let her know that coming out in Society was her chance to settle her own life, and raise him permanently from that stigma of trade. If she married a young man of birth—though Uncle Hamilton preferred to say "when" and not "if"— then he could be allowed to forget that he had once bought cheap and sold dear. The members of Society, whom he would join, inherited their money pleasantly, or married it. They never earned it.

Caroline had found her entrance to Society through Aunt Millie's connections. Aunt Millie was the impeccably born daughter of the impecunious Ogilvie family. It was because of that very impecuniousness that Aunt Millie had married Uncle Hamilton. Uncle Ham was the sort of man who came up with phrases which he imagined people would think witty, but which were actually to be taken seriously, for they were much to the point. He had always taken care of his money, he said, so that when he was old the money would take care of him. But even Uncle Ham had seen the necessity of placing Caroline in the world, he had also seen the advantages to himself, and he had told Aunt Millie to make a careful estimate of what it would cost to bring Caroline out.

Uncle Ham had gone over the estimate, had cut out anything he thought could be considered not strictly necessary, and then, feeling very generous (and, for him, he *was* generous, Caroline reflected), had taken a small furnished house in Belgravia. Caroline had tried to thank Uncle Hamilton and Aunt Millie. Uncle Ham made a gruff acknowledgement, and Aunt Millie had looked embarrassed.

But they must love her, she assured herself. Aunt Millie certainly did. She had taken a lot of trouble. She had written to cousins and friends and even acquaintances of her own girlhood and had begun to give dinners and soirées, teas and luncheons, so that Caroline would be invited back to débutante parties. Caroline had had a new wardrobe, carefully planned and chosen so that she had not one extra thing, and all of it made by her usual dressmaker. Nevertheless, she now had more clothes than she had ever had at one time in her whole life. She had been duly presented at Court. How she still shivered at the memory of that curtsey, practised over and over for that small minute before the Throne. And then she was "in," a recognised member of Society. She only had to marry into it to be sure of keeping her place.

All this flashed through her mind as she stood at the top of the beautiful, curving staircase and looked down at the people sitting on the stairs below her. The couples were those already engaged to marry, and so allowed to sit "alone"—that is, together, but in company. The clusters of young people were those still looking for an engagement to marry. Or, at least, the girls were looking for a "suitable" marriage.

Like every other girl there, she was on show to get a husband. But unlike every other girl, for her the thought was a real humiliation. Yet her own honesty told her there was no other life but marriage for women, and that she could sit in their country house for ever waiting for a beau. She was lucky to be brought into contact with so many eligible young men in the Season's parties. If she did not succeed in getting a husband, then, without a fortune of her own, she would not get Uncle Ham's promised dowry. She would be put to governessing, she supposed. Uncle Ham had made it clear that his money, after his and Aunt Millie's deaths, was going to a hospital wing, a wing that would bear his name. Caroline shivered at the thought of governessing, with its life of carefully mended gloves and shoes, and worn, well-brushed dresses. No, she did not want that. There was nothing else for her but a husband. And though she was popular enough, this was her second season and no-one except the penniless Harry de Lisle, whom Uncle Hamilton did not count, had yet paid her serious attentions. Sometimes she felt she would just as soon take Harry as have no-one, but Uncle Ham had made it clear that he was not going to give a dowry so that a penniless fool could use it to support himself. No, there was no use in wishing otherwise: it was a false world, but a world she must get used to. To succeed in it, Uncle Ham and Aunt Millie had often pointed out to her, she too must dissemble. From where, from whom, did she get this terrible desire to speak out, to speak the truth? Sometimes she thought that to escape the humiliation of yet a third season she would accept *any* eligible young man. She turned her head gracefully, and looked over the crowded staircase, the milling groups in the hall, searching for a glimpse of Mrs. Smythe-Taylor's peacock feathers. She started down the staircase, picking her way carefully through the laughing, happy groups. She smiled and nodded at acquaintances as her feet found the clear scraps of carpet between the seated groups. Two small feet in silk shoes, silk shoes that along with her gown, her pearl necklace and her earrings, belonged only to the Season. At home, for her, all was care and frugality.

Conscious as she picked her way down the staircase that someone was looking at her, Caroline looked up. Robert de Lisle Devonshire had stood up from a group seated on a low stair. Robert Devonshire, the son of the house. He came up the stairway now, stepping purposefully. A handsome man, well-built, tall, aristocratic, proud, and, perhaps, a little vain. She had danced twice with him that evening. As he approached her, he put out a hand. She instinctively reached out her own hand and gave it to him.

"I've been looking everywhere for you. I thought I

would have trouble getting you alone," he hold her. She knew in a second from the low murmur of his voice, and his intense look, that here at last was the offer. Here was the great moment! Here was where she chose her life. . . . But she hardly knew him! But then, did she know any of the young men she had been introduced to? Had dined with, danced with, supped with? She had never been alone with any of them. In fact, it was up to her chaperone to see that she was never alone with young men, and Aunt Millie had taken her chaperonage duties seriously. Reputations were fragile and needed to be well guarded, as all chaperones were never tired of telling each other and their charges, though the latter did not always agree.

Now, standing there, her hand in his, she knew all in a moment that he was going to ask her to become his wife. She looked down across the hall again, hearing the violins in the ballroom, and being conscious of the velvets, silks and satins of the people. The heavy perfume drifting from the women about her mingled with the scent of massed flowers. The feel of opulence, riches, and the atmosphere of not having to plan carefully, of not knowing care. Caroline had often wished she were rich, as these people were, rich—and free. And standing near her, holding her hand, was one of the best born and richest young men London had to offer. "Marry me," he said, under his breath, "marry me, Caro." She was never to know if it was a question or a command.

In the sound of those violins, with all that glitter about her, she swayed a little. It was such a lovely place, and surely this was the lovely moment she had been born for, surely this was what she'd craved. She pulled herself together visibly and said, "But you'll have to ask my Uncle Ham . . ."

"I already have," he said. "In the billiard room, not twenty minutes ago." In the orbit of her own femininity, she recognised the aura of his masculine charm as he bent his handsome head to kiss the hand he was holding. "Male and female created He them." Engulfed in Robert's tremendous masculinity, feeling her own femininity sharply contrasted with it, she knew now what that sonorous phrase meant.

Yet she hardly knew this man, his mind and heart were blank to her. He turned on the stairway so as to face the way she did. "May I offer you my arm?" he said. "We should go to tell my parents and your uncle. What better time than now?"

She hesitated, but only for a moment, and then with a lift of her head—for all the humiliation she had suffered was safely over—she put her hand through his arm. He promptly covered the hand with his possessively, and so linked they descended the wonderful staircase to the brilliantly lit hall. She was aware of turning heads: everyone knew in an instant that she was engaged. Little Caroline Hamilton, engaged to marry the impossibly handsome, impossibly well born Robert de Lisle Devonshire, one of the grandest names in London, one of the most brilliant "catches" of the Season! She found her heart flooded with relief and gratitude. And what was that other feeling? Yes, she experienced the most dangerous of all human feelings, she felt the sensation not only of pride, but of vanity.

Caroline had done just what Aunt Millie and Uncle Ham had advised her. She had not let things drift. She had said "yes" without consulting her heart. She had used the only thing Uncle Ham believed in. She had used her head.

Chapter 2

Caroline awoke to the small sounds of the middle-aged maid, Sarah, entering her bedroom and softly pulling aside the old blue velvet curtains on their big brass rings. Those curtains had once graced the dining room but had faded in the sun, and had been cut and fitted to Caroline's bedroom. As the curtains were withdrawn, the black of the bedroom gave way to the half-light of morning, pearly grey. Caroline lingered a moment in half-sleep in the warmth of the feather mattress and pillows. The great four-poster bed had been her aunt and uncle's but they had parted with it for the new kind of tester bed, and now Caroline luxuriated in the old-fashioned comfort. The house was newly built, but the furniture in her room was the old pieces familiar to her since she had been quite a child, which had come to her as cast-offs from various parts of the house at various times. All were clean and decent, even if they did not always go together. Only one thing was new: her mahogany dressing table. It had been a surprise gift from her aunt and uncle for her twenty-first birthday, now two months gone. There had been no party, for who wants to advertise that an unmarried girl is already twenty-one?

Caroline luxuriated, still in half-dream, and they remembrance came flooding in. She was soon to be married. She stirred uneasily in the bed and, to get away from her thoughts, turned her eyes on Sarah. The middle-aged housemaid put a light to the paper in the fireplace. "Why are you lighting the fire?" asked Caroline.

"It's a raw day, Miss Caroline, September and all though it is, and this room is chilly—"

"But—" said Caroline, surprised.

14

"The Missus wants the room warm for when she comes up to see the clothes fittings," said Sarah, a little brusquely. "If she wants it warm then she"ll have to have the fire lit now. They always have a fire in their bedroom."

Caroline said nothing. The fire *was* jolly. But it was never usually lit unless she was ill.

"What time is it, Sarah?"

"Seven, Miss."

"Oh, I shall have to hurry!"

"No you don't Miss, not this morning. You just stay where you are and see what a treat I have for you." Sarah waited until the fire caught and the cunningly laid wood, with the coals above, started to crackle. She left the bedroom briefly and returned with a tall ewer of hot water which she placed on the marble-topped wash-handstand, a folded towel over the opening of the jug to keep the steam in. Then she was gone once more, to reappear with a breakfast tray. On it was hot chocolate, toast and marmalade.

"Oh, Sarah, how kind of you!" said Caroline, feeling quick tears prick her eyes. "I thought I might just have to go without breakfast to be on time for the fitting."

"Not whilst Sarah is here!" said the maid, smiling. "Your aunt just didn't think. You couldn't get breakfast and be back dressed for the dressmaker at eight o'clock. The Missus is having hers in her room. That's why there are no family prayers this morning. If Mr. Hamilton wants the dressmaker to start at eight, he has to give something up. You just put the tray behind the curtains here when you are finished and no-one will be any the wiser. Now which dress shall I put out for you?"

"Why, the Scotch plaid," said Caroline. It was not a difficult decision. Her guardian's notion of what a girl needed to capture a husband was limited and none of the pleas of his wife had altered that limitation. Now Sarah dutifully laid Caroline's clothes across a chair and glanced around the room to be sure she had done everything. Then she looked at Caroline fondly. She had known the girl since she was five. "Engaged or not," thought Sarah

15

to herself. "Miss Caroline is still a child," She closed the door softly.

Caroline reached a hand to pour her chocolate. How lovely to have breakfast in bed! As she reached for the pot, her gaze dropped upon her left hand. Her engagement ring was gone. Again! But no need to panic. The great stoned ring would be somewhere in the bedclothes. She would find it presently. But why had it come off her hand? It did not *come* off—she took it off in her sleep, without knowing she did it. And that very often since the day a few weeks ago, when Robert had given it to her.

Why did she do this? Whilst she felt around in her bed for the massive ring, she thought: "Most girls would be proud to wear it!" It was the most beautiful thing, and the only real jewel that she had ever possessed. It would be nice to think it came off on its own, but Robert had taken the precaution of having the circle of gold which held the gems altered to fit her exactly. There! She had found it! As she slipped the ring back on her finger, she examined again the massed diamonds, pearls and sapphires in heavy gold claws, the stones cleverly arranged like the heads of a bunch of glittering flowers. This was no ordinary engagement ring. It was a magnificent heirloom piece. She had heard of this ring long before she possessed it. It was the de Lisle Devonshire engagement ring. It was said to have been passed down the centuries since the Field of the Cloth of Gold, when a Devonshire gallant had first met and wed a French de Lisle girl, and the ring had been made by the French king's jeweller. Its antiquity and its beauty were famous. The present Lady de Lisle Devonshire must have taken it off her own hand that night of the ball to give it to her son to present to that little commoner, Caroline Hamilton. Caroline now reflected that her match was one of *the* matches of the Season. Caroline well knew that many a mother reading of her engagement in *The Times* had said: "Why, the little minx! So she had her cap set for the de Lisle Devonshire son. And she so quiet—and even plain. Who would have thought it! What a catch for the upstart Hamiltons!"

But a great many cards had been left at the Belgrave

Square house, and anyone, but anyone, who could claim acquaintance with the Hamiltons had written a note wishing the young lady well. Everyone congratulated Robert de Lisle Devonshire on his fine match. And that was what bothered Caroline. Why was Robert marrying her when quite clearly he could have married so many others, better born? Robert had told Caroline that he was in love with her. Was he—or was it the notion that her uncle, who was known to be rich, might give the little orphan, his only niece, a good dowry?

"What does it matter," asked her Aunt Millie, when Caroline had told her of her anxious doubts. "He will fall in love with you when he marries you and you will be in love with him when you are his wife." Caroline had tried to believe her. After all, Aunt Millie had come from that world. But was it true? She wished there were some way she could be certain that Robert loved her, that he longed, as Lord Tennyson put it,

> For the meeting of the morrow,
> The delight of happy laughter,
> The delight of low replies.

She remembered now the pressure of Robert's lips on hers, the way he had of catching her to him, roughly and closely, the touch of his hands on her skin. If this was love, why did she shrink from it? She had been surprised at her own reaction. Surely these moments were what every girl longed for? And the more she resisted his embraces, the more she fired him, it seemed. "High spirited, my Caroline, and a trifle—cold? All the more attractive for that. . . . well, I shall have to teach you—" She had turned away from his next kiss, only to find him tighten his grip on her arms. His fine brown eyes, now half-closed beneath sleepy lids, smiled tolerantly. "I like a little opposition in a woman—but not too much." His sharp, white, even teeth showed up against his full-lipped mouth as, smiling, he pulled her towards him again. But this time she broke from his grasp. The amusement went out of his voice as he added, "A little fight—but a little is enough. My wife will do as *I* wish."

"Supposing I don't love you?" she had dared.

"Then I shall make you. Trust me. Leave it to me," he had told her, masterfully. "You have no knowledge of men. Happily I am not so ignorant of women." Nor, she now reflected, was he. Even she had heard whispers of his reputation. But the girls who poured stories of his escapades into her ears seemed to admire him all the more for his philandering. He was a well-built man of six-and-twenty, debonair, dashing, handsome, with an old name and a future title. What more did she want?

Her aunt and uncle knew all about Robert de Lisle Devonshire. They wanted her to marry "up," out of the class into which she had been born. Robert de Lisle Devonshire's proposal had delighted them. Caroline had gone with doubts about herself to her uncle.

"Be glad you've taken him!" Uncle Hamilton had urged. She had felt hurt. Could it be that her uncle wanted to get rid of her? And then she had put the thought from her. How ungenerous she was in the face of their kindness. They only wanted her to do well.

"Robert is of a good—even great—family, and very good-looking," emphasised her aunt. "And this is the end of your second season. You hardly expected your uncle to afford a *third*?"

"No!—no!" Apart from the expense, the thought of enduring a third season was too horrible. In memory she lived again the anguish of being a débutante. She remembered once more the fittings for the few clothes allowed her, the anxiety about the parties her aunt and uncle gave: would those parties go over or not? The small slights and small victories, social victories, when she was asked to a ball she wasn't at all sure of being asked to. Then her fear of not being asked to dance, or of having to go into supper without an escort. That little programme suspended from her wrist with the pink tassel, and her anxiety to see names written in as partners for the dances, even for those extra dances. Her worry as to whether her dress was the right one: she had only two ball gowns and was sure everyone knew the colour, lines, and folds of

18

each of them. And her fear that no one—but no one—all season long would take an interest, a serious interest, in her. And then hearing of other girls' engagements to be married, going to their engagement parties, being asked to be a bridesmaid again, thinking of the joke "always a bridesmaid, never a bride." Knowing that many men compared not only her looks but her possible dowry and family connections with the looks, dowry and connections of other young girls, she felt again her own loneliness and her hope, her wish that there, somewhere, in the midst of all those young men, her husband, her future husband, might be.

"You *will* love Robert," her aunt's voice echoed in her head, reassuring her again and again. "He's a very charming and handsome young man. If you do not come to love him during the engagement, certainly you will love him in the course of the first year of marriage. A woman loves where good sense indicates safety will lie. For a girl, safety and happiness are one and the same thing."

Robert's darkly handsome face came before her again, his cool air, those well-arranged features. The expression of laziness he often wore, though but a mask for the temper and passion which was so much a part of him, was considered by every girl she knew to be immensely attractive. Her cousin Sophia made little pretence of hiding her jealously. "Such an enchanting man," she cooed. "So handsome, I could die for him!" What was the matter with her, Caroline? Of course she wanted to get married. To be an old maid on the shelf was horrible!

She had expected a long engagement, at least six months, so there would be time to get to know him better, to have him know her. But the marriage was to be within the next six weeks and that frightened her. The actual date had to be before the General Election. Robert's father wanted him to stand for Parliament, and a General Election would certainly be held, everyone said, before spring. She was part of the plan to get Robert into Parliament. He had told her he wanted her sitting on the platforms he would speak from as his bride, his wife. She shivered. She supposed it was the cold.

19

But she couldn't just lie here thinking. The de Lisle Devonshires were coming for dinner—to discuss the date of the wedding. They had not seen her *en famille* before. She must get up and get on with her day. There was a great deal to do. Her eye fell upon the magazine she had been reading the night before, *The Englishwomen's Review*. Better hide that. She reached under the pillows and pushed the little magazine out of sight.

Despite the hungry flames which now raced up the chimney, licking at the fat, shiny, rich coals, the big bedroom, with all its heavy mahogany furnture, was still chilly. Caroline slipped out of bed, her feet finding her bedroom slippers on the heavy carpet while she shrugged her shoulders into her strawberry wool wrapper, embroidered in green silk. The colour went well with her black curly hair and her wide grey eyes that had just a touch of green in them. She sat herself in front of her huge new dressing table. Its legs were fashionably draped in white muslin, and white muslin had also been draped over the top part of the looking glass and there tied with a flat pink satin bow. She picked up one of her two big silver-backed whalebone hairbrushes and sat down on the velvet-covered stool. Feeling the stiff bristles against her head she wished again, if only her hair would grow! It was very fine and naturally curly, but for some reason it never grew beyond her shoulders. There it seemed always to break off. Caroline kept the broken-off ends, saved from her immaculate hairbrush, in a hair tidy, and when there were enough of them she made herself another "rat," a clump of her own hair that Aunt Millie had taught her to put inside the deep rolls of her coiffure. Even as Caroline took one of the silver-backed tortoiseshell combs and began so to put up her hair, she reflected how the "rats" bothered her. Robert had admired her hair. Knowing the apparent luxuriance of it to be a fraud, she wished he had *not* admired it.

Oh, to be fourteen again! Then her hair had hung free and curling to her shoulders: how she hated its present up-swept style! Then she had been a tomboy and people had been indulgent of her words and actions. Now her uncle told her, "You think too much! If you can't help conning everything over, at least have the wit to conceal it!" She had felt humbled and a little bit frightened. Why couldn't she be as docile and easy as other girls?

Here she was, thinking again!

From where she sat she could see, through a parting in the white muslin window curtains, a little bit of a tree, high up against the sky, beginning to be denuded now of its leaves. The branches had a ferny look against the sky, which had turned from pearly grey to blue. The sun, coming up, cast a tracery of these branches against a stable wall. The shadowplay of the tree turned the cream-painted wall into a place of light and shade and so of beauty.

When she turned back to look in the mirror, she saw her own heart-shaped face, a little *gamine*, with a small determined chin. She was five feet two-and-a-bit, but so nicely proportioned that she did not look too small.

A stable clock struck half past seven, and Caroline dressed quickly. Today Stroud, the dressmaker who had already been at work for the past week in the house, occupying the sewing room during the day and sleeping in the attic with the servants, would be expecting to fit her. Caroline had told her she would be ready at eight, as her uncle had ordained. There would be many such fittings, for Caroline's trousseau had all to be made by Stroud. Already Aunt Millie was wondering how it could all be ready. George Hamilton didn't understand about a trousseau: there were many things to do with the lives of women which George Hamilton would never bother to understand. Women's lives were frivolous, he said, and that was always the end of any conversation on the expense of houses or clothing.

Now Caroline could hear her aunt's feet upon the close-carpeted stairway, and the muted sound of her aunt's voice accompanied by respectful murmurs from the dressmaker, Stroud.

"Ah," said Mrs. Hamilton coyly as she entered the room, "what have you been doing since you got up? Mooning and moping?" She came over and put a mittened hand beneath Caroline's small chin. "What a seri-

21

ous face, Puss! Not a smile? However, I suppose one must get used to a little mooning and moping, it's all part of falling in love!"

Mrs. Hamilton smiled indulgently and seated herself in a big rocking chair. Her face was long and thin; the soft mouth pinched, the eyes washed empty of sparkle. Only the beautiful small nose and the curved eyebrows remained. Mrs. Hamilton was forty-four and looked fifty-four. She already wore the matron's lace-goiffered cap of retirement on her dark locks so plentifully splashed with grey. She had an apologetic air which she strove to cover with an air of firmness. Actually she was a timid woman forced to take responsibility beyond her ability to command, but determined to do her best.

The third occupant of the room, the dressmaker, Stroud, was a yellowed, thin-drawn woman of uncertain years. She was a woman of some character but life had made her realise that if she showed any sign of character, it would appear that she was trying to be above her station. So whilst Mrs. Hamilton tried hard to command, Stroud tried hard to please and the result in Stroud was that all the small privations of her life, resulting in those gold coins she sewed carefully into her mattress, showed in a pinched face and resigned shoulders.

Caroline slipped off her wrapper and Stroud took the tacked-together dress she had carried on her arm from the sewing room, and slipped it over Caroline's head. It was a tea gown of rose taffeta. Caroline had never had anything so lovely, so unnecessary. Now Mrs. Hamilton put her hands together in rapture. "Oh, that looks so beguiling!" she said with delight.

"It does suit you," said Stroud, and Caroline, facing herself in the big cheval glass, could not help but smile too. The rose tea gown was beautiful, she thought. And her mind flew to Robert and flew away again. It was strange to think she was getting all these things for him. Strange, when she reflected that they were to be married though in so many ways they were unknown to each other.

Chapter 3

Stroud knelt on the carpeted floor measuring carefully to see that the flounce of the tea gown just cleared the floor. She could feel the pain beginning in her hip joints and reaching down into her knees as she knelt. Her fingers were a little swollen too. Rheumatism. She was young to have it, she supposed. She was thirty-four. And if only she'd married! She sighed . . . it would be nice to have her own home. But why even think of it now? She must remember she was one of the lucky people. She had steady work in the Season at an establishment in London under the distant management of Mr. Worth of Paris. She knew many a woman, as good a needlewoman as she was, who was in positive want once the four months leading up to the Season were over, but she had her own clients, of whom Mrs. Hamilton was one. She could go from house to house, six weeks here, two months there, working through the eight months when others starved. At the thought she made a visible effort and pulled herself together. Ignoring the pain in her fingers, she re-doubled her efforts on the flounce. It was pleasant in Miss Caroline's bedroom; the carpet was old but still thick, and one could still see vaguely its design of cabbage roses on a dark brown background. The furniture did not match, each piece being a little uneasy with the others, but everything was solid and in good repair. The Hamiltons were rich, but Mr. Hamilton did not believe in throwing money away, at least, not on others. His own bedroom, which Stroud had briefly entered in order to look at some dresses of Mrs. Hamilton's which needed altering, was the acme of comfort.

The trousseau she was now making for Miss Caroline was as limited as convention allowed. And everything had to be of good lasting material. Other girls had their trousseaux made by dress houses in London. Mr. Hamilton had rejected that idea with a snort. Stroud had always made Caroline's few clothes. Why did she not make the trousseau and save the cost of a visit to London? "A honeymoon is soon over," he said to Mrs. Hamilton. "She can be as extravagant as she likes when she's married. It'll be up to her husband. If he can't control her, that will be his look-out". Stroud, thinking of the careful economy exercised over Miss Caroline's trousseau, supposed there must be some truth in the downstairs gossip that Caroline, orphaned at five, had not a penny of her own. Mr. Hamilton was being generous with the dowry, but then he was getting a de Lisle Devonshire into the family and the cost of that coat of arms for his niece and himself was worth it.

When Stroud raised her head, she could catch a glance through the window of a broad lane, a shrubbery, a driveway, iron gates. The river could be dimly glimpsed, a sparkle of silver when the fitful September sun showed.

Looking out of that very window, Mrs. Hamilton did not see the outside world with the same appreciation as Stroud. To her mind, it was a pity that the house had not been set back more. Occasionally one got some quite ordinary people in the lane, and on Sundays in fine weather she could hear the voices of common people carried from their row-boats on the river. It spoiled things rather, and took away a certain *ton* she wanted her house to have. But there was not much use in thinking about that now. Caroline's wedding was what presently engaged her attention.

Mrs. Hamilton had been dreaming of that wedding since Caroline had turned eighteen. She had taken a house in Hyde Park Gate for the last two Seasons and saw herself having to cajole Mr. Hamilton into doing the same again, when—thank Providence—Robert de Lisle Devonshire had spoken. Mrs. Hamilton now felt a glow of pleasure as she did every time she thought of that second

Season, and the day that Robert had waited on Mr. Hamilton to know if he would approve of his courting Caroline. Approve! Happily, Mrs. Hamilton now reflected, Mr. Hamilton was not a man to lose his head. Remembering his own considerable wealth, he put behind him his uncertain social background and was cordial, but sufficiently distant to make it seem to Robert as if the young man would indeed have to please Caroline before her uncle would give his consent. Of course there was no question of Caroline refusing. She had some foolish romantic notions in her head, but she would be very fortunate to marry de Lisle Devonshire. The family was one of the oldest in Wiltshire and Caroline would be Lady de Lisle Devonshire one day. Then no one would talk of Mr. Hamilton's ever having been in trade.

The fire was not large, nor was Caroline near it, so her small hands as she stood still for the fitting were quite blue with chill. Glancing down at Stroud creeping around her on the carpet, she thought "She must be cold too. Stroud? Why do we always call her by her last name? Is she Miss or Mrs.? Out loud, Caroline asked, "What is your name?"

Stroud, never dreaming that a remark not to do with dressmaking could be levelled at her, continued to work. But Caroline leaning over, caught the thin shoulders in her hands and said low but clearly; "Stroud, please, what *is* your name?"

Stroud gave a frightened glance at Mrs. Hamilton. She had taken out her household account book, was puzzling over it in her rocking chair and had not heard. Mrs. Hamilton dreaded the end of each month when George went over the accounts with her. She seemed always to spend too much. Yet she was so careful in what she bought. "Stroud . . ." began Caroline again.

"Elizabeth, please, miss, if you don't mind?"

"Then why don't we call you Elizabeth? Better still, Mrs. or Miss Stroud. Which is it?"

"Miss," said Stroud in a low tune. "And please, Miss Caroline, don't get me into trouble." Again she looked towards Mrs. Hamilton.

"Were you always a dressmaker?"

"No miss," replied Stroud. "My father was a curate but the living hardly gave us any money and none to save."

"Then why didn't you become a governess?"

Stroud glanced at Mrs. Hamilton again before she replied, "There are more governesses than there are places, Miss. And I could always sew; I like using my hands."

"But a governess is a lady."

"Yes, with hardly ever a penny to fall back on," said Stroud. "You think of those things, Miss, when you're forced to. I'm lucky I could sew."

"What is it?" said Mrs. Hamilton, looking up, suddenly aware of the conversation.

"Nothing at all," said Caroline. "Miss Stroud and I are doing very nicely."

"Miss *who*?" asked Caroline's aunt.

"Oh, don't mind Miss Caroline," said Stroud quickly to Mrs. Hamilton. "She was calling me "Miss" for her pleasure. I think Miss Caroline wants to tease."

Caroline would have retorted that this was not so, but for the pleading look Stroud now cast at her. "You'll lose me my work, Miss," she whispered. There was a moment of silence as Stroud busily pinned. Mrs. Hamilton had gone back to a sum in her accounts.

"But where do you *live*?" Caroline wanted to know.

"Oh, I have two rooms," whispered Stroud, thinking of her two small rooms under the sagging roof of an old house, cold in winter, stifling in summer. Still, many of her acquaintances shared one room, or lived in a basement below street level. Elizabeth Stroud was lucky in her own opinion. But Caroline was saying something more.

"Where *are* these rooms?"

"In London, in Soho, Miss Caroline. Beak Street, Soho. At the Sign of the Geranium—it's a restaurant, a little place, and I live over it. Top floor."

"Beak Street, Soho," repeated Caroline, never dreaming that that particular address could ever mean anything to her.

Caroline went back to her own thoughts and Elizabeth Stroud, snipping and ripping, cutting and stitching, began to dream—to dream of the ten hour day. They talked of having it for women and children in the manufactories. Imagine! Only ten hours. Dressmaking was different. To keep up, you began at first light of day and often fell asleep over your work at midnight. But there was always Sunday. You could sleep a bit later then, and still get caught up on the work after Church. Working for the Hamiltons was like a holiday from London. Though even here she had plenty to do!

She envied Miss Caroline being engaged to marry. Stroud had had a young man of her own once. He had been a baker with a small business of his own. She had been her father's housekeeper at the Rectory, and she had met him in the prosaic business of buying bread. But her father had put a stop to it when he had found out, saying she must marry someone of her own sort. Which meant she did not marry at all; for whom did she meet? Other curates, younger than her father, and so even more genteelly poor. If only she had defied her father! When he had died, she was over thirty and her only respectable prospect was governessing at only twenty pounds per year—a life in the schoolroom with no independence and little chance for saving for old age. She would rather sew. When Elizabeth Stroud thought of her good fortune in getting these weeks of work in a comfortable house in the country, her fingers moved more adroitly over the faille flounce. It would be even prettier when she headed it with the checked *bouillonné* straight from Paris. The bridal gown itself was coming from Paris, from Mr. Worth's own work-rooms, for Mr. Hamilton was determined the wedding itself should be spectacular.

But Mrs. Hamilton was speaking.

"Does Mr. Worth think the crinoline may yet come back into fashion? I'm sure I shall never take to the bustle!" Mrs. Hamilton laughed. "Oh yes, I know I have a few bustle dresses. I am not comfortable in them, as any woman is in the crinoline. What does Mr. Worth think?"

Elizabeth Stroud paused in her work and sat back on her heels. "Mr. Worth says, ma'am, that the crinoline will never return."

"And what makes Mr. Worth so certain the bustle has come to stay?"

"Mr. Worth says it's all this freedom for women, ma'am. In a bustle young girls can now play tennis, even go on shooting parties, and take an active part."

"Tennis?" Mrs. Hamilton looked sharp. Caro must certainly be taught to play, if that were the fashion. But she said placidly to Stroud: "I understand that of bustles, the *Alexandre tournure* is the best. Can you make a bustle like that?"

"Oh yes! I would use *brillanté* and narrow steels, cord and elastic. The medical profession approved of these items as not heating to the spine, as some bustles are."

"Do you hear that, Caroline?" Aunt Millicent enquired. "The *Alexandre tournure*, as good as made in Paris!"

"Yes," said Caroline, "and I would very much like to play tennis. Though I don't believe I'd want to take an active part in shooting parties. I'd hate to shoot to kill."

"Tut! Tut!" said Mrs. Hamilton. "You will have to get used to that. Robert is a good shot. I hear he even goes stag-hunting."

"You can't mean it!" said Caroline without thinking. "Who could kill a beautiful stag!" She shuddered. "I can only bear the fox hunt because foxes kill chickens, though surely it would be kinder to shoot the foxes . . ."

"For heaven's sake don't let Robert hear you speak like that! No gentlemen shoots a fox!"

Caroline suppressed what she wanted to say: "You mean a gentleman prefers to see the fox torn apart by the dogs?" There was a silence.

Mrs. Hamilton compressed her lips over a plenitude of words and fixed her eyes upon the dressmaker. It was obvious that she was not going to say anything in front of Elizabeth Stroud. Stroud, with that sixth sense that made her so popular with the people she served, felt that her presence was not needed. She coughed a little in her throat and then said politely: "Perhaps I should go upstairs, ma'am, to the sewing room. I have this flounce set on perfectly. I should sew it on immediately."

"Oh, perhaps, yes, then," said Mrs. Hamilton, glancing

at her fob watch. Caroline dropped the dress around her feet and stepped out of it.

The bedroom door had hardly closed on Stroud when Mrs. Hamilton began: "That's exactly the sort of thing your uncle means when he says you have too much mind. You don't like hunting; can't you keep that opinion to yourself?"

"Because I think it ought to be stopped. The cruelty to wild animals . . ."

"Yes! Yes! We all know about it. But it is not your business to point out such things. Nobody will thank you for doing it. It distresses people, makes them uncomfortable. A girl must above all be diplomatic—"

"If I were a man I would be allowed to say what I pleased!"

"But you are not a man! Oh, these modern ideas! Girls having their own opinions—that's no way to please a husband!"

Caroline, despite her self-control, make a little gesture of impatience. Her aunt noticed and said, sharply for her, "Why are you so restless lately, Caroline? You can't possibly be unhappy at your age!"

"Oh, I just feel that there is no sense to life!"

"No sense? Why, you are engaged to marry. It has every sense for a girl to make a good marriage and that is exactly what you are doing, not only a good marriage, but a brilliant match."

"But I hardly know Robert."

"You will have plenty of time to know him when you are married to him. I can imagine your being discontented if you were not engaged after two Seasons. Or if you had finally had to accept some inferior sort of person, with few prospects. But Robert de Lisle Devonshire! Really, Caroline, you must thank Heaven for your immense good luck! With him you not only have the security and protection marriage offers women, but are marking a great step up in Society. You will have a title one day!"

"Yes—yes, I know, a title. But I think—"

"*That* is your problem, Caroline, you *do* think. Well,

don't! Leave the thinking to the men! They are better fitted for it!"

"But the things men think, and say, are so often untrue!"

"A good woman—a good wife—can influence a man to think and say what she feels is for the best."

"Oh, Auntie, is that true?" asked Caroline impulsively. "Can *you* influence Uncle Hamilton?"

"That is different." Mrs. Hamilton spoke severely and coldly. "It is none of your business. But since you ask, to attempt to influence your uncle would not be . . . influence but interference. Your uncle is an exceptional man and always knows what to think and do for the best."

Mrs. Hamilton had flushed with the effort of saying this. Caroline, noticing, was silent. She was very fond of her aunt. In fact, she loved her dearly. But looking now at Aunt Millie's beaten, resigned face, she reflected that she did not wish to grow like her, nor to live with a husband who required constant tact and cajolery.

Caroline thought now of Robert's phrase, "My wife will do and act as I say." *Think* and act he probably meant, and she felt sure she could not dissemble, as her Aunt Millie had obviously done all her life, just to keep peace in the house. Then what would she do? Ideas came into her mind and though she tried to keep a guard upon her tongue sometimes those ideas leapt out, almost of their own accord.

As though reading her thoughts, her aunt counselled her now: "I hope you'll produce none of your ideas tonight! I promised your uncle I would talk to you about it. Frankly, tonight, he would just as soon you didn't speak unless you must. Anyway, it is so much easier for a woman to listen. Listening is what most husbands want of their wives. You don't have to take any of it *in*! But if you *do* talk, keep on neutral ground. Don't express opinions, and *never* strong opinions!"

Caroline sighed. Mrs. Hamilton thought it best to ignore the sigh. Caroline was headstrong. There were no two ways about it. One could only hope that life would teach her—as it had long ago taught Millie Hamilton.

"Well," thought Mrs. Hamilton now, "when she is married I shan't have to worry. It will be Robert's responsibility." Meanwhile, there were shoals to negotiate. Tonight's dinner, for example. It had been arranged to set the date for the wedding, and also to get the ball rolling for Robert's political future. Caroline must be made to appear to do her best at it. The de Lisle Devonshires had no notion of how very spirited their future daughter-in-law could be.

So Mrs. Hamilton pulled herself together briskly: "Tonight, you'll wear the white silk. With the puff sleeves out, the new *décolleté* Stroud has arranged, and the change in the sash, I'm sure no one will recognize it for one of your Season dresses. Now, I want you to memorise exactly who's been invited. Naturally, there is dear Robert and his mother and father. Then there is Major Fortescue, M.P. and a young man from *The Times*. His name is, oh, yes, let me see, I've such a bad memory for names!" Mrs. Hamilton dived into her reticule.

"Someone on *The Times*?" asked Caroline, puzzled.

"Yes. The Devonshires invited the editor, but he could not come. He suggested this young man instead. Here it is! Edmund Davis Browne! But you already know Mr. Browne! When you were about fifteen we took a house at Brighton. Edmund Davis, he was then. He was in his twenties. He must be over thirty now . . ."

"Of course! He taught me how to shoot!" She still had the little pistol—almost a toy—that he had given her as a parting present.

"But that wasn't what he was supposed to do. He was engaged to teach you to sing. He was quite musically able. . . ."

"Oh, *yes*," said Caroline, with more emphasis than she meant. To cover a strange sense of confusion in herself at the thought of her former tutor, Edmund Davis, she asked, "But why is he now called Browne?"

"Your uncle tells me he came into a little money. But he only inherited if he took her name—Browne. I mean, his maternal grandmother was called Browne, the one that left him some money. She didn't want the name to die out. Anyway, he'll be there tonight."

Struggling with feelings she could not explain to herself at the mention of her former tutor's name, Caroline asked, "So, he *did* become a journalist?" As she spoke, she felt sweep over her the shy, melting feeling she had had when she took those singing lessons. "Calf love," her governess, observing her, had told her. Yes, she had known he wanted to become a journalist. He was studying shorthand at the time. She remembered he had spoken of the fact that the great Charles Dickens had begun his career in journalism by learning to write shorthand.

"Of course, your Aunt Lucinda and Cousin Sophia will be at dinner," Mrs. Hamilton was running on. "It came to me as a surprise that this is their last night under our roof before they return to London." Mrs. Hamilton sighed. "I can't imagine how my impulsive sister, widowed and all as she is, could have brought up such a sensible girl, a girl with a head on her shoulders. Sophia will make the right marriage without any urging. She only has to meet suitable men. Whilst you——" Mrs. Hamilton broke off, pausing deliberately in the hope that this thought about Sophia would sink into Caro's foolish head. "There! I mustn't scold you. Now, where were we? Oh, yes, the de Lisle Devonshires want to bring their cousin Harry. Remember him? I was afraid he had a crush on you! His coming quite threw out my table, so I asked that widow, Mrs. Erskine, who writes stories."

Caroline began to smile, but not noticing, Millicent Hamilton worried on: "I do hope she has a possible dress to wear. I wouldn't have asked her if there had been anyone else I could ask at the last minute. I shall put her next to Mr. Browne. No doubt, as they are both writers, that will give them something in common."

Caroline looked at her aunt, and wondered if she dared tell her. A *Times* man and Mrs. Erskine! She was sure no two people could have so *little* in common. *The Times* was a Tory paper to its core, and *The Englishwomen's Review*, Mrs. Erskine's paper, was liberal, especially in its views on liberty for women. Caroline glanced over to her bed. The last copy Mrs. Erskine had loaned her was concealed in the bolster case.

"Now, Caroline, I know you've a busy day. There's your painting lesson with Sophia, and your piano practice. If there were time I'd be taking you to visit some poor cottagers—you seem to like that. But I'm afraid we shall have to put visiting off. . . ."

But Caroline was no longer listening. She was thinking of the distasteful day that stretched in front of her, filled as usual with appointments made for her. Could women never do what they wanted to do? Of course Miss Florence Nightingale had, but Caroline had no such courage. She could only leave her family's roof to go to her own home, her husband's home. There really was no way to make a life alone. To do that, you would need money, and some sort of work that would mean more than just whiling away the time.

"Caroline! You're not hearing me!"

"Oh, I am sorry. I was thinking how nice it would be if I could plan my own day—if I could have personal plans."

"Personal plans! My dearest Caroline, you know a girl cannot have personal plans! A girl is expected to devote herself to the domestic felicity of those she lives with—especially the men. You have a splendid engagement but you will not have a happy marriage unless you realise that a woman's life is her husband's life. There isn't, and never will be, room for personal plans."

"I sometimes wish that I was one of the women who could earn my own living!" said Caroline without thinking.

"Oh, Caroline! How can you!" exclaimed Mrs. Hamilton, shocked. "Only failure to marry and destitution could force you to that! Governessing, or worse!" And with this thought, Mrs. Hamilton took out a tiny handkerchief and dabbed her eyes. Caroline, immediately sorry for her wild words, dropped on her knees and put her arms around the frail figure. "Forgive me," she said. "There! I promise to remember everything. I'll please you and uncle completely tonight."

"Oh dear!" said Mrs. Hamilton, sitting up. She put away her handkerchief briskly. "I mustn't encourage you to be sentimental, even with me," she said. She patted Caroline's cheek and got to her feet with determination. "Don't be late for dinner at six. And remember to speak to the man on your right with the first course; then turn to the man on your left with the second course, and so on. Don't—don't, please, get involved with anyone in a serious conversation. In fact, don't speak seriously at all. And please agree with *anything* the gentlemen may think, or at least, appear to."

"Yes, I will remember," Caroline sighed.

Mrs. Hamilton descended the stairs to her husband's study. She was looking forward with relief to relaxing in her middle age. Once Caroline was married, she could forget all that strife with life all that energy she had had to show since she was a girl herself, trying to get a husband and without a dowry: All the energy she had had in her married life, to accomplish a myriad little tasks, heaping each upon the other till she ran from dawn when she rose to that blissful moment when she crept between the starched linen sheets of her bed and her toes found the stone hot water bottle as her disillusioned and weary head found her pillow! Mr. Hamilton was no longer climbing in his business, and no longer interested in being a lover. The placid waters of later middle age and then of old age beckoned Millicent Hamilton to days peaceful at last.

Now, she gave a slight apologetic knock on her husband's door, and hearing a grunt of acknowledgement from within, she entered. Mr. George Hamilton was a man of powerful stature and strong Tory principles. Grave and self-important, he was proud of the fortune his efforts had achieved. He was a man of action and never dealt in introspection about the problems of heart or soul, of love or being. The world was a well-ordered place and God in His infinite wisdom had placed men like George Hamilton in the position to which their natural talents (and the profits of the industrial revolution) had brought them. He had wished for a son in his own image, but his wife had presented him with not one living child. However, the nephew-in-law he had pretty nearly picked out for his niece might very well make up for the lack of a son. A manly fellow, that Robert; ambitious, good blood there. Anyone could tell that on sight.

Uncle Hamilton had been a giant in business, but now that he had been three years retired from it, he felt that he was becoming a withered giant. He had determined to be rich by the time he was fifty, and rich he was. He had put a great deal of hard work and ability into his business, but he had also preserved a little of that willingness to work hard and that natural ability to turn everything to his advantage. All life was a series of advantages, or disadvantages to be made into advantages in Uncle Hamilton's eyes. All life, in fact, was a matter of making good deals, or series of deals, and coming out on top. He was dealing now, for Caroline—and for himself. His money had brought him every luxury, except the luxury of being accepted by the *ton*. What was the use of a fine house, a fine drawing room, a fine dining room, and everything else that went with riches, if he had no one he valued as a friend to go with the things be valued? He wanted only the best people in his home. He had always looked ahead when given the chance. He had married dull Millicent Ogilvie just because he could imagine his own retirement years before he could afford it. Millie, whose family was busy coming down in the world as his was busy going up, gave him a foot in the door of fine society. She was very well-connected. And then his brother's orphaned child had turned up. At first he had not realised that she provided an opportunity, but his instincts held and told him that even this burden might become an asset if properly handled. Now he was properly using her, for was he not doing his niece a favour in putting her into Society with Millie to open the doors? And he felt that the least he could expect from such philanthropy was a place in Society for himself too.

Thinking of this, he rubbed the dry skin of his hands together, making a sound like old rustling papers being dragged over each other, and he cracked each of his finger joints one by one, over and over.

"What is it? What is it?" he asked petulantly as his wife entered the room, a little too quickly for his comfort. He had spent years reproving her for the very eagerness and naturalness which had once attracted him to her. However, he controlled the reprimand that was on his tongue, for he was in a good mood, looking keenly forward to the evening with Sir Ernest de Lisle Devonshire and his lady at his table, and to the political discussion that would take place afterwards when they would decide how best to get Robert into Parliament. So he merely requested that his wife take the tiny velvet fireside chair which was close to the hearth.

He himself stood before the heavy overmantel, with its Chinese pottery dogs and Georgian silver ornaments, and paused, an unctuous moment of suspense, whilst he raised the tails of his frock coat and proceeded to warm the seat of his grey checked trousers. It had been cold at his desk. Then he spoke.

"Well?" he asked.

"I've done it!" she told him with a little air of triumph, and as though she hoped for approbation. "I have absolutely put my foot down and told Caroline that she is to make nothing but the lighest of polite remarks. I do believe I made an impression on her."

Mr. McLeod Hamilton cleared his throat, dropped his coat tails, took off his *pince-nez* and then said: "Good!"

"I'm sure you will be pleased with her tonight."

"I hope so, I have been on the point of great irritation lately. She is such an opinionated girl. I think the fault is partially yours. Allowing her to go to the Young Ladies' Seminary was a mistake. Home governesses were all she needed. Getting girls up like that with education beyond the normal expectation only encourages them to believe they can think."

"Yes, George," said Mrs. Hamilton. She remembered it had been *his* idea to send Caroline to the Seminary; he had thought it would get her out of his way and "improve" her. He had *not* thought it would fill her up with

36

ideas clearly suitable only for men. She wished he would not make her feel that it was unfortunate to have brought up nothing more than a girl, a mere girl, and a wayward-seeming one at that. But once she was married. . . !

That evening Caroline saw that she was the first down waiting for their guests. She also could not help but notice in the overmantel looking glass that the white *peau de soie* evening gown with its new green sash and deep *décolleté* did, as Aunt Millicent said, suit her. Her eyes seemed almost sea green, perhaps because of the ivy-leaf shade in the deep velvet bands which circled the bodice. The mass of her curly black hair had been piled up on her head and tied with green velvet ribands.

The big oblong room looked beautiful with the Aubus-son rug, the great, romatic, white-marbled fireplace, the huge mirrors lighted by candles in which Caroline could see herself. The grand piano shone, a pool of dark rose-wood and mahogany. The silver set about the room gleamed amidst the great bowls of flowers, giving the room an appearance of *richesse, richesse* that charmed.

Caroline did not ring to have the gas lights turned up, but lit the many candles on the chimney-piece and about the room, and was pleased with the romantic glow they cast. She felt an urge to waltz. She pushed a few pieces of furniture back, wound up the music box and began to dance the Viennese waltz. Turning and smiling she closed her eyes to imagine some charming man for a partner. Listening to her own dreams and to the music, she did not hear the butler open the door and let someone enter. And then an arm was about her waist and the man who had come in took the outstretched hand she had pretended was clasped by a partner. "Oh!" she said, and would have stopped, but this stranger propelled her on. "Every touch of fingertips tells me what I know; I'll be true to you, to you, I love you so!" he half sang, half hummed. He reversed her beautifully, her white gown billowing, his coat tails flying. For the life of her she could not help it, she laughed with sheer *joie de vivre* as he sang again: "I love you so!"

She was dancing with a tall, broad-shouldered young man with deep blue eyes in a tanned face and a shock of brown hair—a stranger who yet felt as though he were no stranger at all! The music wound down to a stop. The tall young man, still holding her hand, stepped back from her and bowed low.

"I am Edmund Davis Browne. I think you used to call me Edmund."

"Edmund Davis! But the beard! The moustache!"

He laughed. "And you are little Caroline Hamilton, but oh, so changed!" Still holding her hand he began to sing softly:

"Shy as the squirrel that leaps among the pine-tops,
Wayward as the swallow overhead at set of sun,
She whom I love is hard to catch and conquer,
Hard, but oh, the glory of the winning were she won!"

Remember?" he asked teasingly, and as he said that word he reached for her left hand to raise both to his lips, but as he did so, his eye fell upon her ring. The teasing look left his face, "Good Lord, Caroline," he said seriously. "You're not engaged? Are you? I didn't know . . . I had no idea . . . I knew your uncle's name, of course, and eagerly accepted to come—but are you engaged?" She nodded quietly and he immediately let her hands go. She had the curious feeling that he was—no, not angry, but disappointed with her. For no reason she felt as if she had lost something—something precious.

Edmund, for his part, had had a sort of shock. He had never realised before what she had meant to him—that in all those years, without his noticing it, she had been in his mind. He had seen her still a child, as one is wont to see others, unmoving in their lives whilst one's own life moves on.

So she had turned into a very pretty girl, a débutante. And gotten herself engaged in a very proper way. She was marrying for money, he presumed, and position. Why should he quarrel with that? Yet, he felt disappointed. And couldn't think why. Except, perhaps, that the fifteen-year-old had had spirit and heart, and he had had a small hand in encouraging both.

Now she asked him, "Why did you not come to see us before?"

"I've been working in Berlin for *The Times*," he answered. "And then Paris. I was in Spain for a short holiday, and then I got posted to London. I'm so newly arrived I haven't had time to catch up with the social gossip yet, or I suppose I'd have known of your engagement. You know, I'd forgotten you'd be growing up, Caro, and that life would be changing for you. Who is the lucky man?"

"Robert de Lisle Devonshire."

"The man who wants a safe seat with the Tory Party?"

"Yes."

"He says he will take even a rotten borough if he has to."

"I know nothing of politics."

"Well, a rotten borough, Caroline, is a seat in the Commons that rich men literally buy."

From loyalty to Robert she made no comment.

"And do you love him, Caroline?" She turned away from his question. "Do you?" he insisted. "Do you?"

"Don't most girls love the men they're betrothed to?"

"I didn't ask about most girls," he told her, "I asked about a special girl—you." There was a long pause in which he looked at her with his blue eyes. How changed she was and yet how unchanged! The lively little girl had become a lovely young woman, eager and pulsating with life. What was she doing marrying this de Lisle Devonshire? From what he had heard, Robert Devonshire was a spoiled, vain man, something of a bully when he could get away with it, and without an original thought in his head; whereas Caroline had always been both original and unspoiled, a girl quite unconscious of her own charm.

"Why are you marrying this fellow, Caroline?" Edmund persisted boldly, as though he were still her tutor.

She might have tried to find an answer for him, but at that moment they both became aware of noise outside the drawing room door. Someone was coming across the hall.

Chapter 4

Mrs. Hamilton looked around the drawing room. "Why, what has happened to the furniture? Who pushed it to one side?"

"I did," said Caroline, "I was waltzing."

"Waltzing? Alone?"

The question came from Robert de Lisle Devonshire. He had come into the room with the air of a man very sure of himself, very certain that his handsome, male presence delighted women, young and old. Now he took Caroline's hand.

"Waltzing?" he asked again.

"Why, yes," said Edmund Browne. "Waltzing with me. For old times' sake." He bowed to Robert Devonshire: "My name is Edmund Browne. Edmund Davis Browne. Your fiancée was once my singing pupil. She has a very pretty voice, as I'm sure you know."

Seeing Robert's slight frown, Mrs. Hamilton said hastily: "Caroline was just a child then. I don't believe that she knew how to waltz or really to ballroom dance in those days!"

"Well, she knows now," said Edmund, smiling and looking at Caroline directly. For no reason at all Caroline felt the blood rising in her cheeks. She thought of how she had felt about Edmund when she was scarce past fourteen—over six years ago—indeed getting on for seven. But had he grown into a different person? He looked such a man of the world now. Certainly she had changed. She was a grown person now, engaged to be married and that very soon. But Robert was speaking in that tone he used for servants, or persons socially inferior to himself.

"You were a tutor?" Yes, Caroline noted uneasily, there was that edge of contempt.

"I earned my living where I could," said Edmund blandly. "I'm here tonight—to earn my living." His voice was suave but it too managed that edge of contempt which Robert felt he alone had mastered. A faint colour rose in Robert's handsome face, a sure flag of rising temper, but before he could give vent to the smallest word, Edmund added quickly: "I represent *The Times*." Robert quickly forgot the words on his lips and bowing stiffly to Edmund said, "Honoured to meet you—*sir*." Instant antagonism had flared between the two young men and Caroline rushed to cover it up with social chatter. She put her arm lightly on Robert's and gushed with girlish chatter about how pleased she was to see them all in her home. Mrs. Hamilton's eyes rested on her with appreciation. Caroline was going to be all right. She was already recognising that a woman's role, and especially the role of a wife, was to smooth out any social difficulties and keep peace at all times around the men-folk.

Lady de Lisle Devonshire responded to Caroline's efforts by bestowing gracious social smiles on everyone present. She was in a very good mood. On the way over from Devonshire Court to the dinner party at the Hamilton's deep within the fur-rugged recesses of their carriage, Sir Ernest de Lisle Devonshire had given her the final details of the dowry that had been discussed with Mr. George McLeod Hamilton. The sum was very satisfactory—in fact, so satisfactory that it had put a sparkle into Lady de Lisle Devonshire's normally cold grey eyes. Her eyes indeed tonight were diamond-bright to match the diamonds of her bracelet, necklace, rings and bob earrings. Small sized diamonds all of these, suitable for a dinner that, but for one or two outsiders to fill up the table, was, she understood, *en famille*. Her lips now curved in a constant smile, and she cooed at her future daughter-in-law, telling her how well she looked in white. Caroline knew in a flash that despite Stroud's efforts to alter it, Lady Devonshire recognised the dress and thought it dowdy. But Caroline also recognised that for some unguessed reason

Lady de Lisle Devonshire was making herself uncommonly pleasant: she was being kind and, surely, it was kindness she sought in her new family. Kindness would make all the difference to Caroline, who had known such chill from Uncle Hamilton and such endless exhortations to better behaviour from Aunt Millie. Aunt Millie she knew loved her, but Aunt Millie was frightened of Uncle Ham and was therefore no one to rely upon. Lady de Lisle Devonshire looked as though she had known nothing of fright throughout her entire life and was unlikely to encounter it now.

Lady de Lisle Devonshire had not thought much, indeed, of her son's choice of a bride. Then she had heard of Mr. Hamilton's fortune, his investments, and the dowry his niece was to bring with her. She was his only niece so far as Lady Devonshire knew, and that would mean that upon his death not only would Caroline inherit his fortune, but the very house they now stood in, the very Aubusson carpet her feet now rested on, the great Park that lay behind the house would also all come Caroline's way.

The de Lisle Devonshires were not without money, but enough was never quite enough when Lady de Lisle Devonshire contemplated her own ambitions. Robert must finish in the Lords: a baronetcy did not carry the social or political power that Lord de Lisle Devonshire would carry. He had the looks and manner and with much money and the right connections—that man on *The Times* for instance—could be pushed far.

Sir Robert de Lisle Devonshire was of ancient lineage and was not himself old. His wife, Fanny, twenty years younger than himself, had cause to treasure her own blood connections. But Fanny de Lisle Devonshire had more than blood connections. She had immense determination, vitality and will. The desire for money and power were the source of that determination and will. Every fibre of her being was in sure pursuit of ever more money and every more power.

Lady de Lisle Devonshire did not care to save money. She preferred to spend it. And especially did she prefer to spend other people's money. Lady de Lisle Devonshire was still glowing from the satisfaction of having given the last expensive ball of the Season. But she would like to feel that when she gave a ball again someone else would be paying for most of it. She had not been pleased when Robert, her only child, her son, had found the little Caroline Hamilton among all those eager débutantes. The girl had no looks—well, she was no great beauty—but when Lady de Lisle Devonshire realised the young creature did have money, she understood Robert. Of course she believed in marrying for love—why, there was hardly a more romantic woman anywhere. But money and happiness are synonymous, Lady Devonshire would have said, and to love where money is, is merely taking reasonable precautions that the marriage will be a happy one. Bless the boy, Robert only needed a little leading. She was proud of him. She was glad he was not going to waste his gifts of good looks, of masculine charm, but to use them. Together they could go very far. Of course that little iceberg, Caroline Hamilton, would have to be melted. Fanny Devonshire sensed a certain obstinacy in the girl; but Robert, given time, would change that, and meanwhile she, Fanny, could work to put him on the first leg of his political life. Robert was a little bewildered at times, of course. It was hard for the young to accept all the ramifications, all the checks and balances that older people had long grown used to if they were to make a success of living. He wanted to continue just to enjoy life. But no one of mature years believed that life was for mere enjoyment. Life was a battle, where the spoils went to the conquering. He would get over his bewilderment when he discovered that it was normal not to be happy. In fact, unhappiness, correctly used, was an excellent spur to ambition. It was like having a burr beneath the saddle: hard on the horse and disturbing to the rider, but bound to get action. The acceptance of unhappiness, the calm, poised adjustment to it, was the final proof that one had grown up, had stopped being soft and foolish about the world and was prepared to use oneself and others in the furtherance of substantial ambitions. Of course one always had heart, but not at the price of head, and that really was the hard nut to grasp in the business of growing up. Robert was quite clearly coming to recognise these solid values. Fanny de Lisle Devonshire had been a good mother. She thanked God that she had always seen the light clearly and had never faltered in knowing what was best for her son.

Lady de Lisle Devonshire now descended upon Caroline, all perfume, aigrette plumes, powder and diamonds. She put her arms around Caroline with every effect of tenderness, but still managing to hold the girl away: she couldn't stand anyone being close. The little Caroline would have to learn a lot of things, not to be so kind to servants, for instance. She would have to develop more "manner." The little thing carried herself amazingly well for a family with little blue blood in them. The way Caroline carried her head with unconscious pride could not very well be faulted. But Lady Devonshire had heard that Mrs. Hamilton's family had fallen into the sin of poverty. In fact, that was how George Hamilton had married into blue blood. Lady Devonshire had a fine appreciation of George Hamilton, which he ardently returned. She understood that he had married the colourless Millie Ogilvie so that he too someday might have the opportunity, once his fortune was secured, of stepping into the only classes of English society that could count. It made the arrangements for the dowry—the exact amount it would come to, and the present disposition of the money (a lot of it was in London properties, Fanny Devonshire had been delighted to know)—so much easier to discuss when one knew that there was a genuine bargain to be struck on both sides. As for the commoner blood, Fanny Devonshire knew perfectly well that the upper classes in England had always been willing to admit a little newer blood—always supposing that blood brought with it the good sense of money.

Now Caroline must be shown how to become a great lady. She must learn how to adopt the haughtly manner, to give that impression of pride and pomp which would sit well on Robert's wife as he climbed the political ladder to a seat in the Lords. Yes, everything would go well, Lady de Lisle Devonshire thought to herself, purringly pleased with her part in the arrangements for the forthcoming wedding.

"Charming gel!" said Caroline's future father-in-law, Sir Ernest de Lisle Devonshire, greeting her with a peck on the forehead, "Charming!" He might have kissed her more roundly, but he had to think of his wife. Deuced goodlooking gel, though. He brushed his moustache from his full pink, well-moulded lips and stood off to view Caroline as though she were a spectacle, whilst he re-settled his neck against his white, starched collar of elaborate and old-fashioned design. This had the unfortunate effect of causing him to look as if he had three chins, all running down into his neck and clothes, the fat appearing again in his droppy, pear-shaped stomach. His valet kept him bathed and barbered and his tailor was the best in London, so he gave off the solid air of old wealth and consequence. What he lacked in conversation he made up in many "Harrumphs." He was not a man without ideas. He had plenty of them—none of them his own, but all of them tried and therefore true, and none of them ever risking being replaced by a new idea. He resented people who presented him with new ideas. He knew what he knew and he took it as a personal affront if people did not immediately acknowledge the supremacy of his knowledge. When Ernest Devonshire thought something, that was enough; it WAS.

Caroline managed to look suitably demure as Sir Ernest surveyed her. To avoid the stare of Sir Ernest's lingering eyes, she turned a sweet face up to Robert's profile. Robert was talking about the relative values of guns sold for self-defense. He was Chairman of the Jermyn Street Club and Gun Range. He was speaking to Edmund, who, it appeared, had a reasonably knowledge of firearms: a knowledge unsuspected by Robert, who presumed that journalists never defended themselves with anything other than a waspish pen, a somewhat effeminate way of holding one's own. He was agreeably surprised. Caroline could not help but reflect that if Robert was good-looking in the daytime, he was really handsome in evening clothes. She understood now why they said that evening clothes made a man look like either a footman or a prince. Decidedly Robert looked like a prince, a dark and lowering prince maybe, but a prince, with his brooding grey eyes, so heavy-lidded, his full-lipped, well-made but sometimes sardonic mouth, his handsome nose and well-cut face. His eyebrows were black to match his heavy hair, and this, with a certain touch of olive in his complexion, added to that dark look so many girls had raved about during the Season. He was a man eternally holding himself in check. His moods, his angers, his passions, came from his strong-willed mother, but she had long ago sublimated her tempers to the pursuit of success. Robert's passions had not yet found a safe channel, and so they struggled beneath the surface of the excellent manners in which he had been trained. He was taller than Edmund, but where Robert's personality radiated a man big of bone and quick to anger, Edmund's effect upon the world was of an equal strength, but a strength of finely moulded bone and muscle and finely tuned mind and manner. With Edmund's attention directed elsewhere, Caroline could observe his deeply blue eyes under the thick black lashes, the pleasant firm mouth, the flash of white, white teeth, his crisply curled brown hair matched by a neatly trimmed brown moustache and beard. Edmund was neither tall nor short, but walked with such easy, unconscious grace that one didn't think about his height one way or the other. Caroline idly reflected that whilst Robert was a man who radiated enormous physical appeal on the surface, Edmund's charm lay more in the depths: there was little of the surface here beyond, again, the easy use of great good manners.

The party had been growing as new arrivals came. There was Aunt Newcombe, or as Caroline preferred to call her by her first name, Aunt Lucinda. Aunt Millie's younger sister and now a widow but in well-to-do circumstances. Aunt Lucinda's daughter, Sophia, Caroline's only cousin, was with her. Until tomorrow morning when their train left to carry them back to their home in Knightsbridge, London, Aunt Lucinda and Sophia were house guests. Cousin Sophia, plump and pretty in a rather too *jeune fille* dress (Aunt Luci could not be brought to notice that Sophia was not still a little girl but a grown girl of eighteen), now smoothed that dress over her hips, touched the pink roses in her hair that matched the pink dress, and then, because it was a part of her always to want to touch, moved her closed fan against Caroline's arm and said low, but loud enough so that she could be sure Robert would hear it: "Oh Cousin Caroline, I repeat you are a lucky wretch! I vow I could die for him!"

Sophia now gazed pointedly at Robert, her brown smooth head with the out-of-date middle parting and the old-fashioned curls (Aunt Lucinda certainly didn't dash ahead of the times) cocked to one side, and her smile roguish. Not for the first time Caroline thought: she had the features and expressions of a pretty doll. "He's so—so overpoweringly masculine!" Sophia murmured again. The remark, directed ostensibly at Caroline, was accompanied by a look at Robert, and this time it was Robert's arm that received the light touch, the playful, flirtatious touch of her folded fan.

"Sophia!" said her mother warningly. Sophia, with a little pouting thrust forward of her pink lower lip, so that she appeared to change quickly from roguishness to the edge of hurt, sensitive tears, dropped her head appealingly and said to her mother in a would-be puzzled tone: "Why, whatever am I doing wrong now?"

Aunt Lucinda ignored her daughter's rebellious question, and taking that young lady by the arm in a grip that expressed no-nonsense annoyance, gave Sophia a little shake, accompanied by a frowning look. "Stop these tricks," she said to the young girl, but in a very low tone. Sophia merely deepened the expression which suggested her childish pout would dissolve into tears. From under her lowered eyelids she cast on Robert another admiring look. He seemed totally unconscious of her, for his conversation with Edmund had progressed as far as the use of side-arms in the western parts of America.

Then there was a diversion.

"Why, what a pleasant surprise: of all people, Harry de

Lisle!" It was Edmund Browne who had spoken, and now he strode forward with hand outstretched to greet the young man the butler had just shown into the room. Harry de Lisle's response was not only to take the proffered hand but to put his other hand affectionately on Edmund's shoulder.

"You know each other, then?" Mr. Hamilton said, also giving the new arrival a handshake. Mrs. Hamilton bowed a welcome and Edmund Browne said heartily, "Know each other? I should say so! We went through school together and finished up at Cambridge in the same College. The first time I met Harry I must have been about eight or nine and I'd taken on more boys in a fight than I could handle. Harry came to my rescue and got his nose bloodied, too!"

"Well, I declare!" said Mrs. Hamilton, and added foolishly: "Boys are rough!"

"I didn't know you had any intellectual friends," said Robert nastily.

Harry, unaware of the nastiness, or unwilling to notice it, said with good temper: "Oh yes. If I hadn't had Edmund here I would never have made it to Cambridge. But with him doing all my homework—"

"And Harry fighting all my battles," said Edmund, laughing, "we both made it."

"Pity you couldn't take a degree for me!" said Harry. "I left with nothing to show excepting a good acquaintance with the gentlemen of the Turf, and you left with honours in French and German."

"Don't make me blush," said Edmund. "Whatever honours I ever got I had to work dreadfully hard for."

"Whatever did you learn such languages for?" Sir Ernest asked. "I thought most foreigners spoke English these days."

"I'm afraid, Sir Ernest, that that isn't quite so. Many do put one to shame by speaking our language, but they do also prefer it if you know theirs."

"Humph!" said Sr. Ernest. "Dammit, I've never had to speak anything but my own tongue. Of course, everyone knows a little Greek and Latin. But after all, why would one want to speak to foreigners? If they come here they know that if *they* want to talk to *us* they must speak English!"

Edmund's mouth remained grave, but his eyes began to dance with amusement. "Unfortunately, Sir Ernest," he said, "I had to go to them. I lived in Paris and in Berlin for the better part of the seven years I have not seen the Hamiltons."

"Really?" said Sir Ernest on a note of surprise and faint disgust. However, this was a *Times* man. *The Times* must know what they were doing. Very good business heads there. He looked at Edmund with a little frown. Could he have had anything to do with Scotland Yard? The Yard often had to deal with foreign malefactors. Spies, and all that. Sir Ernest had little use for the continent. A place where people ate frogs' legs and garden snails and never could learn to govern themselves. He had not too much use for Harry de Lisle either, but nearly every family he knew was stuck with relatives they didn't want. And Fanny found him useful as an extra man, sometimes. Thank heavens he had a small income of his own and a Trust Fund he could never touch. He would never actually be a *poor* relation.

Quite unaware of Sir Ernest's low opinion of him, Harry put a hand now through that shock of fair hair, hair that however much he brushed it always finished up looking as if it needed a comb. He had the brownest of brown eyes in a rather ruddy, out-of-doors fact, a face that was as rugged as Robert's was beautifully regular, but a face that with the brown eyes, the red-brown skin and the shock of blond hair, stayed in your memory, if only because the expression was one of such ingenuous frankness that in a world of sophisticates its sheer lack of guile and good temper could startle.

"I do hope I didn't throw out your table," said Harry candidly to Mrs. Hamilton. "It was terrible of me to want to invite myself at the last minute. The truth is, I wanted to see Caroline before I go up to Town tomorrow. I'll be there ages."

"Oh, yes! Yes!" said Mrs. Hamilton, a little bewildered

by this innocence and a little taken by it. "I mean, of course not! You did not throw out my table. We are delighted to have you." And then she flushed slightly, remembering that it was exactly because she feared he would throw out her table that she had been annoyed to have to include him.

"And here you are, Caroline! You heard me say I only really came to see you." Harry had turned to Caroline and now made her an elaborate bow. Caroline smiled at him with genuine affection. She remembered his attentions to her in both her Seasons. Where another young man wanting to dance with her would have boldly written his name straight across all those dance numbers in her pink, pencil-hung dance programme, Harry waited around until he felt everyone else who would ask her had done so, and would then humbly look in her programme to see if there was even an "extra" left open for him. He made her uneasy and, at the same time, she laughed at him. He reminded her of an overgrown puppy, full of good feeling but given the slightest encouragement apt to lunge forward in the absolute certainty that everybody was as good natured as he was himself and, if he only found the right way of putting it, even a lovely girl like Caroline might accept him after all. Time and again he had come to the brink of proposing to Caroline, but she had never given him that little bit of encouragement a man essentially humble in his opinion of himself would need. When he had read the announcement of her engagement to Robert he had roundly cursed his lack of nerve, but had accepted that the handsome Robert had some appeal to Caroline, which he had never imagined Robert could have. Now that Caroline was wearing Robert's ring, he accepted his defeat and brought to his relationship with Caroline what he thought was circumspection, but it was the circumspection that a puppy dog who has been punished exhibits when he next sees the human being he most loves. He adored Caroline and he could not hide it. Robert did not find Harry's attentions to Caroline worth bothering about. In Robert's opinion, Cousin Harry was a boor, happier around stables than in the drawing room. Men liked him, but what woman would put up with him? And not all men liked Harry. Robert, for instance, detested him.

Caroline, wanting to take Harry from under Robert's cotemptuous look, moved to take him over to where Sophia now sat and introduced him to her and to Mrs. Newcomb. Perhaps Harry could get Sophia out of the sulks: at least she would have to play at good manners with him.

A quiet lady with tightly swept up black hair, faintly tinged with grey, came into the room. Under the general hum of conversation nobody noticed her at once, excepting Caroline, who hurried to her to say: "Oh, Mrs. Erskine, how nice of you to come!" Caroline's pleasure was genuine. Mrs. Erskine was somewhere in her later thirties, a widow of slender means and passionate beliefs. She dreamed of a world in which women would have equality with men. She dreamed and worked for it on that thin paper which championed the unpopular Cause. Mrs. Hamilton, who had no idea what she really did, was sorry for her. Whenever she had a tiny moment of rebellion against George Hamilton she would remember Mrs. Erskine. Better any husband than no husband at all! There she was now, in the puce gown Mrs. Hamilton had dreaded. Caroline had met her at some charity affair, a party of some sort to give funds to clergymen's daughters, middle aged spinsters now without father or brother and with the slim chance of marriage long past, who depended on what they might earn and such gifts as could be got together. Mrs. Hamilton had sat down for a moment in the tent, wondering what she could do with a sick headache coming on, and Caroline, in search of a glass of water from one of the various ladies leading the bazaar, had encountered Mrs. Erskine. Caroline had seen her from time to time and Mrs. Hamilton had had to admit that Mrs. Erskine was quite a nice woman, even if she did write. "Children's stories," she had assured Mrs. Hamilton hastily, on being asked. The minute she had said that she had wondered where she got the idea. And then it had become the truth for her. She beamed on Mrs. Erskine, thinking of her in terms of goblins and fairies and good little girls and good little boys. If she had known that Mrs. Erskine had a neat hand at political commentary for *The Review*, she would have not been happy—that is, thinking of Mr. Hamilton's views.

Following Mrs. Erskine came the last guest, Major Fortescue, M.P. He had little concern for his Commission, which had been bought for him in the Guards by a kindly uncle who was a retired General, and was much more interested in becoming a junior Minister, determined, dogged, devoted and faithfully reactionary, a solid member of Her Majesty's Government—Heaven willing.

The dinner went well. Caroline remembered to drop an innocuous remark every two minutes or so to her neighbor on the right, Major Fortescue, and then to her neighbor on the left, Edmund Davis Browne. Edmund Browne seemed rather willing to engage her in one of those conversations that did not come under the heading of mere remarks. But Caroline kept her head. Her fiancé sitting opposite beamed approval across the centre bowl of flowers, and between the tall, wax candles Caroline smiled back at him. It was true what her aunt had told her: if she did not make this marriage happy, she would be a fool. In the warmth and luxuriousness of the delightful dining room, with its noiseless servants and its wonderfully cooked food, adventurous women like Mrs. Erskine seemed foolish. What could be better than to be mistress of her own lovely home? Yes, it would be good, and so very safe, to be the much loved, treasured wife of an important and ambitious man who would look to her for help. It was good of Uncle Ham to enable her to make her début, and to give her a dowry just as if she were herself an heiress. His cold manner undoubtedly covered a warm heart. It was possible he was one of those people who just did not know how to express love except in tangible gifts. Well, he had supported her, educated her, launched her and endowed her. She ought to feel humbly grateful: and she did.

Glancing across the table at her young cousin, Sophia, she realised that it was natural for Sophia to be a little jealous. Robert was a wonderful looking man, indeed so handsome that, to be fair, it would be difficult for any girl to take her eyes from him. Sophia at the moment was not trying to. She was seated between Robert Devonshire and Harry de Lisle and though she did not neglect Harry to any extent that would make Mrs. Newcombe afterwards take her to task, as a girl watching a girl Caroline could not but notice that most of her gaiety was showered on Robert, at whom she looked with frankly adoring eyes. He seemed to be enjoying himself. She, Caroline, had never thought that Robert or Harry were either of them wits, yet Sophia was continually laughing, showing her sharp, white little teeth. She hardly ate any of the many courses put before her. She was apparently too delighted by the mere presence of masculine company to pay much attention to her dinner. Yet she was a girl who frankly liked food. Sophia was a truly feminine girl, people said approvingly. Why couldn't she, Caroline, be truly feminine too? Caroline put more animation into her remarks and presently turned upon her fiancé across the table such a dazzle of a smile that not only he caught it, but Mrs. Hamilton too, and she inwardly breathed a sigh of relief. She wanted Caroline to marry but she also wanted her to be happy. Perhaps Heaven would be good to her and the child would come to care for Robert de Lisle Devonshire. She earnestly hoped so. She glanced down the table at George Hamilton and the smallest of small sighs escaped her. A loveless marriage was a very hard cross to bear.

Later in the drawing room, when the gentlemen rejoined the ladies, very relaxed now and included to be a little somnolent after the port, George Hamilton, feeling in a happy and expansive mood, said: "Sing something for us, Caroline."

"Willingly, Uncle."

"May I accompany you?" asked Edmund. She smiled a "yes" at him and he seated himself on the heavy mahogany bench at the beautiful, intricately carved mahogany Steinway.

"What would you like me to sing?" Caroline asked her uncle.

"Oh, something light and pretty."

"What about those Meredith verses someone put to music?" suggested Edmund. "Remember, Caroline?" He struck a few chords on the piano but as she did not immediately begin to sing, imagining her a little shy, he began in his charming baritone voice:

"Under yonder beech tree single on the greensward,
　Couched with her arms behind her golden head,
　Knees and tresses folded to slip and ripple idly,
　Lies my young love sleeping in the shade. . . .
You see, Caro' (he had slipped into her childhood name) "I remember the song I taught you. Have you really forgotten it?"

A rosy glow came up into Caroline's cheeks. She hoped it would not be noticed. "No, of course I remember," she said, striving for an even tone:

"Darker grows the Valley, more and more forgetting,
　So were it with me if forgetting could be willed,
　Tell the grassy hollow that holds the bubbling well-spring,
　Tell it to forget the source that keeps it filled."

"Charming! Charming!" said Sir Ernest, clapping his hands together a few times, hands old and dry as withered reeds. He had not followed the words at all, but the drawing room was pleasant, his future daughter-in-law appeared very biddable which was what he wanted in a wife for his son, the food and wine had been good, and the port still lingered on his palate—superb. "Is that all there is to the song, m'dear?"

"No, there's—there's a lot more," said Caroline, suddenly conscious that the song was not the impersonal little ditty she should have chosen to sing in mixed company. Lady de Lisle Devonshire unconsciously expressed Caroline's thought:

"That's rather an intimate song, isn't it? The words—"

Her words had been addressed to Caroline with a touch of reproof in them, but it was Edmund who took the reproof lightly on himself by saying agreeably:

"Yes, it's a love song." He leaned back on the piano

54

bench to look over his shoulder directly at Fanny Devonshire. "The words are from one of the most beautiful love poems in the English language—if it is not indeed the most beautiful."

"Harrumph! Harrumph!" said Sir Ernest obligingly. Caroline went and sat down near Aunt Millie. A little buzz of conversation had sprung up under the cover of which Caroline heard Sophia say, as she leaned forward to tap Edmund on the cuff of his evening coat, "You taught that to Caroline? I wish someone would teach it to me!" Her eyes slid around invitingly until she found Robert, but he was not looking in her direction. "Why did he have to get engaged to Caroline?" Sophia thought. Sophia was sure Caroline did not appreciate this beautiful looking man in the way she, Sophia, would have done. However, engagements were engagements, and very few broke up. Sophia signed. She was just out of luck.

Robert had frowned over the words of the song, too. He agreed with his mother that it was not a suitable song for a nearly total stranger to choose to sing with another man's fiancée. This fellow was a curious sort: he began the evening by waltzing with Caroline alone in a room and then went on to sing the sort of duet only a man engaged to a girl should sing with her—and then not in the company of others. Still, the fellow knew something about guns. That at least was in his favour. Yet he felt he should spike any flirtatious ideas that might exist in Edmund Browne's head. Perhaps the man had been in France far too long and had forgotten that an engagement to be married was a solid matter in England, almost as binding as marriage itself. So he said:

"It's a song I should sing with you, Caroline."

Edmund shot him a quick look.

"Why not?" he said coolly. "I'm sure Caroline would be glad to teach you how it goes."

Caroline nodded agreeably. She was sitting and awaiting that moment when her uncle would nod to his wife, on which Aunt Millie would say something about "beauty sleep" and Caroline would know it was time for herself and Sophia to say their good nights and slip away. After they had gone she knew the political "business" which was the main reason for the dinner party would be put afoot, business that young girls were not expected or encouraged to understand. Now Caroline had seen her uncle nod to his wife and was awaiting the right lull in the conversation to follow Aunt Millie's indicated, but unspoken, direction to rise to her feet and make her curtsey. And then the catastrophe happened!

Chapter 5

Sir Ernest had fallen into a monologue on his parliamentary experiences. He sat with his feet crossed at the ankles and thrust out before him, and wagged them to and fro with the unconscious wage of his head. His interlaced fingers rested easily on the bulge of his pear-shaped stomach and it looked as if he were set to go on for ever. The ladies wore a fixed smile of interest and the men, led by George Hamilton, paid respectful, silent attention to the old man. Even Edmund Browne kept his eyes on Sir Ernest for politeness' sake, but those same usually sparkling blue eyes wore a glaze of boredom.

Suddenly Sir Ernest lost interest in his pendulum-swinging feet and, glancing upwards, his eyes fell upon Edmund Browne. That reminded him. Abruptly he switched from his accounting of all the restrictive legislature with which he had been so happy to associate his name and said:

"I must say, Mr. Browne, that I could not agree with you editorial more if I had written it myself. And the style! I wish I had a copy of this morning's *Times* with me. It caused me immense amusement at the breakfast table."

"Oh, allow me!" interjected Mr. McLeod Hamilton. "I, too, was amused, and I have had the page folded back ever since I read it. Perhaps, Ernest (how Mr. Hamilton loved pronouncing that name without the title to it, as he was now entitled to do, being so close to becoming kin) "you would care to read the editorial aloud to us. You have such a fine reading voice."

"Well, George, that's a pretty compliment," said Sir Ernest. "And since you insist, yes, of course I will!" Sir Ernest pursed his over-full pink lips, and taking *The Times* from his host's hand, began to read:

"ARE WOMEN REDUNDANT?
Marriage is woman's sole profession and to this life her training—that of dependence—is modelled. Of course, by not getting a husband, or losing him, she may find she is without resources. All that can be said of her then is that she has failed in business and no social reform can prevent such failures."

There was a titter of laughter and then the room heard Mrs. Erskine, who had been so quiet and unobstrusive all evening, sitting on her little gold side chair, very upright, too upright, saying: "That is all very well, Sir Ernest, if there was husbands to go around. But since there are more women than there are men due to the slaughter involved in gaining an Empire for the Crown, those women who have no husbands must starve or find work."

"Oh yes! Yes! That is dealt with here, my dear lady. Let me continue. Or why don't you, Browne, who wrote this quite wonderful editorial, read aloud your own witty words. Here you are! Begin here." And Sir Ernest tapped the paper and proffered it to Edmund. Edmund Browne with some embarrassment took the folded back *Times* and somewhat reluntantly began to read:

"Assuming that women are redundant let us export those surplus women to marry overseas. It needs only a little courage and a little scheme and all the redundant ones can be landed in the Colonies. This might quiet those dinturbing elements who seem to imagine that a single life might be made remunerative for women. If that happened then marriage would presently be a matter for cold philosophic choice—"

Edmund paused, embarrassed. It had been one thing to write this in the impersonal offices of *The Times* and at the direction of his editor. It was something else to read it aloud to a group including women, one of whom was Mrs. Erskine, that somewhat formidably able woman from *The Review*. On meeting Mrs. Erskine, Edmund had realised in a flash that the Hamiltons had no idea they were entertaining a militant feminist, and she had under her breath enjoined him to silence for Caroline's sake. Now her agate eyes regarded him with a cold start, challenging him to go on or not.

"Yes. Yes!" said Sir Ernest. "Why are you stopping? There's more. There's more. Do go on, man, do continue."

So Edmund had no alternative but to fix his eyes on the print again and continue:

". . . marriage would then be a matter for cold, philosophic choice and would be more and more frequently declined. Then what would happen to our homes? On the other hand, why don't these surplus women become domestic servants? These happy creatures fulfil both essentials of a woman's being: they are supported by, and they minister to, the comforts of men . . . . Nature has not provided one too many."

Again a titter went round the room. The only person who did not laugh was Aunt Lucinda. All she managed was a vague smile. Sophia giggled delightedly. Mrs. Hamilton, following her husband's cue, laughed with him. Mrs. Erskine looked tight-lipped and white-faced. But she was a guest and too well brought up to make controversy in a home where she had accepted hospitality, and especially hospitality which would not have been extended to her if her hosts had known her views. She had come so that she could continue to keep in touch with Caroline. She had a genuine interest in the girl. Caroline, looking at her, and knowing her feminist views, guessed what anger she must be enduring in keeping silent. Little realising where her next remark would take her, Caroline generously said now what she imagined Mrs. Erskine was longing to say: "Oh, but you can't mean it! Exporting women like—like so much merchandise. *The Times* can't have thought! Training the ones who can't get husbands to be domestic servants—"

There was a silence. Mr. Hamilton looked shocked. Was it Caroline who had said this? But before he could sputter into speech, Edmund said, "*The Times* did not intend that the editorial should be taken too seriously—"

"But the question of women who don't marry and must work should be taken seriously," said Mrs. Erskine in a quiet voice. "Many women, as I can only suppose you gentlemen are aware, live on pittances, hardly eating enough to stay alive, and only because they have never been taught to earn for themselves."

"I've been abroad on the Continent and have not followed all that is happening here at home." Edmund addressed her seriously. "I presume you are speaking from information *The Englishwoman's Review* has gathered?"

"*The Englishwoman's Review?*" Sir Ernest did not gather any of the portent of Edmund's question, for his glare would have descended upon Mrs. Erskine had he caught Edmund's suggestion that she had to do with this journal. He only heard the title. "Is that scurrilous little sheet still coming out? Somebody had the temerity to send my wife a copy!"

"Yes," said Mr. Hamilton angrily. "And I, too, had a copy sent me. But by a good friend. It has had the gall to suggest that landlords are responsible for the filth and squalor in which the poor live. Whatever next?"

"Indeed, yes!" said Sir Ernest. "They attacked owners of country cottages, too!"

"I wish they had the job of letting rooms to the scum I

have to deal with!" said George Hamilton angrily. "Lazy lot! Always complaining!"

Mrs. Erskine was heard now saying quietly:

"But there is a shocking overcrowding, Mr. Hamilton. And many of the houses let to the poor are simply not fit for human habitation."

"My dear Mrs. Erskine." Sir Ernest took up the conversation in a voice of condescension. Who was this damned woman anyway, in that ugly-coloured dress? "I really cannot believe you know of what you speak. Surely a lady like yourself does not visit London *slums*?"

Mrs. Erskine opened her mouth to protest his presumption of her ignorance, but Sir Ernest now continued just as if she had never spoken or had vanished into thin air. "I know what you mean, George. Some of my farm labourers are eternally complaining that the thatch lets the rain in or the walls are continually damp. Good Elizabethan cottages at that—cottages people come to gaze at just for the sheer charm of the old places."

The word "damp" had caught George Hamilton's attention. "Damp?" he repeated now. "I get tired of hearing that word. Why, only last week some of the wretches in one of the houses I look after in Leg Iron Court chopped up the wooden banisters for firewood, and *their* excuse was wet and damp. Well, they'll wait a long while for a new set of banisters. To read that *Review* article you would think that all that landlords had to do with their money was repair. Repair!"

"*The Review* usually checks its facts," said Mrs. Erskine, still in a quiet voice but now with a faint blush of anger in her cheeks.

"Don't believe it!" said Sir Ernest rudely. "What would a lot of women on a magazine like that know? I'll bet none of 'em have ever put their noses inside labourers' cottages—"

"Or ventured into a London slum," added Mr. Hamilton. "It takes all the courage I have sometimes to go into places like Leg Iron Court. The women sit around drunk on gin, the men are fighting and nothing on you is safe from some brat's thieving fingers."

"Quite!" said Sir Ernest de Lisle Devonshire. "I believe in giving charity, of course, but I believe in charity for those who deserve it. My wife could not be kinder to the *deserving poor* whenever she comes across any of them." He cast an approving glance at Lady de Lisle Devonshire's erect figure. Except for levelling her lorgnettes at Mrs. Erskine when that lady spoke, she had made no comment or remark whatsoever. The subject bored her.

"Deserving? Oh, of course, quite," she said now.

"Deserving?" asked Caroline unexpectedly. "Surely charity shouldn't be confined only to those who deserve it. Isn't *need* the only thing necessary to appeal to our charity?"

"Need? Need!" spluttered Sir Ernest, nettled to think that he was being questioned in any way, first by that unimportant woman in the ugly dress and now by this bit of a girl. "Need, indeed! You'd have every thieving, low, drunken family asking for help if *Need* was all a Christian thought of!"

But Caroline continued obstinately: "But maybe families would not continue low and drunk and thieving if they had our help. Surely it's a matter of conscience. Of course, if one has neither conscience nor heart—"

Caroline broke off in mid-sentence. Too late she could see that the effect of suggesting that Sir Ernest of all people lacked conscience was to make him feel insulted. He looked at her now as though he was on the point of apoplexy. George Hamilton's mouth was shut tight like a trap door. Lady de Lisle Devonshire levelled her lorgnettes at Caroline. Aunt Lucinda held a shocked hand to a shocked mouth. Mrs. Erskine's eyes fixed on Caroline blazed with gratitude and a Crusader's warmth. Mrs. Hamilton had given up being alert since the singing. She had thought Caroline had done her credit all through the evening. She had nodded through the editorial reading because George was so evidently pleased with it. She had not actually taken in a word that was read. Now she became uneasily aware that something awful had happened. Caroline had come out with some remark a girl should never make. Sophia looked like a cat before a saucer of cream. Clever Caroline had gone and muffed it again. That tongue of hers!

The only people who were calm were Harry and Major Fortescue. Harry because he did not follow what had gone on, and Major Forescue because, being an M.P., he always tried to wear an impartial air when things controversial turned up in his neighbourhood. Why risk making enemies anywhere? Now Edmund Browne said in a half-tender, half-mocking way, "So the little mind still thinks for itself?"

"Yes, it does," snapped Caroline. She felt all nerves, and from that very nervousness added: "And can judge editorials and their authors quite well."

"Imagine," she thought, "that I could have found Edmund Browne romantic or in any way attractive, even if I *was* only fifteen at the time."

"I suppose, Miss"—Sir Ernest was nearly stuttering with fury—"you will next be telling me that we should repair *your* property, do it over for damp, no doubt!"

"My property? I don't own any property!"

"Oh yes, you do! Some of that very property we're talking of! In fact, Miss, the very house in which they demolished the banisters."

"My property!" said Caroline, in real astonishment. "How can it be my property?" she turned to her uncle.

"Your father left it to you when he died," said George Hamilton, obviously begrudging the information. "I have been managing it for you without any charge to your estate—for years."

"Why did you not tell me?"

"The law only requires that I tell you when you reach twenty-one. There is nothing to oblige me to do so before then. You were twenty-one recently, but you are soon to be married. I have discussed the property thoroughly with Robert, and he will lift the burden of management from my shoulders."

"But I want to manage it myself!"

"Whoever heard of a girl managing slum property? Or any property? It's not to be thought of!" Uncle Ham was furious.

Two high spots of colour now warmed Caroline's cheeks. Her heart beat fast. And her grey-green eyes sparked with surprise and anger. Edmund Browne found himself looking at her with renewed interest. She had been a forthright and honest child. She was being forthright and honest now. But, looking around the faces in the room, he thought she was not being wise.

"You had no business not telling me I had property of my own," said Caroline now. "No business. No business at all!"

"No business—! No business! What's the matter with you. Miss? I have been your legal guardian all these years, and when you marry your husband will be your legal guardian. In fact, your business *is* no business of yours!" At this sally he looked around the drawing-room as though delighted with his little joke.

But Caroline persisted: "What else did my father leave me besides property?"

"Some money!" snapped her uncle. "But you are wanting to discuss these wholly private matters with everyone in this room?"

"Nearly everyone in this drawing-room knows more about my inheritance than I do," said Caroline. "I presume that all this is the very dowry I thanked you for?"

"I've had enough!" said George Hamilton. "You need a lesson in manners, Miss. Go to your room and try to recover yourself!"

"There's no need to order me," said Caroline quietly. "I will be glad to go." She rose to her feet and looked towards her fiancé, thinking he would give her some support. But that handsome young man seemed to have found something faintly amusing in the dialogue, for all his lazy length now lolled in his chair perfectly at ease, and a small smile played about his well-cut mouth. "Robert?" said Caroline.

There was a moment of silence, or was it hesitation, and then:

"Yes, dear Caro," said Robert, his small smile breaking

into a full one. "I'm sure your uncle has only your good at heart."

"Did you know about this?" she asked him in her direct way. "That I had money of my own?"

"Why yes," he told her. "I'm surprised you didn't know. Everybody else knew. It's the sort of thing people do get to know about."

"I've told you to go to your room, Miss," her uncle said.

Robert made to get to his feet, but Edmund, quicker than Robert in his movements, was there before him to hold open the door. He looked at Caroline as she prepared to pass him and his dark-blue expressive eyes were alight with interest.

"Bravo!" he said in an undertone as she prepared to go by: "The little kitten turns out to have claws!" Caroline checked her step, and looking up into his face, said in the same undertone he had used: "Claws that would cheerfully scratch your eyes out, you writer of editorials, you!" The heavy mahogany door closed behind her. It opened within a second for Sophia to follow her. Sophia looked pleased, yet scared. She was supposed to accompany Caroline upstairs.

Chapter 6

As they left the drawing-room Sophia made for the stairs, but Caroline turned towards the conservatory.

"You're supposed to go to your room," Sophia said, as though she were in charge.

"Why not go to yours?" Caroline answered. "I'll come up—presently."

"But—" began Sophia.

Caroline stamped her foot. "No", she said, "not you. Don't *you* start ordering me about. You get to your room if you want to. But I'll come when I want to."

With a frightened start at Caroline's white face, Sophia ducked her head and scurried upstairs like a rabbit.

Caroline was in a difficult mood, she thought to herself. Like someone in revolt. Of course, now that she was rich—Sophia's mind scurred away again. How could Caroline be rich? Sophia had always felt sorry for her cousin, brought up by the ill-tempered Mr. Hamilton and by the frightened Mrs. Hamilton; but she had always reflected that for an *orphan*, Caroline was lucky. Sophia's father might be dead, but she had her mother still, and *she* had never been made to feel that she had eaten the bread of charity. But now Caroline was rich *in her own right*! Sophia had difficulty grasping this. Why couldn't she, Sophia, turn into an heiress overnight? Sophia was angry and jealous.

Alone in the conservatory, Caroline circled the little path. It was silent in the humid air of the hot-house, perhaps too silent. Water dripped somewhere, slowly, stealthily. She could almost feel the plants breathing in the heavy air. Something in that close atmosphere, something in that silence, reached through to Caroline. A dry sob rose in her throat. She was alone, those who should have understood her—Aunt Millie, Uncle Hamilton, and Robert—didn't understand her at all. Or if they did, then like her aunt, like Robert—the man who was to be her husband—they said nothing; they made no attempt to stop her being humiliated in public! Without warning, the tears came, filling her eyes and rolling down her cheeks from those wide-open grey eyes so that she saw the world swimmingly as through a pane of rippled glass. She put her aching head against one of the supports of the conservatory and leaned there, feeling outraged but at the same time weak and deserted. What could she do now? What could she even think?

She was just an ordinary with ordinary attainments. She was lucky to get married—and to get married to such a man. In the outer orbit of her thought she could see

65

Robert clearly; he was a very masculine person, breathing the attraction of the opposite sex, all shoulder, slim hips and long muscled legs, conscious of his charm and then careless of it.

According to Aunt Millie, marriage offered the only protection for girls. Aunt Millie was "protected" by Uncle Hamilton, yet every day she paid for that "protection" by going down before him, humbling herself to keep him in the right and superior to her, as though she was a child or a dog, to be spoken to sharply or brought to heel. Oh, Caroline mustn't think like that, for money or no money, she had no choice but marriage, and to Robert.

Only then did she begin to take in the fact that she had money of her own. Money of her own! It made her feel so differently! She had always supposed that her aunt and uncle were keeping her, and she had felt grateful but wished she had not had to. She had seen her aunt wheedling money from her uncle, and she had thought unhappily: "She must often do that for me." The few dresses bought for her, the carefully spaced parties in the Season at the Belgravia house—these had not come from a generous steak in Uncle Ham's flinty nature, but from her own pocket!

Caroline had never forgotten to thank him for each thing. And he had always accepted her humble thanks. She had longed so for a little money of her own! But she had never even had more than a little pocket money—a very little at a time. Uncle Hamilton could not have loved her at all or he would long ago have told her that her father, his brother, had provided for her wants. She must have been just a duty to Uncle Ham. What a mean-hearted man!

Aunt Millie Caroline understood. She would never dare to go against Uncle Hamilton; she was much too frightened of that taciturn man. And Robert? What had been his part in it? Had he never intended to tell her that her dowry was her very own? Of course he had never spoken of a dowry. A man in love is not supposed to speak of dowries.

The door opened and she looked up, surprised, even alarmed.

It was Harry de Lisle. "Can I do anything to—help?" he asked lamely. He came towards her in his frank, yet awkward and difficult manner. He put out his hands and pulled her small, gauzy shawl tighter about her shoulders. This simple gesture of protection brought fresh tears to Caroline's eyes.

"Caro!" he said. "Poor little Caro!"

Why had she ever thought Harry made her feel awkward? Dear Harry, the only one who realised she had feelings and suffered.

And now he said: "Let me help. I don't know how, but I want to help you." At these words she found that she was in his arms, sobbing against his broad shoulder. He gently kissed the top of her head where the smooth hair had been swept back from her face to meet in a torrent of ringlets falling the nape of her neck. He found he was holding her closer. "How fragile she is!" he thought. "And what a lot of courage for such a little thing!" He had a sudden tremendous desire to take care of her, not just for now but for life . . . Of course Caro had ideas that were crazy for a girl, but they could be cozened out of her presently by a loving husband. What was he telling himself? She was Caroline Hamilton, engaged to marry his cousin Robert. But even as his common sense told him this, his arms tightened about Caroline. How much did Robert really care for her? Robert, who flirted with every woman he met, or had done before the engagement. Was it Caro he cared for, or the money this marriage would bring? Knowing Robert as he did, Harry could not help but wonder. Caroline clung to him like a lost child. She was one of these young, wild colts Robert liked to break. Robert was very good at that. He gently kissed her cheek. "What a darling!" he thought.

He bent his head to kiss her more nearly and suddenly a hand grasped his shoulder and swung him around, and in a thick voice, one choked with anger, Robert said: "What do you think you're doing with *my* fiancé? Or could it be that my future wife—"

Before Robert could finish the sentence, Harry found that he had released Caroline, and almost at the same moment doubled a fist and swung it with all the force of his compact frame into Robert's beautiful if savage face. There was a horrible sound of impact on flesh and cartilage and bone and then Robert staggered backwards, hitting his head on one of the shelves supporting the plants.

He fell with a thud.

"You've hurt him!" exclaimed Caroline, shocked. "Is he—Is he—?"

"Oh no! Not dead. Just out. It was the shelf more than my prowess."

Caroline sank to her knees beside the prone Robert. "He must be in pain," she said. She felt anxious but also bewildered. It was so strange to see Robert lying there. She had thought of him as invincible. To see him lying hurt, weak and unconscious touched her heart in a strange way.

"You shouldn't have hit him," she said to Harry.

"I thought he was about to insult you," Harry said in his simple way.

Robert was bleeding from a slight wound in the head. Caroline was tearing the flounce from her beautiful dress and staunching the wound with the silk. "But he said nothing."

"Yes, he did. He suggested that you were about to kiss me, and it was me that was trying to kiss you! Anyone could see that!"

"Yes, anybody could," said another voice, and there stood Edmund Browne in the doorway. "Really, Harry, if you have courting to do you should be a little more discreet. Especially when the lady belongs to another. Conservatories are made of glass." His voice was friendly, but also a trifle amused. He did not look at Caroline. She felt the blood rising in her neck and face.

"Oh," said Harry, "then I suppose you saw me hit my cousin?"

"Yes," said Edmund Browne, and added with an elaborate courtesy that infuriated Caroline, "and I don't have to be asked. I do believe Caroline is worth it!"

"Now, see here," began Harry, not at all sure of what was being said to him by this old friend. Harry knew that women could change a man's relationship with another man. Was Edmund being friendly or not?

"Oh, no, Harry," said Edmund quickly, seeing Harry's fists almost automatically clench. (Harry was not good with words; blows were more direct.) "No fisticuffs with me, please! You know I'm far too cowardly for the manly art. And Miss Hamilton's reputation is quite safe in my hands. I'm beginning to realise, though, just how much my former pupil *has* grown up." He looked deliberately at Caroline for the first time since he had entered the conservatory. To his own astonishment he had felt jealous at seeing Caroline in the arms of a man—any other man. And in that second she suddenly felt she hated him. There he was, leaning against the door jamb with that mocking, smiling air! Hate him? She loathed him. Was it not his horrible editorial which had begun the whole terrible thing? But now he was going on:

"I think the party is breaking up. Nobody seems calm enough after Caroline's speech to settle on how they will get a safe seat for our now recumbent hero. You certainly did touch upon a fiery topic, Caroline, one that has Sir Ernest determined you will eat humble pie before him for his forgiveness, and that without delay. But do I hear footsteps of the paterfamilias?"

"Oh!" said Caroline. "Uncle will see that I didn't go to my room; that I disobeyed him!"

"May I suggest the back stairs, then?" asked Edmund Browne in his horribly amused way, rather as though Caroline were a little girl and of little consequence. He continued to lean on the jamb of the conservatory door in leisurely fashion. What a really odious man he had become! Nevertheless she took his suggestion and used the small door at the back of the conservatory, which she knew led to a narrow corridor and then to the back staircase which the servants used to get to their own quarters and to the family's bedrooms. Reaching her own bedroom in this way, Caroline shut the door behind her. For a moment or two she leant against the heavy wood of that door and tried to get her breath and find her wits. Then she opened her door a crack. She could hear her uncle's voice in the hall as he saw off the de Lisle Devonshires, and the bustle of getting on greatcoats and wrappings in the big front hall, and the jingle of the horses' harness as the large front door was opened to find that the Devonshire's carriage had already been brought around. Now she could hear the smart trot of the horses as they wheeled around the curving driveway, now the bang of the great front door and, once, it was securely closed against his being overheard, she heard the angry voice of her uncle in full tirade, against the bleats of her Aunt Millie, begging him to be considerate. Caroline's heart banged painfully as she heard her uncle's feet mount the front stairs. She heard him say to her aunt, whose cries intermingled pleadingly with his furious words, "No, I *won't* listen."

Mr. George McLeod Hamilton felt justifiably infuriated. He had managed this young woman's money very well, never losing a penny of it, indeed greatly adding to it, and applying the income to her upkeep. He had kept books, and could prove it! Taking care of money was hard work—and this was how she thanked him! He knew that as a female she must be married, to be "placed" in life, and he had put up with two Seasons, enduring the company, in his Belgrave house and at his table, of all sorts of young whippersnappers; he had got rid of the spendthrifts who had courted Caroline merely to get her money, and spend it. He had singled out Robert de Lisle Devonshire himself. He had then hung on in London when the Season was an an end and it was getting uncomfortably hot, just to give Robert that extra little time he needed to have the courage to come to him, George Hamilton, for permission to propose to Caroline.

Of course he had hinted to him of the money. That was the card to play when a young man seemed interested, but hung back. If Caroline had remained a spinster, she would have had the money placed in trust for her, so that she could never waste the capital—the income would be ample to keep a female in great comfort. Even a man! Caroline had embarrassed him by thanking him for her dowry, but there seemed little point then in telling her the money was her own. It would be passed to her husband, and what did it matter that it was titularly hers? She was not entitled to handle it whilst her uncle was still her guardian, and it would become her husband's when she married. So why put her in a bother about it meanwhile? Sir Ernest had had little sense in bringing up the subject. It would so soon be Robert's duty to fuss and worry over the money. No female was fit to look after money, anyway. Undoubtedly Caroline would by then have replaced the burned banisters which upset her so, only to have them burned again by those ungrateful poor. Evil poor! Yes, evil. In Mr. Hamilton's mind, to be poor was to be evil. God gave to each his just deserts.

The sound of her uncle's hand on the door of her bedroom caused Caroline to retreat instinctively to her dressing-table. And there she clutched the back of a chair.

Her Uncle Hamilton advanced upon her, followed by her aunt, who begged: "Do not be harsh with her. She is like your own daughter—my baby!"

But Mr. Hamilton ignored his wife's pleas. His bulk towered above Caroline. She felt physically threatened. Rage was in her uncle's face. He felt he had been humiliated at a time when, having aristocracy at his table at last, he should have been proud and elated. Aristocracy that was nearly kin to him, too, but for this stupid girl. This little chit was risking his scheme to raise himself—and even herself—in the social scale. By dint of terribly hard work and endless scheming, he had achieved riches. But he wanted to lose the label of "tradesman."

The girl was strong-willed. That was all right in a man, but in a woman—no, it was unbearable. "She needs a good whipping, that's what! A really good whipping!" he thought.

Mrs. Hamilton, who had been letting out little wails of anguish, was cut short by a contemptuous snort from Mr. Hamilton. He fought for breath, for control. Caroline, looking at his face mottled with anger, found she was trembling.

"Well, what have you got to say for yourself?" he demanded.

Caroline gripping the back of the chair so that her fingers hurt, said: "What I've said before. That I don't understand why you did not tell me that I had money. You always treated me as if I had none, as though I were a burden to you. All through the Seasons I have suffered—"

"*You* have money! What would the knowledge of it have meant to you? You would have spent it. I have looked after your money and your property, and little thanks do I get for it!"

"You should have told me," Caroline answered doggedly.

"Why should I?" he asked. What would *you*, a slip of a girl, have done? Spent the money and mismanaged the property."

"Mismanage? I wouldn't own to a building with the banisters gone—"

"Oh, wouldn't you?" he said contemptuously. "I suppose you would have replaced them so that the lodgers could chop them up again. Half of your lodgers don't pay their rent until I get after them, and few ever pay on time."

"But why should they if the place is in need of repair?" Caroline stood her ground.

"Repair! Repair! It's all I hear. Well, it's now your property, Miss, and we'll see how much repair Robert puts into them."

"He shall put them all into good order—"

"And if he doesn't, Miss?"

"Then I shall. It's dishonest—"

"Dishonest? Are you now telling me I'm dishonent—" Mr. Hamilton struggled for breath, in the kind of silence that comes after lightning and before the clap of thunder.

Indignation flooded Caroline's heart again. Was is not dishonest not to have told her she had means? So she said: "Aren't you?"

The next thing that happened was that one of Mr. Hamilton's big hands reached out, and Caroline tasted her own blood as one of her teeth cut the inside of her cheek.

Her uncle had struck her, and hard. It was not the first time he had done it, and she realised it would not be the last. When Uncle Hamilton lost his temper, he struck out; she had seen Aunt Millie trying to hid bruises from the servants with lies about knocking into doors. She herself had known what it was to be forced to pretend she had hurt herself, fallen when skating on a nearby pond. She did not want to go on like that. But she was frightened of him. Nonetheless, this time she stood her ground.

"Apologise!" Mr. Hamilton was demanding. "Apologise!"

Caroline put a shaky hand up to her bloodied mouth.

"I ca—can't, she said. "I have said nothing wrong. I can't apologise."

"Then you shall stay in your room until you do!" Mr. Hamilton yelled. A vien stood out upon his forehead, a big, purple rope. "I have had enough of her impudence." Mr. Hamilton added, turning on his wife. "She's a bad, ungrateful girl."

"Caroline!" begged Mrs. Hamilton. "We've taken care of you all these years!"

"I know," Caroline answered. "It's not easy now for me. I *am* grateful. But why didn't he tell me—I've often felt like a burden—"

"You have been a burden," said Mr. Hamilton. "A strong-minded self-willed, unwomanly—"

"Oh, please, don't say that," said Mrs. Hamilton. "You don't mean it, George."

"I do! I do!" exclaimed Mr. Hamilton. "And she must apologise not only to me, but also to Sir Ernest. 'Neither conscience nor heart,' she said. You don't leave this room until you make abject apoligies, Miss. You can stay here on bread and water; *I'll* break that obstinate will of yours!" Caroline had heard all this before, and had been through such scenes before, but this time he added something new: "And if you don't like it, you can leave—get out from under my roof, lock, stock and barrel!"

He turned abruptly and strode towards the door, pushed his wife out before him and shut the door with a bang. Caroline could hear the key turning in the lock and then his heavy feet retreating, and his voice savage now with complaint, his low growl interrupted by little yelps from his wife. Then all was silent. He would be sorry later, and would make it up to her with some small attentions, some permission granted, such as skating. But what would be the use of that?

Caroline was alone. She could still feel the imprint of her uncle's hand on her cheek, and as the house grew quiet for the night, she realised that now, indeed, unless she came out with an abject apology, she was alone in life. Except for Robert. But Robert had not stood by her in the drawing-room; would he, learning of all this, stand by her now? Doubt of his love for her came to her again. When had he heard about her money? Had he known all the time? Had he waltzed with her, gone driving with her in the park, danced attendance on her, and, finally, proposed to her, all because of the money? She was not such a fool as not to know that the fact that she had money of her own added to her charms. But was that the *only* reason he had been interested in her? She writhed with hatred at the idea. The Season did mean that you were husband-hunting, but there was also meant to be love. Supposing there were not? Robert had proposed to her at the last moment, just before everybody who was anybody left Town. Did this mean that he had not proposed until Uncle Hamilton had baited the hook cleverly with mention of her fortune? Did she love Robert—or was it just dread of not being asked, of facing a third Season, or of being an old maid which had prompted her to accept him?

But there *was* her fortune. And she had turned twenty-one. She was entitled to have her fortune put in her own hands, at least whilst she was still unmarried.

She must do something. She could not stay in this room for days, or maybe weeks, living on bread and water until her will was broken and she gave in once again. She had gone through this so often—Uncle Hamilton's will against hers. But the trouble was that Aunt Millie would be red-eyed with tears until Caroline gave in. And so far, Caroline had always given in. Her uncle had always been so certain of his victory! Well, this time he was going to be mistaken.

She slipped off Robert's ring now, and held it in her hands. That ring represented security in Society and she must suppose it represented affection. Certainly it represented position, an enviable position as the future Lady de Lisle Devonshire. Robert was ambitious, too. Was she going to give all that up because she had quarrelled with her uncle? But, "Apologise!"—Uncle Hamilton's words came back to her. No. She could not apologise. "Then you can get out from under my roof!" was what he had said.

Caroline needed time to think, and time to be alone. Time perhaps to talk it over with—who else, Robert. Time to get to know him. Time in which he should know her. She did not want the hurried marriage which they all wanted without even consulting her.

She was being treated like a child, punished like a child. All right. He had said: "Get out from under my roof!" He had never dared to think she would. But why shouldn't she? To leave would take an awful lot of courage, but to stay would mean giving in to her uncle. She had money, or would have money when she demanded it.

She was grateful to Uncle Ham for having given her a home, but she should *not* have been made to feel grateful also for the money she was supposed to have cost him. She had cost him nothing!

Aunt Millie must have known about her money, but had not dared speak. Aunt Millie had no say at all. Caroline knew her aunt spent many a wretched hour chasing small sums through those household accounts which Uncle Hamilton watched with such a hard eye.

Caroline was twenty-one. She would get out from under George Hamilton's roof. It would be painful, hard and difficult, but she would do it!

Caroline had been pacing the room up and down, up and down whilst she thought. Now she stopped at her writing-table and wrote two little notes: one to Mrs. Hamilton, which she left with a kiss on her own bed (poor Aunt Millie would spend most of the night awake in her bed beside her husband staring into darkness and praying for God's help, whilst her husband slept, secure in his own certainty that everything *he* did and said must be right and good for the women under his control); and the other for Elizabeth Stroud. It simply said: "Dear Miss Stroud, Please go on with my trousseau. Payment will be arranged by myself. Truly yours, Caroline H."

For now Caroline knew what she would do. She would go to Aunt Lucinda's little house in London in the morning. Aunt Luci had always been kind and understanding. She was much more modern in her views than Aunt Millie and Uncle Ham. Aunt Lucinda would know that Caroline had to have time to understand Robert, and to find out how much she cared for him. To find out, in fact, if she cared enough for him to give her whole life into his keeping.

The ring Caroline now held in her hand was the kind of priceless ring a woman travelling alone did not wear unless she wished to attract thieves. So now she took a white thread and a needle, found one of her white petticoats with a little pocket at the knee, put the ring into that pocket and firmly stitched it up. The ring would be quite safe like that. Then, as the household settled into slumber, Caroline quietly got out of her crinoline gown with its torn flounce and put on the white petticoat, with a travelling dress of a grey-blue wool which had a much smaller hoop. Then she packed a few necessities in a small basket. She added the little pistol Edmund had given her, not quite sure why she included it, but feeling that she needed something to take care of her.

The moon was up, a silvery wafer, and leaning out of her window, Caroline threw the dress basket so that it landed in the shrubbery. Then, following the tomboy habit of her early years, she slipped out of her bedroom window and down by the old tree.

She had but twenty guineas of her own to use—twenty guineas saved up from the pin money allowance Mr. Hamilton had grudgingly made her each year, and now her total wealth in the world until she had her fortune put into her hands. This sum resided in a gold chain purse with a sapphire clasp. She held it in her hands, determined that no one would see it, or be able to take it from her.

Before she turned her back to it, she looked up at the great red brick house. It looked shut away from her. Its windows were all shuttered—that is, all but hers; and the great door was locked and barred. She shivered. Where did a solitary girl, running away from home and with no friends nearby, spend her first night on her own? Not a creature stirred. It was as if Caroline, standing there in the shadow of the shrubbery, were alone in a world totally empty of life. The wind rose threateningly. There was the sudden spatter of heavy drops of rain. Far off in a tree an owl hooted. Again Caroline shivered. She was not cold; she was full of fear.

Chapter 7

As she moved across the lawn, keeping to the shadows, she glanced back once at the pile of red brick which had been her home. *Had* been?

She thought of growing up there, the pains and yet the joys, for there had been joys. And her heart smote her at the thought of Aung Millie waking, probably from an almost sleepless night of muffled weeping, to find her niece gone. Sentiment arrested Caroline's feet for a moment, and then with a resolute shake of her head, she moved on. She must get away from Uncle Hamilton, from the pressure he would bring to bear, a pressure signally able to make her feel guilty and then to make her give in. She was borne up by the thought of how he had made her feel beholden to him throughout her life when actually her father's money had paid her way all the time. At the back of her mind was a recognition that Uncle Ham, with all his grudging ways, had shared his home with her, when the last thing he had probably wanted was to be bothered with a female child. But she suppressed thoughts of any generosity in him now because she needed her anger, her rage against him, to carry her on.

How vast and high was the dome of the night sky, star-spangled though it was. She reached the big gates of The Grange and stumbled through. The black road stretched before her. Her little feet felt its hard stones through her thin shoes. She clutched the small dress basket and the chain purse tightly. That money would have to last her until she could get some of her own. And she had no ideas what her rights were in that, or how long it would take before she could touch her inheritance. The pocket in her petticoat which held the heavy ring with its glory of stones banged against her knee, a constant reminder that Robert offered her a safe, secure life. If only she knew him a little better! She meant to ask him to come and see her at Aunt Lucinda's. Surely if she talked to him she would begin to know him and he her. If they were to spend a life together they must begin by knowing each other better than they did. She had been hurt that he had not stood up to her uncle in her defence tonight, though she guessed why he had not. She realised that he still stood in subjection to his parents, and more particularly to his dominating mother. But she could not live in subjection to them, too. On the other hand she had offended him by putting herself in a compromising situation with Harry de Lisle, a situation which had ended horribly with Harry punching his cousin and the fall which would be particularly hard for Robert, with all his pride, to accept. She imagined him coming to consciousness on the floor of the conservatory. How angry he must have been to find that he had struck his head and fallen ignominiously in front of her and of Harry. Decidedly she owed Robert an apology, and perhaps if she were sufficiently gracious in making that when she saw him at Aunt Luci's, *then* he would be able to talk with her about their future lives together.

The wind started up, in little gentle gusts to begin with,

hardly fluttering the leaves of the high hedges, and then in greater sighs and sweeps of sound so that suddenly branches and even frailer saplings were bending in its fierce thrusts. She leant forward into the rising storm, her small mouth set in determination. Whether she liked it or not, her mind told her, the world was huge and empty of welcome for unmarried, unattended girls. If she could see a life with Robert it would be the best thing for her. A sudden gust of wind hurled grit from the road and the grit hit her eyes and cheeks. For a moment she wished to return to her safe room. It was not too late. And then she straightened her shoulders and tried to reason with herself. She was frightened because she could hardly remember being out, even by day, unaccompanied. She began to remember the murder of a young woman, the details of which had been splashed across *The Wiltshire Gazette*, a young governess whose horribly mulilated body had lain for three days and nights in the falling rain.

The boughs of the trees creaked and swayed in the wind and cast eerie shadows. The wind was getting worse and the noise of leaves being torn along the dusty gullies of the road terrified the girl. She was alone in a midnight world, empty of everything but herself, the soughing branches of trees, the indifferent, cold moon and the rising, threatening wind, which howled ever louder with each passing minute. She trembled at every shadow, shied away at every looming tree, and at times her heart beat so loudly she felt ill with fear. The far-off moon lit the scene, a pale, watery globe, veiled in cloudy wreaths, distant, cold, so far from giving human comfort as a thin wafer is far from stilling the hunger that cries for help. She must manage alone. She bent her girl's body against that violent wind, walking forward into it with that resolution which was a part of her and which so often forced her forward in life when it might have been more prudent to hold back. "Oh God!" she prayed, "help and protect me! O dear God!" But no voice in her heart or mind comforted her. Her fear persisted, a choke in her throat, making her mouth dry.

She thought of her comfortable, safe, four-poster bed,

her flannel nightgown, the security of the little night light burning steadily if she wished on the night table beside her bed. Then she remembered the locked door, her uncle's towering rage, felt again her lip now swollen where it had been cut. Courage, a little courage, and her uncle would realise she meant to manage her own life, not merely to accept the life he chose for her. She had money of her own. It made all the difference. Money, the key to at least some freedom!

Was it going to rain? As though her question had brought it into being, there was a sudden spatter of huge drops of rain, and they a downpour, getting rapidly worse as though the skies had opened to deluge her alone. Caroline realised quickly that nothing she wore was suitable for wet weather. But what could she do but press on? If she could manage to get to the tiny country railway station, there would be a coal fire in the waiting room. She would wait there and dry herself off and then take the first train that ran to London in the morning.

But the rain grew heaver, coming now in great sheets of water. Caroline realised that even her shoes were squelching with wet. Her coat had suddenly become paper-thin, and her clothing clung to her, so much thin fabric easily soaked.

The moon, still well above the rain clouds, continued to light the road through the grey downpour, and for this Caroline was glad. But where the moonlight did not directly fall, beneath the overbending high hedgerows, the blackness of the night held menace. Peering a little fearfully into the shadows, she suddenly started back and froze. Before her appeared on the road a shadowy, cloaked figure of a man, and then, too, she heard the panting of a great dog. Who was it? But whoever it was, the figure came closer. Fumbling in her reticule, Caroline found her pistol. It was meant for just such a moment as this.

But she hesitated to shoot blindly. Who could it be? Caroline's heart was now beating in great leaps and bounds of fright. All sorts of people who had made money rapidly in the busily expanding economy were buying up the houses with their new-found wealth. With them came furtive hangers-on, thieves, murderers who liked the easy pickings of the country towns. These people had begun to infest the country roads, too. Only a few days ago her uncle had observed that there were footpads about at night. He had been telling her that there was no question of her being allowed to go for country walks alone. She must have a man-servant with her, and as he could not spare one from the house for such a silly pastime, there would be no walks.

Whilst she aimed her pistol, trying to make out in the rain and gloom of night something of the person approaching, Caroline could now hear the slavering of the huge dog as he panted and pulled against the chains and straps his owner held him by. They the dog was suddenly upon her, his great claws tearing at her shoulders; she could feel his breath upon her face. She was knocked to her knees with his weight and fell into the roadside ditch, the big dog atop her. Then a man's voice called firmly: "Down, Hamish! Down!" Caroline was vaguely aware that she knew that voice, and they she fainted. When she came to, her head was resting on the man's knee. His hand held her pistol.

"It's all right, Caroline!" a masculine voice was saying. "It's Edmund Browne. Hamish won't hurt you!"

Her eyes opened wide and she looked up into a handsome face, a concerned face. "Edmund!" she moaned. "Oh no! Not you!" And she struggled to her feet.

"Not so fast, Caroline. You just fainted. And you're soaking wet. Let's move closer under the dry of the hedge. That's better. What has happened to cut your mouth? And what are you doing at this time of night upon the road, and alone?"

"What are *you* doing here?" she countered.

"I'm walking my dog."

"That awful brute!" She cowered away from the mastiff, who had begun to sniff her clothing out of curiosity.

Edmund Browne laughed, showing even, white teeth. "He's not a brute, Caroline. He's just affectionate. And the best protection against night prowlers. He undoubtedly thought you a footpad, and so did I! See, he's sniffing you now just to get to know you. He's an Irish wolf-hound: he looks formidable, but he really thinks of him-self as a lapdog."

"Well—" she put out a small hand and gingerly petted the dog. Hamish's tail promptly began to wag with pleasure.

Edmund had been shocked to see Caroline lying there in the ditch; shocked and puzzled. What could have hap-pened to bring about such a thing? But now the most necessary matter was to bring her where she could be dry. "You haven't answered my question, Caroline?"

Still she did not answer him.

So he said again: "Where are you going, and at this time of night?"

"I've left home," she said low.

"Left home? Caroline, why?"

"You saw the way my uncle spoke to me in the drawing-room. He came upstairs afterwards to my room and threatened me. I was to apologise humbly or get out. I got out!"

"And your lip?"

"It's not the first time he has hit me. He has these tow-ering ranges. But I am no longer a child to be locked in my room on bread and water, locked in until I finally give in and apologise. Not this time!"

"It's happened before?"

"Oh, yes. And it seems the older I get, the more often Uncle seems to think I need punishment. He treats me like a foolish child, a child in need of correction." Her voice was angry.

"But where can you go?"

"To Aunt Lucinda's. She's leaving for London with Cousin Sophia in the morning. I want to be on the first train in the morning and go to her house to be there when she arrives. I'm sure she'll take me in."

"But Caroline, where will you spend the night?"

"In the station. I thought it all out. There's a fire in the waiting room. And it will be empty of people at this hour."

"But this is impossible! Caroline, you can't run away like this! And, anyway, the waiting room at the railway station will be locked up until tomorrow morning."

"You'd sooner I were home and ready to be chastised again? I'm not going back! I'll find somewhere to spend the night!"

"But Caroline, I must take you home."

"Then you'll have to carry me there! And be responsible for what happens when Uncle Hamilton finds I disobeyed again!"

"Surely you exaggerate."

"I didn't cut my own lip." she reminded him.

There was a silence. Then Edmund said:

"Why don't you go to your fiancé's home, then? Why don't you go to Robert's mother?"

"Because his father is someone I'm to apologise to, also. And he would return me at once to my uncle. And then you can't imagine the beating about my room I would get!" Edmund was silent. He knew that women were often struck by angry men in a family. He was not shocked, for a beating was considered by many husbands and fathers necessary to teach a recalcitrant woman good sense. But he could not bear to think of Caroline being treated like that. For all her spirit she was anything but formidable. He felt sick at the thought of her small frame under the impact of blows. Perhaps if he saw Mr. Hamilton it might be possible to draw his rage upon himself in some way and maybe get Caroline out of a tight corner? He didn't know exactly what he meant, but something could surely be done to help her. Anyway, she could not spend the night under a hedge!

"What about Mrs. Erskine, then?" he tried. "She seems very fond of you."

"I thought of her. But I can't go to her. She lives in London, you know. But down here she is, herself, staying with friends. I can't impose myself upon her there."

"Well, we can't stay here talking in the rain. You'll get pneumonia in those wet clothes. And so will I. It's raining much more than when I left my inn. You'll have to come to the Fox and Hounds where I'm staying the night and,

83

at least, get dried out. Come on Caroline, we'll work out something there."

She protested. She did not want to go. He wished to be masterful with her, as he was used to being with both men and women, but something about her produced in him a feeling of the impossibility of mastering her. And this in turn both left him uncertain and then made him brusque. She was tired, and wet and cold. "Come along," he said again, in a much less gentle tone than he would have used if she had been any ordinary girl. "Come along! I'm getting more and more wet, even if you don't think *you* are!" And he pulled her to her feet with a show of force. In a flash he understood her uncle wanting to slap her. But then Edmund pulled his cloak from his shoulders and, despite her protest, wrapped it around her. He found himself both enchanted and irritated by the very fragility of her form as he enveloped her. She was at once so feminine and yet so unlike the rest of her sex. So uncomplaisant.

In silence they walked the quarter mile to the inn, Hamish's throaty coughs as he strained against his dog collar and against the firm hand which held his lead, the only sound between them.

When they got to the Fox and Hounds the landlord was closing up for the night, it being now long after midnight. He was astonished to see Edmund with a girl. He stared at her bedraggled appearance.

" 'As there been an accident or somethink?" he asked, all jowls and eyes.

"No," said Edmund. "The young lady got caught in the rain and was sheltering under a hedge. I'm afraid my wolfhound, Hamish here, frightened her. I think a little hot, buttered rum, landlord. And then if you have a pony and gig?"

"A pony and gig? At this time o'night, sir? Lord love you, sir, I don't know anyone as 'asn't put up cart and beast by now on a night like this. It'll blow into a storm, I'm thinking, much worse than we 'ear now. I could manage something for you in the morning."

"But you have to get me something. I must see this young lady to her home."

"Sorry, sir, I'd be willing to get you anything I could. But this ain't Lunnon, sir. This 'ere is the country. You can't find anyone up at this hour. She'd best stay 'ere until morning. I'll just stir up the fire so the young lady can warm 'erself a bit, and then quick with the 'ot buttered rum." The landlord had poked the fading fire to a blaze with the addition of small nuggets of black, shiny coal and then a well-dried log. The red sparks flew up the wid chimney and Caroline shivered in the sudden warmth. She stretched blue hands towards the blaze and realized she was soaked through with the rain. Still she said, obstinately:

"I'm not going home. I'll spend the night anywhere but I will not go home."

The landlord brought the hot buttered rum.

Edmund looked worried. "What about a room for the young lady?" he said.

"Room, sir' No room either. Not a 'ole in the 'ouse that ain't taken. If you come from these parts you'd know we have the Wiltshire Fair tomorrer. Everyone and his Missus is 'ere in the inn that don't live locally."

"Haven't you got any kind of a shakedown that I could use?"

"No, sir, I 'ain't. Could you take a cold supper in your room, sir? You've got a nice fire there, and maybe that would get her dried out. The dog could do with a drying out too."

"I can't take your rooms," Caroline spoke for the first time. "And you can't sleep just anywhere. You told me at dinner what a hard day you are going to have tomorrow when you return to London."

"Well, you can't sit about the inn, either. Heavens knows *who* may wander down to these public rooms during the night! You need to get dry and get to bed somewhere. Why not come upstairs to my sitting room and see if we can make you a little less wet? When we've had a little supper you can tell me what you think."

As she climbed the stairway she realised that her teeth were actually chattering from the wet clothing.

"That's it?" said Edmund. "Out of those clothes! When I return you to your guardian in the morning. . . ."

"Return me?"

"What else can I do? But I will reason with him. A girl can't run around the countryside like this! Heaven knows whom you might have met with tonight? Lucky it was me."

"I am not going back."

They had reached his rooms.

"Look," he said, "Let's talk about that when you are out of these wet clothes. "Here." He tossed her a dressing gown, green fleece lined with blue silk. She was contemplating this when he opened the bedroom door and pulled her in by the arm. He threw a shirt of his on the four-poster bed. "I think that will fit you better than my sleeping things," he said. "Supper will be served out here in the sitting room. I'll knock on the door to tell you when it's ready."

His white silk shirt came to below her knees, the shoulders dripped off her shoulders on to her arms; she had to tuck up his sleeves by folding the cuffs back and back again. The frilled front of the shirt, with its touch of lace, became her, though the collar opening looked enormous around her slender throat with its slight bones.

"A little, young, wild thing," was how he thought of her, surveying her in his dressing gown. Her grey-green eyes, wide with anxiety, and her curly black hair looked marvelous against the green wool. One could catch a glimpse of the blue silk lining and her creamy-white skin looked so velvety against the combination of soft green and silky blue. What a voluminous robe the dressing gown was on her, and his bedroom slippers fell off at every step! Despite himself and the knowledge that she was feeling dreadfully self-conscious, Edmund laughed. She went a bright pink. "I suppose I look dreadful." she said.

"No," he said. "Dreadful would never have been the adjective I would use. What do you think, Hamish?" Edmund put his hand on the dog's shaggy head and the dog waved his large tail. "Ah, you agree with me, then. She looks adorable. Adorable."

The supper was served on a table with a white cloth before the big fire in the sitting room. The table was lit by candle light. Candles which threw a strange soft glow on both her hands and arms and on her delicate neck and showed the outline of her small chin. But her eyes, her forehead and the hair which looked so massed, pinned still over the heavy rats concealed in it, were just beyond the circle of light, almost in shadow. The drawn curtains, the wood fire, the vension pie with salad, the dark red velvet claret wine, the coarse brown bread, the yellow butter, the smell of the cheese and apples waiting by the table for their dessert, made the room intimate. Outside the wind soughed in the trees, the rain spattered on the closed window panes, the dark lay unfathomable, but inside there was warmth, even, at such a moment, a feeling of affection. Edmund looked so handsome. The damp rain had made his crisp hair even more crisply wavy. His deeply blue eyes, with the thick black lashes, regarded her with great kindness. Caro, lulled by the cosiness of the room, and by the good red claret she had taken with her meat, began to talk confidingly of her uncertainties with Robert, her doubts as to whether she loved him or not, or even how much he loved her. And then she stopped herself in the middle of all that confidence, remembering something: "But, I'd forgotten: you don't think the way women feel counts. You think we'd all be perfectly happy shipped off to the Colonies like criminals if we don't marry. When I was a child I thought you wonderful because of your idealism. . . ."

"And now?"

"Well, you're hardly an idealist now. You are prepared to write things now you don't really mean, to work for an editor who can speak of women as though they were merchandise. Do you know what it's like to feel you are merchandise?"

"I don't think of women as merchandise," he said. "But should we go into all that tonight?"

He felt his temper rising. He was tired and so he tried

hard to remain reasonable. She was not herself, either. She had been through a terrible evening and she was in his room, a situation she would never have chosen.

Gently he explained to her, hoping to make her feel less angry, "Editorials are not one man's opinion, you know. They are the opinion of the newspaper itself. I have to write what I'm told when I write an editorial. But whether you believe that or not, let's call it a truce for tonight. And let me add that I wish I could help you in your decisions about life. But you, and only you, can resolve whether you want to marry Devonshire or not."

"Then why do you want me to return to my uncle's, where I will be made to marry whether I want to or not? Uncle Ham is determined I shall do exactly as *he* likes!" Her grey eyes with the green flecks in them sparkled anew with anger.

"Because I can't help you to go against your legal guardian's wishes. He is your uncle and he has cared for you nearly all your life. He must know better than I—and maybe better than you do, what is best for you."

"My uncle! That man! Do you realise that he has duped me all my life? He brought me up as if I were a pauper! The times I've thanked him and the times he has accepted my thanks and left me feeling that everything was his, and everything I had was begrudged!"

"But surely, Caroline, it's a little beneath you to quarrel with your uncle because he has been parsimonious with you. I'm sure he was adding to your capital by his thought."

"And would have let me believe that that capital was *his* dowry for my marriage. He has accepted thanks for that, too. Do you know what it's like constantly to have to thank someone for everything and then to find out that you didn't owe any thanks?"

"But you do! He must have wanted you to take you into his home—"

"He doesn't want anyone! He always made me feel I was a cross to bear. Now Aunt Millie—" her voice softened. "Yes, Aunt Millie loved me, and loves me, but she is so scared of him. . . . When I have an establishment of my own I shall have her to stay with me."

"You mean, then, when you do marry Devonshire—"

"I don't know what I mean. But I shall have to live somewhere. And now I do have money I can afford a house even if I don't ever marry—"

"Oh, come, Caroline. You are too young to start living alone."

"If I were a man no one would consider me too young to live alone. I know women who do." She was thinking of Mrs. Erskine.

"Yes, Caroline, But they are either widows or elderly spinsters. And even they usually do not live alone. They have another woman to live with them. And most of them would be glad to have a man about the premises—"

"Nobody could be glad to have a man like Uncle Ham!"

"Now, Caroline, you are being harsh. You'll regret it. I'm sure when you know more. . . . You know, to understand all is—"

"—to forgive all! Well, I wonder how I can ever forgive him, and not just on account of me. Imagine his leaving poor tenants so miserably cold that they burnt up banisters for warmth—"

"I don't think they should have burnt the banisters."

"Oh, don't you! Well, I'm sure when Robert—*if* Robert—comes to be in charge of those buildings he will care for tenants and put everything into good repair."

"Don't be so certain of it. Like me, de Lisle Devonshire has probably come up against the practical side of things. You can't always do everything you'd like to do."

She was restless with this reply, but he continued doggedly: "If you replaced those banisters at once they would probably burn them up again."

"Oh you're just like Uncle Ham. He never can believe that poor people are just as human as we are. If you explain to them that you will supply firewood—"

"But it's no part of a landlord's business to supply firewood. Besides, giving people firewood might not be appreciated. Look how much you were enraged to think that your Uncle Ham gave you everything!"

"But he didn't give me anything! It was all my own. I was giving *him* thanks. You don't seem to realise that."

"Maybe he deserved thanks. He was handling your money, I'm sure, cautiously and I'm certain had a lot of labour turning it over professionally and well."

"You're on his side!"

"No, I'm not. But I do know the world a little better than you do. You don't know the circumstances of the banisters—"

"I shall! Since the premises are mine and I'm now twenty-one, I'm going to look into everything."

"Capital! Good! Good! And when you do I'd be interested to see what action you take about it. Things which look simple, like charity (as you seem to know), are not always so simple."

"Now you're muddling me all up You make me feel that you have no charity towards others, towards the poor, and no principles either. When I think of that article on exporting women. . . . The Edmund I knew as a child would never have written such a dastardly thing. . . ."

"I'm paid to write—I am not paid to make the policy of *The Times*."

Suddenly she felt tearful and said out of the blue, out of the tension of the last hours, out of her own tiredness:

"Why are you being so horrible to me?"

"I'm not being horrible," he replied firmly. "I'm being reasonable." How like a woman, he thought, to take cold reasoned argument as "horrible." "You seem to me to be talking like a childish romantic!"

"Childish! Romantic! Oh!"

"Not like an adult person," he said.

"Oh" she cried again. "Oh!"

They sat and glared at each other. He recovered himself more quickly than she did. "She knows nothing of the world," he thought. "I shouldn't blame her—it's one of her charms that she imagines everything can be fair, or, if not fair, put right. She'll learn it isn't always so." He began to smile at her. "Look," he said out loud, "we'll talk of this later. As I suggested before, let's call truce tonight." His blue eyes were soft and kind again, and she felt that maybe she had been harsh. She was tired.

"Now," he said briskly. "You should get to bed—it's late. Even for me, it's late. Meanwhile I'd advise you to get a lawyer. I'm sure your uncle will not keep the money from you if he knows you are determined. But you will need a lawyer to help you get it. If you want a good man, there's a Mr. Joachim connected with *The Times*. You'll find him at the Inns of Court."

He moved back her chair for her and she rose awkwardly, pulling the folds of his dressing gown around her. She shuffled in what seemed to her his great shoes over to the connecting door to the bedroom and there turned to say goodnight to him, proffering him her hand in thanks. He took the small hand in his big one.

The landlord had come in to remove the table. They had forgotten him. He took in the little tableau they made.

"Well, good night, sir, and madam," he said, and added with a slight wink at Edmund, "A very good night to you, sir."

"There's nothing like that," said Edmund angrily. "I met the young lady on the road."

"Oh, yes, *sir*," he answered. This time there was no denying his wink. "Well, I hope it all turns out right," he said, and with that he moved the last of the supper things out of the room. As he leaned in to take the door handle and close the door, he was grinning hugely.

"There!" she said. "You see, the landlord thinks it's wrong for me to be up here with you."

"Nonsense," said Edmund. "The landlord merely needs a good drubbing to teach him his manners." He felt furious, but there was nothing he could very well do about it then.

She was saying, "No, I can't stay here tonight. I would be compromised."

"If you don't stay here, you will be dead. You forget the storm. I'd insist on your going home, but we can't find any conveyance so late at night and in this rain. Now let's both try and behave sensibly. I'll settle with the landlord in the morning. He'll say nothing of your visit here: he won't dare! I shall ask your uncle to come here and get you in the morning and to thank me, in the landlord's presence, for my insistence that you stay the night. That will stop any gossip the landlord has in mind."

Caroline smiled. But she was not going to *be* there in the morning!

"Well, at least the landlord got up a good blaze in your bedroom whilst we supped," he said. "If I were you, I'd spread out all the wet clothes to dry in front of it. I'm sure everything is soaked. That's why I loaned you my things."

"And what will you do?"

"Make myself very comfortable on the couch outside on the sitting room here; don't worry about me," he told her. He closed the door.

Caroline had hardly got into the great four-poster, with its enormous feather pillows and feather mattress, clutching his shirt about her, when there was a knock on the communicating door and Edmund came in.

She retreated on her pillows. "What are you doing here?" she asked. He came towards the very side of the bed and reached out and pulled something towards him. "A pillow, if you don't mind," he said, "and a few other things." He picked up a small dressing-case, took a folded rug off the ottoman, and turned to say good-night.

How tiny she looked in his big bed! How young! He stopped at the foot of the four-poster and looked at her. An immense tenderness arose in him. How could they think of marrying this infant to de Lisle Devonshire—that handsome, spoiled, bullying lout! She put a brave face on it, but she did need taking care of. She needed it? Well, not precisely she. A self-truth came uppermost in his mind, as self-truths will come unbidden and at the oddest moments. It was a need with him to make her safe. That was it! He wanted to be the one to make her safe. "My little feminist!" he murmured now. He could feel her getting tense at the note of affection in his voice, tense and frightened. She shoved up against her pillows harder and said in a voice she wanted to make firm:

"I'm not a feminist particularly. I just want to be free. Please go away!"

For the life of him he couldn't help but laugh. She looked so deliciously small. But: "I'm going," was all he said.

Before he left, he reached forward to where Caroline's small feet stuck up in the coverlet of the bed, and squeezed her toes with his hand. "Sleep tight!" he said with a boyish smile. And he was gone. There it was, that maddening charm of his. But he *had* written that editorial. He thought her feminist because she wanted to live her own life! He was glib with his explanations now, but she could not forget the words of that editorial, words he had written and then read aloud. She could not trust him.

Caroline slid out of bed, softly padded over the carpet and locked and bolted the door between the rooms. She then spread her clothes before the big fire, and now she timed her inward clock to make herself wake up around 5 a.m. She noticed with relief that her room not only gave upon the sitting room but also had a door leading into the inn corridor. She could leave and Edmund would not know when she went.

What a strange day it had been! To have re-encountered Edmund Browne. To have been sentimental with him, and then to have discovered who wrote those horrible editorials her uncle loved so much, taking a slap at women, editorials written quite frequently of late. To have Edmund be so very odious when Harry was being so kind, and now to be in this embarrassing situation with him, she curled up in Edmund Browne's bed, wearing his shirt, his dressing gown. If anyone ever knew that she was in his room, in his very bed, her reputation would be ruined for life.

Edmund stood for a long time outside the bedroom door. He did not know what was happening to women, or to some of them. Something was definitely happening. Like Caroline, some of them had got ideas in their heads about their own lives. And men like John Stuart Mill, whom Edmund respected, stood up for them. Things were changing. He did not know if it would be for the better or worse. But maybe better. After all, he himself had no desire to marry a stupid wife, a woman such as the Berliners described to him when they said a woman's total interest should be *"Kinder, Kirche, Küché."* Children, church, home. Edmund felt that when he married, he'd like a wife to match him: a woman with a will of her own. Not too much will perhaps, but enough to challenge him. Now Caroline was not showing will, but merely the petulance of a spoiled child. He hoped she would learn from experience and not suffer too much in getting that experience. But whether she liked it or not, he was taking her back to her uncle in the morning. He could not be responsible in any way for his one-time pupil running off from home.

Sighing a little, he grasped the pillow and the rug and thought about where he would sleep. In his ears came the gentle turning of the key in the lock of the bedroom door.

"Silly girl!" he grinned to himself. There was a second door from the inn corridor straight to the bedroom. He grinned to himself, threw up the pillow boyishly and caught it, and then made the decision where he would sleep for the night.

Chapter 8

In the morning Caroline woke whilst it was still dark. Her little watch told her that it was not yet five o'clock. She stole to the door leading into the sitting room and listened. Not a sound. She dressed stealthily. Her clothing was quite dry. She re-packed the dress basket. Then finding paper and a quill pen on a writing table, she wrote:

My dear Edmund:

As I told you, I am not going home. I have thought it over carefully and I must go to London for a while. I enclose a note for my uncle which I beg you to have delivered. I don't want Aunt Millie to worry. I will get into touch with you if only to express my thanks for your kindness.

Please do not tell Uncle Hamilton I spent the night here. He would never understand. By the time I see him again I will have thought of something—if I am asked.

Again, my thanks,

Caroline

Opening the door to the corridor, Caroline, quiet as any mouse, went downstairs. Grey veils of the half light of another day's disclosed the entrance hall of last evening, an entrance hall which was quite deserted, she believed. And then she started. Curled up most uncomfortably in a big armchair was Edmund, the pillow and rug about him. He must have spent a wretched night, for he was still dressed, and the fire had long gone out so that the big room was chilly. Lying on the far side of his chair was Hamish, snoring horribly. She was touched by his thought for her reputation and could not help stealing up a little closer to look at him asleep. He stirred a little and the big dog made sounds in his throat, as though he were on some chase or hunt and was re-living it in dreams. Caroline froze. How boyish he looked asleep, how thick was the brown, crisp, curled hair, but if those dark blue eyes of his opened! What could she say for herself then? Or the dog might stir. She stole to the door hardly breathing. The heavy bolts had been well-oiled and the big door opened almost soundlessly. She held it only wide enough to let herself and her dress basket through and then she pulled it softly to behind her.

She saw nothing and no one on her way to the station, unless you could consider a wild grey cat, with half his tail missing, someone.

There was a train for London in the station. "You won't want it Miss," said the solitary young porter, a new man, for he did not recognise her as Miss Hamilton. "It's what we calls a milk train. Stops every place. You'd make it faster on the 8.05 in about two hours. It'll get you to London before this 'un!"

But it was a train for London and it was in the station already. That was all that mattered to Caroline. This milk train would take her safely away from her uncle and even from Edmund who might wake and, finding her gone, come after her to make her go back to her uncle's with him. Caroline smiled at the porter and shook her head when he offered her the waiting room which he had just unlocked. With determination she got into the train.

Caroline had bought a third class ticket. If there was a first class carriage on the milk train Caroline did not even look for it. Her twenty guineas was a great deal of pin money, but her commonsense told her that, inexperienced as she was in fending for herself, indeed in paying for anything, she could easily get through twenty guineas before she would be able to touch any of the money that was hers. And she did not know how to work. She could not earn a single penny, for she had no notion how anyone could, let alone a girl. "Fingers run through money," her uncle liked to say, and quite probably, he was right about that.

All the time the heavy ring in her petticoat skirt pocket reminded her of her engagmeent and her dreadful uncertainty of the wisdom of such a marriage. The heavy gold, encrusted as it was with the beautiful stones, hit her knee whenever she moved, so she did not have to think of Robert to be reminded sharply of her promise to him. That promise, given him on the wondrous staircase at that fabulous Season's ball, seemed to have been given a long time ago now, but actually it had been only a few weeks. The ring not only hit her knee, in some way it also hit her heart. She was an honest girl, and if she did not intend to become Robert's bride she must release him from his promise quickly and return his ring to him. But what alternative was there to marrying Robert? Having some money of her own was not the complete answer. She wanted to be married. She wanted to be a wife. To have a husband and a home. But she had to come to terms with herself on the question of love. Aunt Millie had told her that few brides began by being in love with their bridegrooms. That came later, came with marriage, with the years. Or if not love, at least an understanding, so that one was resigned to the married state.

As she sat on the narrow, dun-grained, varnished seat of the none too clean third class carriage, she could not help but remember the times she had been to London with her aunt and uncle in all the elegance of first class. That had not been so very many weeks past, but already she felt different. She supposed this was because she was actually travelling on her own. And the wheels of the train said endlessly over and over: "Run-away; run-away; run-away. You're a fool, a fool, a fool—" She put her hands over her ears, but how to shut out one's thoughts? She imagined her poor aunt presently finding her room empty, the bed not slept in, and the little note Caroline had left her. She imagined her tears and was swept with a pang of love for her. Her aunt would be anguished and in his haughty, autocratic way even her uncle would be anxious. But it would be easier to forget her uncle's reaction to her going away, for Caroline was up-borne, when she thought of that man, on a wave of anger against his treatment of her. She felt it horrible that he had allowed her to feel herself so poor, when she could have been happy in the knowledge that her parents had provided for her upbringing. Thinking of all the times she had thanked Uncle Hamilton for his generosity strengthened her in her resolve to make him realise that she was going to take time to talk things over with Robert, and to know what she was doing, so that if she married Robert the marriage would be of her own choice.

Of Robert himself she could not think. She felt too confused by the onrush of recent events. Why, only this time yesterday she had been safe in her own comfortable bedroom, sipping her hot chocolate and with nothing more on her mind than a little wonderment about her mind's unconscious attitude to her splendid engagement ring.

Presently, as the dark quite faded before the light of the new day, the train's rhythm affected her and though she tried by sitting bolt upright to resist fatigue, she must have fallen asleep. Suddenly in the carriage she jerked awake. A dreadful thought had come to her. Supposing Uncle Ham heard from Edmund Browne, found out at the station that she had taken this milk train, and then took the fast train, the same train as Aunt Luci had planned which arrived before the one she was on? He could be waiting for her on the station in London! It was a crazy idea, but it set her heart to hammering, and fear roused itself again. A scene on the platform would be horrible. He was much stronger than she was. The only thing she could do would be to give in to him.

Oh, surely her imagination was exaggerating? He would never pack his bag all in a minute like that, and have his affairs straightened out, and leave Aunt Millie so quickly, too. No, he was too methodical a person. A deliberate man, yet the thought of his being on the station was enough to stop her sleeping again. She remained wide-eyes with worry until the train slewed into Paddington Station and a porter unceremoniously opened her carriage door, leaned in to yell: "Everybody out! London!" and left the carriage door opened to the platform.

She looked quickly around the crowd for Uncle Ham. No, he was not to be seen. She sighed with relief, only to imagine him waiting at Aunt Lucinda's. Now she was becoming ridiculous! He was never the man to quit the station when the train with his quarry on it would be in a minute or two after his. No, if he were there at the station in London he would have been waiting for her right on the platform at which she was now looking nervously, still standing in the open carriage door.

London! The great dome of the station rose over her, all glass and wrought iron, newly built and resembling a soaring Gothic cathedral of iron and glass. But what a dreadful bustle on the platform!

"Carry yer luggidge, miss?" Some boys, ragged and

dirty, surrounded her as she still stood in the carriage door, though now she would have alighted but for the press of people below her, all gazing up at her. The boldest of the small boys put his hands on the leather strap of her dress basket and endeavoured to take it from her by main force. She raised the basket above her head and looked around her, wondering how to escape these people and how to find and take a hansom cab to Aunt Luci's.

"May I be of assistance, Madam?" A middle-aged man with big, yellow, tobacco-stained teeth under a fiercely waxed moustache, dressed in loud tweeds, grinned familiarly at her.

"Don't go with 'im, Missy," a stout ugly woman with a growth of some sort on her upper lip advised. " 'Ere, you give me the basket and I'll put yer on yer way."

" 'Aven't anyone ter meet yer?" asked a sluttish girl of about her own age, with tangled hair falling from a dirty straw hat and torn *chignon*. " 'Ere, I'll take yer where ye'd like ter go!" She winked broadly.

Caroline, clutching the remains of her twenty guineas and her dress basket, and holding firmly on to her cape when eager hands tried to take it from her, looked around her desperately. Was there not one respectable person there? What was she to do? Just as the ragged group about her pressed in more closely. Caroline saw a square-cut woman with a tall thin man making resolutely towards her. At a glance Caroline saw that their looks and clothes were impeccably conservative.

"You need help," the woman told her. "We are from the Girls' Friendly Society. We come to the stations just to help girls from the country like yourself." The man handed Caroline a card which bore the name Howard M. Spence. He brushed the crowd from him saying firmly: "Be off! You ragamuffins! Be off or I'll call the police!" They scattered. "Now tell me where you wish to go and we will take you there by omnibus."

Caroline breathed a sigh of relief. She had heard of this Society, which had been formed with the object of meeting all trains in order to protect innocent girls arriving in big cities from just the harassment—and even worse—that had happened to her.

"Mr. Spence has given you this card," said the square woman. "I am Mrs. Denham. What, please, is your name?" Caroline told them and gave them the address of Aunt Lucinda. "That'll be very easy from this station," the man assured her. "It's really a short distance. Come along, Miss Hamilton. It was wise of you to remain in the carriage door so we could see you, but the next time I suggest that you keep the carriage door shut as a protection against people like that."

"The porter opened the door," said Caroline. "Of course I never expected anything. But next time I shall close it." She smiled gratefully at the two.

"Have you any preference for a horse-drawn omnibus, or would you be willing to try one of the new steam type, so much cleaner and faster?" Mrs. Denham wanted to know.

"Either will do," said Caroline. "I'm so glad to see you. But now all I want to do is to arrive at my aunt's house."

"Well then," said Mrs. Denham. "If you will give me your dress basket and take Mr. Spence's arm . . . ?"

Mrs. Denham marched in front. She seemed to take some pleasure in clearing a path for her new charge with her folded umbrella, for at the approach of anyone of a ragged sort, she lifted the gamp like a spear and even the most hardy gave way before this threat. "You have to be firm with these cutthroats and thieves—for that's what they are," Mr. Spence assured her. He seemed to be rather proud of Mrs. Denham's prowess. "Public places are infested with every sort of low person looking for the unwary. Not enough police; not enough police by any means."

They were soon in a steam operated omnibus, sitting on a long bench, facing another long bench, passengers to right and left of them and passengers opposite them, men and women and children with parcels and packages everywhere.

Caroline looked through the windows of the omnibus with amazement and delight. Though London was not new to her, she had only seen it from the vantage of the Season surrounded and protected, always in a carriage, with her aunt and a maid, very often a groom. She had never been free to look as easily and eagerly as she now did, or to feel that she was really mingling and moving amongst genuine Londoners. The people who really lived there. Not the ones who took a house, or opened their own town house, just for the Season. How busy everyone looked and how intent on his or her affairs, as though each person had been pre-programmed for a hurried and diverse day, and each one was a little late in getting started, so they must now walk quickly and earnestly. No strollers here. Men on horseback were everywhere, many on the way to their offices, stray dogs crossed the streets, and sometimes made the horses shy. Hansom cabs, landaus, four-wheelers, victorias and other private and public carriages of all kinds filled the streets coming from Paddington to Marble Arch and then along Park Lane to Hyde Park Corner. Thence the omnibus went to Knightsbridge, where Aunt Lucinda had her small house in Wilton Crescent. Marble Arch, Mrs. Denham now told her, had been originally designed for the entrance to Buckingham Palace, but had quite lately been put up at Hyde Park instead and now led directly into Hyde Park Gardens. Omnibuses with horses drawing them were whipped past their steam omnibus at every chance, the drivers applying their whips vigorously to the backs of the horses pulling them. "They vie with each other for pride of place," Mr. Spence explained. "Some people feel that the steam omnibus is not as safe as a horse-drawn vehicle, but the drivers are fearful that the steam type will take over completely from the horse-drawn ones. But I hardly think so. As a nation we love horses and London would never be the same without them."

"But you chose to take a steam omnibus," Caroline thought, though she did not say what Mr. Spence might find disagreeable. She contented herself with nodding brightly.

Advertisements on the passing omnibuses reeled past Caroline's tired but excited eyes. Pear's Soap, Oakey's

Knife Polish, Mellons Food, Reckitts Blueing, were some of the familiar products advertised. Many people walked, raising occasionally anxious eyes to the uncertain September skies. Would it rain or not? Hawkers called their wares and plied for trade noisily. And suddenly Caroline became aware of two street musicians, one with a recorder and the other with a violin. The song they played, with the sweet notes of the recorder and the violin bringing in its plaintive and poignant lament, was the one so lately sung in the safety of her family's drawing room, with Edmund Browne at the piano. For some reason her eyes filled with tears as she heard in memory his mellow baritone blending with her mezzo soprano. The words came back to her, too:

"Had I the heart to slide an arm beneath her,
    Press her parting lips as her waist I gathered slow,
Waking in amazement she could not but embrace me,
    Then would she hold me and never let me go?"

Hating herself for her weakness, her mind slid back to herself at fifteen. She must have been in love with him! Puppy love, of course. How she had dreamt of love then. Of a love that would last her life. The heart at fifteen knew nothing of good sense and reason, but what of her heart now? It was still a traitor. For she wanted romance in her marriage. Was romance to be found with Robert? She had thought so on the night of the magic staircase. She had felt she was stepping into a world of wonderment, of joy. But that feeling had lately become less and less.

She gave herself a little impatient shake. As for Edmund Browne, what was he to her? A man who brought back sweet memories of her adolescence. A man who had sheltered her at the inn for a few hours. But she remembered, too, the moments in the conservatory with Harry when Edmund Browne had stood in the doorway with his mocking, leisurely voice and horrid knowing smile. And there had been nothing to know! She hoped Harry knew that too. But surely he could not have any illusions about why she had clung to him on that dreadfully unnerving night. True, he had made to kiss her, but remembering his kiss now, upon her head, she supposed he must have meant to kiss her as any kindly brother would. It was Robert who misunderstood things like that—wilfully misunderstood them. She suspected he chose to misunderstand because in some way he hated his Cousin Harry. They were such different types of men and she could imagine that brusque, bluff Harry got on Robert's nerves. But there was someone else who had given an air of misunderstanding to that conservatory scene. Edmund Browne! However, why worry about him? Look at the opinion he had of unmarried women: shipped off to the Colonies, no less!

Passing by streets of slums that knifed into the broad thoroughfares along which the omnibus travelled, Caroline caught glimpses of ragged children, women lying in doorways, workless men and occasional signs creaking over doors of ramshackle houses, signs reading: "Lodgins for Travilers;" "Gud Beds." Mrs. Denham, seeing Caro's shocked face, said "There are terrible slums in London behind many streets, especially Oxford Street. Slums stretch all the way from Great Russell Street to Marble Arch. Best never to go near them: they're not safe. . . ." She went on talking, but Caroline only took in what she said with half an ear. The streets of London were too exciting for her to take in everything Mrs. Denham said. And anyway, Caroline devoutly hoped that however sad she felt about it, she would never have occasion to go near those slum streets. Obviously her property was not in the best of neighbourhoods, but nevertheless it couldn't be in such neighbourhoods as that.

They descended from the omnibus at Hyde Park Corner. It turned out to be just a short walk from Hyde Park Corner to No. 70, Wilton Crescent.

"Just listen to the birds singing," said Mr. Spence cheerily. "There are trees and gardens here. A bit more like what you're used to I dare say, Miss Hamilton, than the slums of Marble Arch."

The door opened to them at No. 70 Wilton Crescent revealed Mrs. Lucinda Newcombe herself. She had arrived from the train station but a short time before and still had her pelisse and bonnet on.

"Why, Caroline! Thank Heaven you are here! I've only just arrived from Paddington myself. I found this telegraph awaiting me with a message for you from your uncle. Well, it's for me but it's really for you," said Aunt Luci, a little confused at the group of three standing in her doorway. "Come in! Come in! Do!" She handed Caroline the message, which read:

Kindly advise safe arrival Caroline. Will be obliged if you keep her with you few days. Writing instructions.

George Hamilton.

"Instructions!" burst out Caroline, forgetting for a moment the presence of the representatives of the Girls' Friendly Society. "I trust you don't think I will obey any of his instructions!"

"Now dear, don't take on so. Your uncle was never too diplomatic in his use of language. He does care for you and shows a great sense of responsibility towards you."

"And treats me as a child as to get his orders obeyed!"

"Yes, I know," said Aunt Luci, with a quick glance of embarrassment at Mrs. Denham and Mr. Spence. "I know how much his authoritarian manner must seem difficult for you to accept. But let us talk about it later, Caroline. I'm sure these dear, kind people can't want to hear all our private troubles."

"Oh, I'm sorry," said Caroline. "What dreadful manners I have! I'm just too upset! This is Mrs. Denham and Mr. Spence from the Girls' Friendly Society."

"I had guessed as much," said Aunt Lucinda, giving each of them her hand. "What an inestimable work you do! But for your Society many a young girl arriving alone in London would find herself astray in one of those horrible lodging houses and unable to get out!"

Caroline shuddered, remembering the "lodgins" she had seen advertised. How was she going to get along in a London as difficult as that? No wonder people talked of the necessity of having a male protector, a husband, a father, a brother. She had a fleeting glimpse of why Uncle

Hamilton and Aunt Millie were so anxious to get her a husband and so willing to let her risk marrying one she did not necessarily love. Male protection was a necessity for a young girl. Well, she would have to manage without, if Robert could not convince her that he did love her and that she could grow to love him.

"I think now that you are safely received," Mrs. Denham was saying, "that Mr. Spence and I will be on our way. Our services are probably in demand back at the station."

"Oh yes. And thank you! Thank you!" Caroline said fervently.

"Can I offer you some refreshment before you go?" Aunt Luci offered, "Some chocolate perhaps? Some tea?"

"Oh no, thank you. To know we have delivered your niece safely is thanks enough," Mrs. Denham assured her. Smiling and nodding, with Mr. Spence lifting his top hat, the two Good Samaritans stepped away from the door. As Aunt Lucinda closed it after them she said: "What good people those are!"

"Yes," said Caroline. "I was lucky they saw me," and she explained her arrival at the station and the ragged crowd about her.

"Perhaps now you are beginning to realise that your Uncle Hamilton was doing only what he thought was best for you. He was very upset when he found out you'd run off. And your Aunt Millie—poor Millie!"

"How is Aunt Millie?" asked Caroline anxiously.

"Dreadfully upset, poor dear. She cried a great deal when she found you'd gone. But she was relieved to read in your note that you had come to me. We enquired of you at the railway station and one of the porters remembered that a young girl had gone up on the slow train. That Mr. Edmund Browne came by early. I understood him to say that he had sat up all night with you: that was very thoughtful of him. Of course if there had not been a storm and he could have got a horse and trap he would have seen you home. The idea that, after all, he had been your tutor reassured Aunt Millie, for she was sure that with Mr. Browne there, no harm could come to you."

Caroline thought, "If they knew the truth, would they be so happy? But no harm *had* come to her, and she was grateful that Edmund Browne had let them believe what they did. It was in a way very nearly the truth.

The room that Caroline was given by her aunt was charmingly furnished with tartan bedcovers and window curtains, reminiscent of Balmoral and the Queen's taste for Scottish things. It looked out upon a small reas garden in which the trees were just turning from green to rust, reminding one that it was September.

"Oh Aunt Luci, I love it here!" said Caroline. "It's like being home—" She stopped herself, because it was not like being home. Home was home, however unhappy she had been there. She had grown up in it. It was a familiar place. However cold Uncle Ham had been, Aunt Millie had always made her feel that she was loved. Of course Aunt Luci loved her, too. But it was not the same thing. They did not share a thousand little secrets, secrets hardly remembers but little happenings, nevertheless, which made the woof and wrap of life, gave background, made a girl know there was a place in the world which was especially hers.

If her decision should be not to marry Robert, Caroline recognised she had a real difficulty on her hands. She could not just go tamely home to tell them she was back on their hands, unmarried and not likely to get married easily once she had thrown over such a catch as Robert Devonshire. She could not stay indefinitely with Aunt Lucinda, no matter how hospitable that kind woman might be. Aunt Luci's income was such that she just managed the little house on it. Caroline was not at all sure that Aunt Luci would let her pay her share there. And even if she did there was the nearly open animosity of Cousin Sophia to consider.

But meanwhile Caroline was glad to be in the small house. It had been Aunt Luci's house when her husband died and Aunt Luci had managed to keep it by the judicious sacrifice of many small luxuries she had enjoyed in her husband's lifetime. She had even managed to keep the two servants, Jerome and Rosie, who had been with her since her marriage. There was a young person, Katie, to assist with the hard work. The servants had been glad to stay, for Aunt Luci was the most considerate of employers. Caroline was grateful now for the long service of those two domestics, for it meant they had known her since she was a child and now would not make her self-conscious about running away from her home.

"Well," said the voice of Sophia, "so you've ruined your life, Cousin Caroline?"

"Oh," said Caroline, turning to meet Sophy, who had now entered the bedroom, "and in what way have I ruined my life?"

"I should think your fiancé had better explain that to you," said Sophia. "He told me what he saw in the conservatory and that he was so shocked he couldn't react in time and that is how Harry came to hit him. I went downstairs, you know, in search of you."

"Oh did you? Well, let me tell you, Harry hit him, but it was a shelf—"

"Yes. I know about the shelf. Otherwise Robert would have made short work of Cousin Harry. Harry is a weazel compared to Robert."

"And what did Robert say was the reason Harry hit him?" Caroline asked coldly.

"You know as well as I do," said Sophia, equally cool. "The only difference between me and Robert on that score is that Robert cannot believe that you—"

"Be careful, Sophia," warned Caroline.

"Careful? It's you who must be careful. You may hoodwink Robert and my mother but you can't hoodwink me!"

"Girls! Girls!" said Aunt Lucinda. "Sophia, please remember that Caroline is a guest in this house."

"An unwanted guest, so far as I am concerned," said Sophia rudely. And then as if to herself: "I wonder where she *really* spent the night. Up all night talking! One of these days Robert will wonder about that night at the inn, too!"

"Are you going to start him wondering?" asked Caroline.

"Please!" begged Aunt Luci again. "Even if not for your own sakes, then for mine. I can't bear this quarrelling. I don't know what has got into your head, Sophia, but whilst Caroline is a guest—my guest if you like—in this house, you will please keep a civil tongue in your head. No, Sophia, no another word from you," said Aunt Lucinda to her daughter, with an authority which she could unexpectedly show.

"Well, I was just wondering," said Sophia in a tone of great sweetness, "whether Caroline's engagement is broken. She isn't wearing Robert's ring."

"No!" said Caroline, suddenly furious with this pert young woman who felt she could pick a quarrel with her cousin, "no, my engagement to Robert de Lisle Devonshire has not been broken. If and when it is I shall announce it myself. And I'm not planning on doing that, Sophy, so don't count on it yet! Or maybe ever!"

Sophia retorted: "Well, since I can't seem to say anything to please Cousin Caroline, let me go." She made a stiff little inclination of her head and left the room.

Aunt Lucinda shut the door after her daughter. "I don't know where Sophia gets her temper from. Not from *my* side of the family. I assure you. But Sophia, my own daughter though she is, often appears to me to want to be unpleasant."

"Oh, Aunt Luci, it's my fault this time I'm sure. I only seem to create dissension lately. I don't mean to!"

"Now, don't bother your head, Caroline. Let's talk a little about you, instead. You may well say that you are none of my affair, but of course you are. I love you very much. I do hope you know what you are doing in running away like this, in defying your uncle—"

"I have thought about it, Aunt Luci, most long and painfully since yesterday evening. Great heavens, it already seems such a long time ago! So much has happened. But my uncle treats me as if I had no wishes of my own. He seems prepared to pass me and my inheritance like a package from himself to Robert, and Robert treats me like a—like a possession already his."

"I'm sure Uncle Hamilton means only the best. He

knows that women need male protection. He has been like a father and a brother to you and he wishes to see you married—Oh, Caroline, surely you are not thinking of breaking your engagement to Robert? Sophia seems to think that there might be cause—" Aunt Luci broke off in confusion. "What am I saying! Sophia does seem to want to make trouble lately—"

"Oh, it's nothing to do with Sophia. Or anyone else. It's only me." Caroline began to walk up and down the small room as she talked. "I realised only a little while after my engagement was announced that I really don't know Robert. I somehow let myself be engaged because it was the last big ball of the Season. It was a lovely one. Everyone was waiting for me to get engaged. Robert is, I know, a wonderful opportunity for a girl. But Aunt Luci, what about love? I know you loved your husband— you've told me so so many times."

"Yes, I did," said Aunt Luci. "But I was unusually lucky there. And I didn't know I loved him until we had been married quite a while. You know, you can't always expect marriage to be founded just on love."

"But I want my marriage to be founded on it. Even if I don't love Robert as first, I'd like to feel he asked me to marry him because he loved me. I'm willing to try from there—to love him back, I mean. I've got to talk to him. I'm asking him to come here, to this house. Is that all right?"

"It's perfect," said Aunt Luci beginning to relax. "I am glad, and I am sure you will discover that he is the best man for you. Half the girls in London would gladly marry him, you know."

"I know. I should feel I'm lucky. Why can't I feel just happy and glad? I don't want to be miserable. I certainly don't want to live by myself—"

"Then why this quarrel with Uncle Ham?"

"Because I can't let him continue to feel he can treat me like a child. I could get over his always making me feel like a pauper, because I suppose he can't help his own closeness with money—apparently with anybody's money. Even mine. But not to have told me of my inheritance! Obviously he still thinks me too much a child to be told anything. And Aunt Luci, I *am* twenty-one."

"I know, my dear, But you must realise Uncle Hamilton thinks of all women as children—"

"But we're not!"

"A great many men still think we are. And I must say I feel lost at times without any husband. I am glad to have a *man* servant. I just feel safer that way."

"But Aunt Luci, girls aren't packages to be handed over from one man to another, in marriage for instance. Sent off to the Colonies—you heard that *Times* editorial . . ."

"Yes dear, I know. And I don't know the answer. Life is so much pleasanter with a man about the house—" Aunt Luci signed. "I think I'm too old," she said, "to have these new ideas, though I can understand *you* having them. But don't let them spoil your engagement, dear. You really ought to get married."

Caroline, once alone, sat down at the small writing desk. She was very tired but she knew she could not rest until she had made some effort to tidy up her affairs. She sent Mr. Joachim a letter in care of *The Times*, and then crossed off that and wrote to him at the address Edmund Browne had given her. Writing the title; *The Times*, made her think of Edmund. What a puzzle he was! Writing an editorial that made her angry and then being so gentle and helpful with her when he found her in distress on the road. What sort of man was he really? She would probably never know.

In her letter to Mr. Joachim she tried to be as factual as possible. She told him of her inheritance and also gave him the address of Uncle Ham's lawyer in Essex Street, off the Strand. She remembered Mr. Bumbry very slightly but she was sure he knew all about her fortune. Uncle Ham never did anything in business without lawyers, accountants and banks.

She sent a short note to Mrs. Erskine. She would like to know some of the other women on *The Review*, she felt. She would be able to talk to them and find out how much she agreed or disagreed with them. It would be nice to be understood by others for a change.

She thought of writing to Harry next, but put off doing it for the moment. She must not seem always to turn to him in her troubles. It might give him wrong ideas. But there was Edmund Browne. She would have to see him, to thank him. It did not have to be a long interview: just a few words. She was certain he would never disclose that she had spent the night in his room. Sophia might conjecture all she could, but she would never know. The truth was really beyond imagining. But the letter to Edmund Browne was not easy to write. It seemed to her that when she thought of him she thought of two widely differing men, and he was both of those men at one and the same time. He was the charming man who had sung so romantically to her, who had waltzed with her, who seemed at times to have a *tendresse* for her. Even in those minutes at the inn when he had stood at the foot of her bed, the man who had stolen downstairs to a cold, public room to sleep uncomfortably in a chair so as to protect her as much as possible from gossiping tongues, seemed to be a gentle, considerate person. And then there was that other Edmund Browne who could write such editorials as to make one very angry as a woman, and this was the same Edmund Browne who stood in the conservatory and seemed to mock her distress.

But finally the letter to Edmund Browne was finished. It was just a brief note asking him to call upon her at her aunt't house when convenient.

Thinking of Edmund Browne made her think of the absurd, ridiculous little scene in the conservatory. She had been a stupid ninny to cry all over Harry. And when she thought about it she felt a little uneasy that Harry might imagine her tearfulness to have stemmed from something warmer, some feeling other than sisterly for him. She remembered now his kiss on the top of her head, and his attempt to kiss her on the lips. No, she could not pretend that those kisses of his had been just brotherly. Well, she would have to make him realise that he was mistaken in her when she saw him again. A little reserve, a little coldness, and he would understand that she had nothing but friendship for him.

She wrote a note to Robert Devonshire. It was merely a dutiful note, an account of where she was, with the assumption that he would come and see her and then they would have a chance to talk about things—really talk as they never had before. There seemed to be always someone coming in so that any real conversation was impossible. How she herself really felt towards Robert she could not say. She was not in love with him—no. But then, maybe she could grow to love him, as Aunt Millie and Aunt Lucinda said brides did grow to love the men they married. She hoped Robert did really love her. To be wanted would be such a great help to her in sorting out her own feelings and making her decision about the future.

She rang for Jerome. Jerome had been with Aunt Lucinda so long that without anyone really being conscious of it, he had become to some extent the man of the house, discreet, kind, understanding and helpful in many a situation Aunt Lucinda might have found difficult to handle quite alone.

Aunt Luci was a very different woman from her sister Millie Hamilton. The two were very devoted, but Mrs. Hamilton was by nature a totally dependent woman. Necessity and temperament had developed in Lucinda Newcombe a self-sufficiency that she was not always aware of. The training of dependence that she had received as a girl was still there, and when things became difficult that training made her look around for a man to cling to. But, having listened to their advice, she was just as likely to go and do the opposite of what they suggested if she felt she had a better plan. She had developed some skill in the dual role of being independent in a dependent manner.

Jerome, entering Caroline's room, stood waiting for her instructions. He did not know what the trouble was but he was a kindly man, he liked Caroline and he could see for himself that she was tired and distressed.

"Do you think you could deliver my letter to Mr.

Joachim—look, this one—by hand? Would Mrs. New-combe be able to spare you?"

"If I may take a cab, Miss, I could do it. I'll hardly be missed. That's not far, the Inns of Court."

A sign of tiredness escaped Caroline. Jerome immediately responded by saying: "Now don't you worry, Miss. You just rest yourself and if there's anything old Jerome can do, you just let him know and he'll do it."

Tears stood in Caroline's eyes at these kind words. She was almost too tired to take kindness as ordinary.

"I'm going to take the liberty of sending Rosie in with a nice, hot brick for your bed, Miss. Straight from the oven and with a bit o' flannel wrapped about it, it'll take the chill off those linen sheets. And I do wish you'd get between them, Missie. You need rest, Miss Caroline. A cup o' tea, too, would do wonders. Now, lie down, do. It's always blackest before the storm is past. You remember that now."

The bald-headed bewhiskered manservant left her room.

"The poor little chick!" he thought. "There's something really wrong."

But when Jerome had closed the door Caroline thought: "What am I doing?" She went over it in her mind. She was writing a note to a man she did not quite like, Edmund Browne, and she was writing a dutiful note to a man she was not sure she could ever love. Shouldn't she write a note to a man she did like and who did like her? Of whose regard she could be sure? Why *not* write to Harry. He was so basically kind and affectionate and once he had understood that she did not care for him in any special way, she was sure he would be just the kind of friend who would give her honest advice on her situation. She had to talk to someone of her own generation. And Harry, above all the men she now had in mind, was a gentlemen in the truest sense of that word. Her note to Harry merely told him where she now was and said that a visit from him would be welcome. She gave this note to the smiling, elderly Rosie, who had just brought her the promised warm brick and put it in the bed, and also a pretty tray with a pot of tea on it.

If Jerome had not been so anxious to please Caroline, this letter would have been delivered by penny post in the course of a day or two. But he was anxious to help and so he took the letter around to Harry's room in Jermyn Street. Harry was at the Jockey Club, the servant there said, but was expected back in the late afternoon. So Jerome told the servant that the letter was urgent and asked him to be sure Mr. de Lisle got it before he retired for the night. The servant promised this. On such trifles of behavior can the success, or failure, of a life depend. Having delivered Harry's letter, Jerome jumped back into his waiting cab and saw to it that the other letters were hand delivered too. Then, feeling that he had at least tried to do something to help Miss Caroline, he returned to the Wilton Crescent house.

Unconscious of these efforts of Jerome on her behalf, Caroline had taken his advice and gone to bed. The bed felt wonderful; she had not realised until she sank back against the pillow how truly tired out she was. Now the murmur of London traffic came from far away, distant but never-ending in its hum. How smooth the old linen sheets were, how pretty the room, how comforting the tea had been and the warm brick to her feet was now! How welcome, more than any other feeling, was her sense of security! Maybe she could not stay many days in Aunt Lucinda's house, but whilst she was there she felt safe. Her eyes closed drowsily on the drawn curtains, the tartan bedside chair, her own tartan coverlet and the down-soft eiderdown. The faint sounds of the house came to her, someone drawing water somewhere, someone singing—probably in the kitchen—"After the Ball is Over", all those noises of a house contentedly being taken care of. Caroline drifted off into sleep. When she woke she was much refreshed. Looking at the clock beside her she saw that it was just after luncheon. She was glad that they had not woken her to eat. But now she felt she could get up and stir about a bit, see her aunt again and perhaps try to make better friends with Sophia. Presently she would go back to bed again in that pretty room with a long night's sleep before her and, for the moment, no more question of responsibility for her own life, at least until after she had breakfast tomorrow morning.

She slid out of bed and padded over to her dress basket to find the only other dress she had brought with her. But it was not in her dress basket. The basket was empty and Caroline found that, whilst she slept, Rosie had stolen in and taken all her clothing to be pressed. The Paisley wool dress, banded in black velvet, which she had planned to wear was hanging in her wardrobe freshly ironed.

"Oh Rosie, bless you!" was all Caroline could say to herself. And the tears started afresh at this sign of love and kindness. She dabbed her eyes dry and began putting on her clothes. When she at last stood before the mirror she felt she now looked a lot more like herself.

Jerome evidently thought so too, for his face lit up when Caroline passed him on the landing. He told her that her aunt was in the morning room catching up on correspondence, but he would tell her Caroline was up.

"Oh no, please don't disturb her," said Caroline. "I've taken too much of her day already."

"Something for lunch, Miss? Rosie kept a little hot luncheon for you," Jerome offered.

"No! No! Thank Rosie, but tell her I'll wait until teatime now. I'm not hungry."

"Then maybe you'd like to sit in the drawing room, Miss. It being a bit cold in there. I've lit the fire, and it's drawing nicely now."

"Thank you, Jerome. Yes, I'll sit there for a while now. Is Miss Sophia in?"

"No, Miss. She got her mother to let Rosie go out with her. She's at Whiteley's. She does love the shops, Miss Sophy, and she had the need for some new embroidery threads."

Caroline entered the drawing room. A pretty room, all pale greens with touches of red in cushions and candle shades, the floor bare of rugs but polished to a honey colour of shining parquet. Family portraits mostly in oils, but some in water colours, decorated the walls. The windows at one end of the room overlooked the small walled garden and the similar gardens of neighbours, whilst those at the front of the house had a tiny iron balcony and overlooked the Crescent, with its green gardens in the middle, surrounded by high iron railings. Each household had a key to those gardens and Caroline had often sat in the cool shade of the trees on the velvet lawn watching children and their nursemaids take the air. How pretty the houses in Wilton Crescent were, all grey stucco with white trim for windows and shining black doors with even shinier brass knockers and letter boxes. Even the stairways of iron that led to the basement kitchens had touches of shining brass on them. The Crescent did not have an air of wealth so much as of pride and care in the homes. From where she was standing at the windows with the iron balcony, Caroline could hear the bell of the muffin man already alerting each cook that he had freshly made muffins and crumpets on the wooden tray he carried on his head, covered with a fresh white cloth. Already there were a few maids in afternoon starched white caps, waiting for him at their area steps. The muffins would be warmed up and served with tea at four o'clock.

The serenity of it all struck Caroline and should have given her a sense of peace, but instead it struck an uneasy chord in her conscience. This was how Wilton Crescent looked on an afternoon. But what did her property look like—the property with the unpleasant name: Leg Iron Court? She supposed it to be a place like Fetter Lane where, in the old days not so very long ago, they had put on, or struck off, the iron fetters for the poor wretches sent to prison. How did the people of Leg Iron Court get along on a day like this? Suddenly she felt full of a desire to know, and at the same time a spurt of nervous energy. She could not sit still like this, waiting for her aunt, waiting for Sophia. She had business to do and she should be about that business.

She rang for Jerome.

"Did you deliver my letter to Mr. Joachim?" she asked him.

"Oh yes, Miss, and waited in the office until the boy came back to tell me he was already reading it."

"Could you get me a cab—a four-wheeler will do?"

"Why yes, Miss. Could I know where you are going in case your aunt—?"

"I'm going to see a Mr. Joachim, a solicitor at the Inns of Court—the man you took my letter to, Jerome."

"Oh, of course, Miss. But should you go alone?"

"I'll go straight there in the four-wheeler and Mr. Joachim will get me a cab and I'll come straight back here."

"Someone should go with you," Jerome said worriedly.

"No!" said Caroline sharply. "I don't need anyone. I'll not take one of you from your work in the house."

"Well, there's little Katie . . . ?"

"No, Jerome. I'll be all right, really."

Mr. Joachim's office was up a set of very winding wooden stairs, stairs that had never been varnished so that the wood was grey and old and worn in many places by the feet of all those who had used it. But when Caroline finally reached the solicitor's rooms, almost under the roof, they were charming, with sixteenth-century panelled walls and mullioned windows. A great number of books covered the chairs, sofa and tables. Two law clerks sat in an outer room, thin, pale, hard driven, but full of alacrity at her entrance, and a boy of perhaps twelve stood tying up a parcel with much application of red sealing wax. Mr. Joachim's own room was hardly less free of huge law books, rolled documents, tied in red, briefs ready to hand to barristers.

He hastily cleared a chair for Caroline by the simple method of putting the books on the floor and then sat opposite her, pink, white-haired, benign.

"You certainly don't lose any time, my dear young lady," he said. He took off his glasses, folded them fussily and then promptly put them on again. "But I can claim to be almost as precipitate as you are. I have already been in touch with Mr. Ethelbert Bumbry. I wrote him a letter, sent my boy with it, and Mr. Bumbry kept him whilst he wrote me a reply. Couldn't be swifter. Of course I shall presently have to pay him a visit. But it appears from his letter that your father left his affairs in excellent condition, his Will most clearly expressed. You are to inherit the whole of what he left when you attain the age of twenty-one. So your guardian can raise no barriers to your having the control of your property now. But, of course, if you marry your husband will have the ordering of your fortune. And I understand from Mr. Bumbry's letter that you are engaged—"

"But not yet married," said Caroline firmly. "Meanwhile I would like to know what monies I have and what properties."

"There is a sum of fifty thousand pounds, some odd shillings and pence at Coutts' Bank which can be, and shall be, transferred to your name as you wish. It has been held by your uncle Mr. George Hamilton in a separate account, and the properties have been held in trust for you by that same gentlemen. He has stiven to conserve and increase your assets and has, so far as I can judge from a cursory glance at the figures Mr. Bumbry sent me, discharged his duties religiously well."

Caroline felt a moment of remorse. No doubt her uncle had done all he could according to his way of looking at things, and, yes, she should be grateful to him. But her mind still smarted under the remembrance of the times she had felt she was nothing but a financial burden to him. Would he not long have told her of her wealth if she had happened to be born a boy?

"About these properties," Caroline began.

"Why, yes," answered Mr. Joachim. "Some very valuable slum properties, houses built on land that is worth twice what it was when it was bought for you. The property itself is in something of a decline, but then it is slum property."

"Where are the properties?" she asked.

Mr. Joachim hesitated.

"I don't know how well acquainted you are with London," he began. "But looking down from Marble Arch, down Oxford Street, but keeping your mind upon the smaller streets, you will find your buildings there."

"There!" Into Caroline's mind came the dreadful signs: "Lodgins for Travilers," "Gud Beds." "But that is a terrible district!" she exclaimed. She had seen that very district in the early morning, never dreaming it could have anything to do with her!

"Slums," said Mr. Joachim quietly. "Some of the best slum property in London. The rents of Leg Iron Court come to a tidy sum every year, and nothing has been spent on the buildings for years."

"My father bought *that*?"

"Not your father. He had his money invested in safe securities, Government bonds, bonds put out I believe for Waterloo. Though that's a supposition: I haven't yet seen the Will, you know. Most of these bonds were redeemed, I think, and so your uncle had to find some other investment for the money. Your uncle shrewdly put the money into a neighbourhood which never lacks for tenants."

"But *slum* property—"

"Do not judge as harshly as your inexperience in business matters dictates." Mr. Joachim said hastily, seeing Caroline's face. "Many a noble lord has done the same. Many a Church draws income from the slums. After all, slum people have to be housed."

"I must see some of these properties at once!" said Caroline.

"It is hardly an area into which a young lady should venture—"

Remembering Edmund Browne's remarks, she said: "Then let us say I am not a young lady for the moment. I am a landlord. Have you anyone, anyone sensible and strong who could protect me? I understand that my uncle used to take someone of that sort with him."

"Sensible? I don't know," said Mr. Joachim. "But strong and reliable yes. There's a fellow connected with the police who does similar odd jobs for me. Name's Brady. Louis Brady."

"When could I get him? I want to go as soon as possible to Leg Iron Court."

"Well, almost any day," said Mr. Joachim. "Brady's work with the police is mostly nights. He is usually available to me in the day. I'll get into touch with him. He lives just beyond Temple Bar, which is very close here. I could arrange for you to meet here. Let me see, this is

Tuesday. Would Friday suit? Surely that is soon enough for you?"

She could not very well say that that was not soon, though she found herself all urgency and impatience.

Donald, the twelve-year-old boy, found another hansom cab for her and she was back in Wilton Crescent in such a short time that her aunt forgot to scold her for going out alone.

But now Caroline was frightened. Had Edmund Browne perhaps told her the truth when he said that she could do nothing for the poor who rented her properties? Now Mrs. Denham's remarks came back to her—those remarks she had only half heard: "No one who doesn't actually belong there would venture into such a warren of Courts and smelly, evil small streets. Why, it would be taking one's life in one's hands!" She tried to shut out the remembrance of Mrs. Denham's bell-like voice: "I work for the Girls' Friendly Society and am accustomed to getting about London, often on my own. But to go into those slums—no, I am not that brave." "Nor I," had added Mr. Spence fervently.

Caroline wondered would *she* have the courage to go? Even thinking of "Lodgins for Travilers," the women lying on the doorsteps. The fighting men, the ragged children, even that memory made her shudder. But they were *her* properties, her tenants. Caroline set her little chin in that way that made her Aunt Millie inwardly groan. She had waxed eloquent in her uncle's drawing room about helping the poor. No, she had to go. She would go. Even if she went, as knew she would, trembling.

Chapter 9

Caroline passed a restless night. She didn't know why, but she had an overwhelming feeling of disaster, some new disaster. She tried to think what else could happen. But no, she could not. It would have to be something she could not imagine. It would not be of her own making; she would keep too tight a hold upon herself and her actions to let anything happen by her own will. Nevertheless, despite everything she could say to herself to calm her apprehensions, she could not succeed. She felt threatened.

Sitting in the little morning room at the breakfast table, so placed that it was impossible to see anything but the tiny autumnal garden, high-walled and pretty, Caroline tried to appear composed in the presence of her aunt and particularly under the sharp eye of Sophia. But Sophia was quickly able to guess that Caroline felt there was something wrong.

"You're not eating anything, Cousin Caroline," she said.

"I'm not hungry," responded Caroline.

"Oh," continued Sophia sweetly. "Did you get into further trouble yesterday? I heard Jerome telling Rosie that you had gone to see solicitors."

"You hear everything," said Caroline truthfully, but unkindly.

"Come girls, don't quarrel," implored Mrs. Newcombe. "It's a most unpleasant way to begin the day." Aunt Luci was sitting in a lace mob cap that hid her hair; her locks had already been brushed and combed, but the putting of them up upon her round head took Aunt Lucinda at least half an hour. Breakfast was at eight o'clock, she was never late, but try as she would, she never got up early enough to complete her coiffure.

"You do look peaked, Caroline," she was said kindly. "Is there anything I can do?"

"No, really, Aunt Luci. It's probably just—just everything. Two mornings ago I was in my own room, waiting for Stroud to fit me with part of my trousseau. Now I am here and I feel under a cloud I never meant to create. Yesterday, Mr. Joachim, the solicitor I saw, gave me to understand I own some of the poorest slums in London. I have said I will visit them—"

"But Caroline, you can't visit slums. It's dangerous!"

"Oh, but I must. I'm not looking forward to it, but if my income comes from there and I'm to continue to use that sort of income, I must see what Mr. Joachim calls my 'good investments'. Maybe I will not agree with him."

"For heaven's sake, Caroline, do not start upsetting your uncle's arrangements. He has the reputation of being a very shrewd businessman."

"But maybe a very hard businessman."

"Caroline, business is not charity."

"You sound like Edmund Browne, Aunt." But she smiled at her plump little aunt. "So far as I can make out from my conversation with Mr. Joachim and with Mr. Browne and now with you, dear Aunt Luci, principals must go out of the window when profits come in."

"We live in a practical world. You can't be too softhearted or you'll finish up without any means of your own!"

"Well, I will have to go to see the premises," said Caroline obstinately. "Mr. Joachim has found me an able man who will protect me—I mean, my person."

"That at least makes good sense," said Aunt Luci. "But wherever did you get this Mr. Joachim? I could have asked Mr. Trimble—"

"Edmund Browne gave me his name. Mr. Joachim works in a legal way for *The Times*."

"So, did Edmund Browne spend all that time sitting up with you that night at the inn discussing just your property?" asked Sophia, spitefully.

"That, and other things," Caroline tried to be cool. But she felt her face flush as before her came the picture of herself in his silk shirt, and his big dressing gown over it, and then the slipslop slippers.

"She's blushing!" said Sophia, triumphantly. "I knew there was something else that happened at the inn—"

"That's enough—from both of you," said Aunt Luci crossly. "Now, Sophy, if you've finished breakfast, there is your pianoforte practice—"

"All right," replied Sophia sulkily. "I'll go. What will you do, Caroline?"

"I'll wait in the drawing-room, Aunt Luci, if I am not in your way there. I'm expecting Robert. I asked him to visit me to discuss—things."

"Oh, I'm glad, dear. I shall tell Jerome to show your visitor in there. I think it's time you met with him. Apart from the plans for your wedding, I think he is owed an explanation of your rather rash act in leaving your uncle's house. If you want me I shall be here in the morning room. I have some bills to see to."

Because Robert was to call, Sophia did her best to dawdle near the drawing-room doors, but Aunt Luci clucked her out of the way to the little library where the upright piano stood. Presently the whole house could hear Sophia's somewhat laboured playing of "Bluebells in the Wood" *after* Chopin.

Meanwhile Caroline sat waiting in the one room that ran the depth of the house, from garden to street—the same room from which she had risen so hurriedly yesterday to go and see Mr. Joachim. Seated beside the old fireplace, but not feeling cold, Caroline was beginning to think over what she would say to Robert, when the door opened and Jerome said:

"Your visitor to see you, Miss."

Caroline arose, astonished, her face full of surprise.

It was Harry de Lisle.

"I didn't imagine you would come to see me so soon," she said awkwardly.

"I would have come last night if I had got in at any civil hour," said Harry. "But it was nearly midnight."

He spoke straightforwardly and easily, and his plain face was alight with happiness.

"I'm so glad you sent for me," he said. "Your aunt's manservant made mine to understand that you wanted me to have your letter at once, so I knew you wanted to see me quickly, and here I am! I confess I am so confoundedly happy I probably won't make a great deal of sense. But let me tell you, Caroline, that I feel profoundly and deeply honoured."

In a horrible flash of understanding, Caroline realised that Harry had totally misunderstood her note. He thought that she had sent for him in her trouble as she would send for the one man in her life. She tried to stop him speaking but, having found his courage after his long wait through two whole Seasons for some word of encouragement from her, he was now in a rush to bring out what his heart had long begged him to say.

"No. Don't stop me now, Caroline. It's clear what has happened. You have broken with Robert: you are not wearing his engagement ring. Thank Heaven for answering my prayers! You realise that we were made for each other. Oh, my adorable Caroline!" And Harry seized her hands and covered them with kisses.

Caroline did not pull away. She thought it best to remain calm and to try to get him to listen to her. "Harry," she said, "I want to tell you—"

But Harry was not listening to anyone or anything other than the message of his own simple heart. The *élan* which had brought him as quickly as he could to her side, carried him along.

"I've been in love with you since your first Season. I wondered when you'd notice. And now I know what you are going to say. But first let me hold you in my arms as I did in your conservatory—let me know that you are really mine!"

"Harry, you've got to listen!"

But it was too late. He had put his arms about her. Then the voice of Robert de Lisle Devonshire was heard, cold with fury.

"Take your hands off her! Let her go, I say!"

But it was Caroline who broke free from Harry. Harry turned to face Robert.

"This is the second time you've forced your attentions on my fiancée," said Robert de Lisle Devonshire, his handsome face contorted with cold, dark anger. "You need to be taught a lesson, Cousin Harry, and with something more civilised than fisticuffs which you so delight in. You won't knock me down again. I demand satisfaction, not as a pugilist but as a gentlemen. I suggest pistols!"

Harry found his tongue. "But this is ridiculous!" he said. "And, anyway, duelling is going out, has gone out, you could say. Why, it may even be forbidden by law—"

"Coward!" retorted Robert. "You can meet me tomorrow in Hyde Park—the Dingle, I'd say, at dawn—or be known as the coward you are."

"I'm no coward," said Harry, angry now. "That's something you can't say about me—"

"Then prove it!" said Robert. "My seconds will wait on yours tonight. Now leave this house—or shall I call my groom from my carriage to eject you?"

"I've seen your groom," said Harry, "and I wouldn't ask him to try a turn with me. But I won't embarrass Caroline or her aunt by remaining. I'll be back, Caroline," he promised, bowing to her, then he straightened his broad shoulders, tried to convey with his eyes that he understood the appeal she was making him at the moment to be silent—he guessed she had not yet told Robert she would not marry him—and he left before the scene should become any worse. Caroline had been through enough. He could see that she was afraid of a scene with Robert, and by coming to see her so quickly he had almost precipitated one. If he left her alone she would be able to tell Robert of her change of heart.

Harry's blue eyes were not even hurt as he left the room. The silly duel Robert proposed was sheer bluff, had to be. It had been a few years at least since anyone had duelled, and no doubt Robert would begin to feel an ass when he reflected on his proposal. Especially when he learned from Caroline that she was breaking her engagement. That would take some of the peacock air out of his cousin. Harry began to grin as he ran down the stairway to the front door. By the time he had reached the street he was whistling softly to himself.

The moment the drawing room door had closed after Harry, Caroline said: "Of course you don't mean it, Robert—duelling? Why, that's an eighteenth-century pastime: we're in the nineteenth. A duel would be so—so silly. Besides, there's nothing to duel about!"

"I think there is," said Robert, stiffly.

"But Robert—it's ridiculous. And Harry can't shoot. You know that!"

"Then all the worse for him. I shall certainly kill him if he cannot defend himself."

"Robert, you can't mean it?"

"Why not? The only thing the fellow understands is pugilism. He almost killed me with a blow the last time I saw him. Now it's my turn."

Caroline looked at Robert's face and took a deep breath. He meant it?

"Robert," she tried again, "supposing I tell you that I do not want this? That there is no need—that it would be murder—"

"I am sorry, Caroline, but in matters of this kind I cannot allow your opinion to count. I will take care of the duel. It is entirely a matter for men and I have men friends who will not find a duel ridiculous when I tell them the circumstances. Of course I will keep your name out of it as much as I can. I am certain you did not encourage the fellow."

"But Robert—"

"That's enough about it," said Robert. "I can't discuss it any further. Rather, let me hear from you just how and why you ran away from your home. I was deeply shocked—"

"I had to run away. My uncle had locked me up before for a week or more at a time on bread and water. Then I thought myself quite penniless, unable to do anything about his tyranny. But knowing I have independent means, knowing that I am not a child but a woman of

126

twenty-one, I could not put up with such schoolgirl treatment any more."

"I see," he said.

"I know you have been informed of my true financial position. I hope you will see that I must take an interest in my own properties and my own money. I have arranged to see the properties. Will you come with me?"

"Come with you? But why go? These places are slums."

"And I am the landlord. I take their rent money. So will you, if—when we marry? Don't you think we should know more about things?"

"Things? What things? You can't mean more about those slums? All I care about them is that the tenants pay their rent. And don't worry—the rents are collected by some minion your uncle found. Let's leave him to it."

"But the banisters! Remember they burnt up the banisters. Aren't we even going to look into the reason for that?"

"Oh, come, Caroline. Why should we bother about such things? We have more things to do with our lives than worry about old slum banisters."

"Things like what?" she said coldly.

"Like this!" he said, catching her to him, and before she could stop him, he had kissed her. Suddenly she felt he was too domineering, too sure that she had no thoughts, no ideas worth his consideration. He was just like her uncle. Women were there for the use of men, just as Edmund Browne had written—were persons who waited on men, either as wives or as domestics. Persons whose whole lives were satisfied if they pleased the men in their lives. She wanted to please a man, her man, but she also wanted that man to please her, too.

He reached for her to kiss her again but she struggled, and when this only made him tighten his arms she struck him. Surprised, he let her go. Then he laughted. "And I thought you a cold little priss miss," he said. "What have I discovered? A woman of fire and, could it be, passion? Let's get married—at once! Or rather, as soon as I have this duel safely out of the way."

"Robert! You've got to listen to me!"

"Please, Caroline. Not now. We have a whole lifetime and I'm sure we'll find time for me to listen to you then. But meanwhile I have two seconds to find, and pistols to prime and polish. This time tomorrow, Caroline! I'm sure you will be proud of me when I tell you how I protected my honour—and of course yours."

Bowing, he was gone too quickly to hear her reaction to his bragging words. "The vainglorious brute!" she said to the empty room. "I'd have liked to throw his precious ring at him!" Heavens, only such a vain man would think of duelling! Of course the duel would be made to look as if it were about her, but the truth was that it was Robert's way of getting back at his cousin, who once too often now had sent him to the floor with a blow—a blow that she could well imagine Harry had often felt his cousin Robert deserved throughout their childhood and their boyhood together.

But the duel? It must be stopped at any price.

Chapter 10

"Oh, Caroline, how dreadful!" said Aunt Lucinda, in an agitated voice. "This has all been so distressing. Your running away—and that only twenty-four hours ago—and now *this* fresh scandal. A duel, and about a woman, you, Caroline! No one has called anyone out in a duel for these past twenty years. The last time, surely, was when the Duke of Wellington called out Lord Winchelsea! We are more sensible now—and leave duels to Continentals and other unreasonable people!"

They were sitting in the drawing room. The tea table had been brought in, but the tea, buttered scones and all, lay untasted. The tea was cold and grey in the cups. No one had eaten any lunch either.

Caroline glanced about the room, full of Georgian furniture, for Aunt Lucinda had not had the means to replace the things she had bought during her married years with the more up-to-date heavy mahogany furniture of Caroline's own home. The result was that though Aunt Lucinda's drawing room was out of date, it held the charm of an age gone by. Many a duel must have been mentioned in that room before.

Now Aunt Lucinda's small figure fluttered on the sofa on which she had settled when Caroline had given her the news. She was deeply upset, and her soft, dimpled hand pressed against her heart as she said: "Now what shall we do?" The question was directed at no one in particular. She was giving herself time to find and keep her head. And she went on talking, fighting for time to think, as she said: "Heaven bless us! Why do the young make the old suffer so! As if life doesn't have enough problems of its own without going out impetuously to drag in fresh trouble! Forgive me, children, I did not mean anything unkind by that. But all this—I feel it could have been avoided with a little more wisdom on all sides! Oh dear, what am I saying? I suppose the truth is, I know that the duel must be stopped. But how? And if it is not stopped, what a tragedy! One cousin killing, or at best, maiming, another. Horrible!"

There was a silence. Caroline could not think of anything to say, and Sophia kept quiet, although her normally plump and indolent figure was upright for a change, and her eyes were as bright and keen as a bird's in search of an unwary worm on some smooth lawn. She looked pleased, interested. They had all agreed that nothing could happen to Robert. To see Caroline in a mess over Harry—well!

"I shall have to send for your uncle," said Aunt Lucinda suddenly.

"That's a good idea!" said Sophia instantly. She had not spoken throughout Caroline's guarded account of the reasons for the duel, but now she smiled and said, "Perhaps he will take Caroline home with him—"

Caroline shot her a glance of anger and then said to her aunt: "No, do not send for Uncle Hamilton. I could not bear it: I would sooner leave this house than see him now!"

"Then to whom, Caroline, shall I turn? Who can I send for? This is men's business! Oh, Caroline, what could you have said to Harry to encourage him so! I know he was interested in you during your first Season, but common sense told him that your guardian would never have agreed to his paying attentions to you. How could he have imagined himself encouraged then?"

"My, I think I could guess!" said Sophia, openly malicious. "Cousin Caroline is full of mystery. Here is Harry de Lisle at her feet, and now there's a duel to be fought! And did you know that Caroline has a pistol, a little silver-handled one?" Suddenly Sophia blushed.

"Then you've been prying amongst my things!" Caroline said, shocked. "Really, Sophia, I hardly think you can be an arbiter of right behaviour! *I* don't look amongst other people's possessions—and I don't impute dishonourable actions to them. Regarding Harry, Aunt, I think it was a real misunderstanding, a *mal entendu* on Harry's part."

"But of course, Caroline!" agreed Aunt Luci. "That bold, rash young man, more used to the easy manners of the Jockey Club or the boxing ring than to a lady's drawing room!"

Caroline felt uneasy now. Should she confess the embrace in the conservatory? Did Sophia know of it? Had Robert told her? No, she hardly thought Robert would want to confide this. And it had not been her fault. She had not encouraged Harry. No, Aunt Lucinda would merely be even more bewildered by the actions of the young people, actions she frequently said she could not understand.

"Caroline," said her aunt again. "We must think. If we cannot have your uncle's advice, then we must get a discreet man, a man of the world, someone with *finesse*."

"Finesse?" echoed Sophia slowly. "I imagine the only sophisticated person Caroline knows who answers that description is that music teacher of hers, the man who is now on *The Times*."

Caroline flushed.

"Oh dear!" said Aunt Lucinda, noticing. "Perhaps not. In a way, he began all this with those wicked editorals of his about unmarried women, girls, and even widows, I suppose."

"But he has *finesse*," persisted Sophia mulishly; Caroline's flush was not at all lost on her. "And Caroline has known him a long time. He would be bound to help. What do you think, Caroline?"

Caroline moved uncomfortably. "I hadn't thought of him," she said. "I don't like to ask for favours . . ."

"Why ever not?" asked Sophia. "I'd say he'd love to have you ask him. He was quite interested in you—or at least, he once was, surely. That sentimental song he sang with you . . ."

"Really, Sophia," Aunt Lucinda said. "There's no need to make Caroline embarrassed. If Mr. Browne wished to make things personal I think Caroline clearly showed she did not. I thought she was cool towards him."

"Well, anyway, what about Mr. Browne?" asked Sophia with her habitual persistence, whenever she wanted something to go her way.

"I must say," said Aunt Lucinda, "Sophia is right in one thing. Mr. Browne is a man of the world, and that is what we need now. Someone who will stop this ridiculous duel—ridiculous, if it weren't so dangerous. Can we not send Edmund Browne a note suggesting he call?"

"Perhaps, since the matter is urgent, such a request would be better coming from you, Aunt. I did write Mr. Browne suggesting that since I was in town, he might call when he had time, but I do not expect that he would respond at all quickly."

"Perhaps *I* could send him a note then, Caroline? I mean, since the matter is urgent. I can understand your not wanting to ask favours of any man now that you are engaged to marry. But there is no reason why I should not ask him to help."

"Why yes, Aunt. If you think so."

Caroline hated the idea of asking Edmund Browne for any more help. It was enough to be in his debt and depending upon his silence about the night she had spent in his room, but now to request him outright to stop a duel being fought over her! She hated to see him about such a thing. But if something were not done, and that quickly, the duel would take place. It would be common news and a common scandal, setting all the drawing rooms of London alive with speculation. She could not hope to have even acquaintances in the fashionable world after that. But more important, there was the possibility of Harry being killed. No, however embarrassing it might be to see Edmund Browne in these circumstances, she must not allow that.

"Help me to my *escritoire*, then," said Aunt Luci. "I feel a little faint. It has all been too much for me. But I will write a little note. Ring for Jerome and ask him to bring candles. It is getting dark. Tell him also that I want my note taken to Mr. Browne's rooms at once. We must hurry."

And it was late. The day had been spent in talking and now the lamplighter was passing down the Crescent, touching his light to each of the gas lamps in the street. So, whilst Jerome made up the fire and brought the candles (Aunt Luci felt she could not yet afford gas), Sophia fidgeted, her eyes gleaming with excitement, and Caroline felt nervous and unhappy that she must involve Edmund. Aunt Lucinda sat down at her Queen Anne desk and wrote a short letter to Edmund Browne. Jerome, the candles now burning brightly, stood at the door until he received his instructions to take the letter at once and to make sure that Mr. Browne got it the moment he returned to his rooms in Albermarle Street.

When Edmund Browne arrived within the hour, Aunt Lucinda had had time to collect herself. It was so much better when there was a man to give advice, Aunt Luci said. Whilst Caroline sat quietly by and Sophia watched eagerly, Aunt Lucinda explained how, when Caroline was in disgrace after the dinner party, Harry had shown her some sympathy and Caroline had not been insensible to his kindness. Edmund Browne quietly flashed Caroline a quizzical look at this, and Caroline felt a tide of crimson coming up over her face and neck. Could it be that a hint of that sardonic smile he had shown in the conservatory now touched his mouth? Caro returned Edmund's gaze without faltering. Her intentions in accepting Harry's kindness then had been honest, and she was not going to let Edmund Browne make her drop her head or lower her eyes. But anger stirred in her heart against him, and she wished she did not now have to ask his aid. She was also conscious of Sophia watching her, and wondered what that young woman would be making of her cousin's blush. Her aunt continued on to the scene Caroline had described to her which had taken place in that very drawing room such a short while ago, when Robert de Lisle Devonshire had stumbled into the matter. Jerome, of course, had not announced him because he accepted Mr. Devonshire, engaged to Miss Caroline, as already part of the family.

"It would not have occurred," Aunt Lucinda assured Browne, "if Harry de Lisle were more accustomed to the society of ladies. Any gentleman used to drawing rooms would have known that unless Caroline were in acute distress she would consider any advances, even of kindness, made by some one other than her affianced, to be merely a trespass upon her good nature and upon her name."

"Yes, I understand," said Edmund Browne; but his voice held that trace of mockery which Caroline recognised, though her aunt's ear did not pick it up. Did Edmund Browne really believe that she had encouraged Harry?

However, he was now saying to Aunt Lucinda, "My dear lady, I will do my best to stop this matter where it is now. But could I be permitted a word alone with your niece? I feel there are one or two points she could best clear up. And if I may say so, I think *you* have had enough anxiety for one day. Surely this is the moment when your charming daughter will wish to conduct you to your bedchamber? A good night's repose . . ." He looked at Sophia, who had kept a seat in a corner and was avidly following everything. Now she bit her lips with annoyance. She wanted to stay and satisfy her curiosity. But with such an invitation to be helpful to her mother, she could only make the best of it, and help her dear mama to her room. Sophia was sharp enough to realise that Edmund Browne was skilfully getting rid of her, and of her mother. Why did he want to see Caroline alone?

"I declare to goodness," she said to herself, "that scrawny little Caroline, with a face that is all eyes, is getting more than her fair share of masculine attention." And Caroline was engaged too, whilst she, Sophia . . . She began to think of Robert de Lisle Devonshire. Imagine! A man fighting a duel over you! The very thought of Robert's darkly handsome good looks sent a tremor through her—well, what was the use? He was going to marry Cousin Caroline who, instead of feeling proud and intrigued that he was willing to risk his life duelling, was all in a pother as to how it could be stopped. Sophia wouldn't have been like that! She would have loved to have something to make London—and especially the *haut monde*—sit up and take notice! So thinking, Sophia bad-temperedly left the room, her doll's mouth making a *moue* of annoyance at her mother's back as they both climbed the stairs.

Left alone, Edmund Browne turned to Caroline and said, "Well, young lady, what a kettle of fish you have managed to cook up! What's behind all this? I was considerably put out when I awoke yesterday morning to find that you had fled like a thief in the night. Can you imagine me explaining *that* to the landlord at the inn?"

"I am sorry," she said. "You had told me that you would take me home in the morning. I had my own plans—"

"But you don't seem to know what you really want, Caroline." His voice was suddenly kind. "Tell me something, Caroline, and tell me true. Remember I know you. You make a poor liar. You could never deceive me at fifteen and I don't believe you'd make much of a hand of it now. So, let's be frank. You do not care for Robert?" There! It was out. He was glad he had freely asked. He hoped she would as freely reply.

The question was so sudden that Caroline had not time to dissimulate. She stood up and turned her back on Edmund so that he would not see her grey-green eyes fill with tears. "Oh, Edmund!" she said suddenly, in the voice of the young thing he had remembered for so long, the pupil who had spent her fifteenth birthday, at her own wish, on a picnic with her family, with himself as the only guest.

"Whatever is the matter with me?" she went on. "Robert is the perfect match, they tell me. My uncle, my Aunt Millie, particularly Aunt Lucinda, everyone. But why do I wish to be in love with the man I marry?"

She had turned around to him on this last sentence, as though facing him would help her to ask the question, and help him answer it. He held out a great folded handkerchief to her as if she had been that little girl again, half child, half woman. "Here, dry your eyes," he said, smiling. "The main question is, is Robert Devonshire the right man for *you*? Do you love him? You sound as if you don't and as if you feel badly about it. Loving, you know, is not a decision of the mind. Love comes unbidden, and it can stay, even unrequited, for years. There are many," he said softly, "who love where they wish they did not, but they have no other choice."

"Am I foolish to imagine that falling in love should be for life?"

"If you are foolish in thinking that, then I am a fool, too," he said. "I will marry only when I know love will be for ever."

There was a silence for a moment. Caroline looked at this young man with the wonderfully blue—dark blue— intent eyes. He was tall and slender but she felt great strength in him, strength of frame and strength of character. If only he were always so kind with her, an Edmund she could appeal to, whose sympathy she was sure of, the

Edmund she had thought such a wonderful man when she was in her 'teens.

And he, looking at Caroline's black, curly hair, her great grey-green eyes, her milky skin and the fire that burned in her small person, a fire wildly determined upon freedom but yet so much desiring love, thought: "How best can I counsel her? I don't like Devonshire but that may be my prejudice. Perhaps he is the best man for Caroline. Perhaps she might yet find happiness with the fellow, and, certainly, she would have a great position in the social world, and financial security as the future Lady Devonshire." Out loud he said, "You confided a little in me the other night. Is there something you would like to tell me now?"

"I don't love Robert," she said quietly. "I knew it fully after Harry left today. I tried to give Robert the chance to talk about our future, but he wouldn't listen. He's so arrogant! I find it hard to believe that he loves me: I think he feels a girl who is engaged to him is bound to be in love with him. He cannot believe I might not be."

"Is there someone else then for you, Caroline?" Edmund asked her gently. As she did not reply, he said: "May I take it that there is?"

"No," she said, "no." She sounded confused, and did not help herself by saying, "It's just that I *know* I don't love Robert. I want to return his ring for the present. I want to be free whilst I take time to think things over. But why talk of that now? I sent for you because of Harry. Oh, Edmund, if Harry is killed—!" She could not go on. She was too overwrought. Tears fell down her cheeks. Seeing them, and her agitation, Edmund thought: "Great Scott! She loves Harry." Into his mind leapt the scene in the conservatory as he remembered it. Whatever her story of today, retold undoubtedly with words to suit Aunt Luci's ears in the conservatory Caroline had lain in Harry's arms as though she belonged there. She had not rebuffed Harry on that occasion, and now her tears told their own tale. Of course she loved Harry! The flame of jealousy which had consumed him when he had seen Caroline in Harry's arms in the conservatory, which had made him speak coolly and unkindly, now leapt up again. Self-knowledge flooded over him. He was in love with Caroline himself! But this was terrible! Harry was his long-time friend. And he was being asked to save him for Caroline. He couldn't do it. And then he knew that of course he must. He could not let Harry be killed. Nor could he stop him from finding happiness with Caroline, as she would with him. Caroline trusted him. He was sure Harry trusted him too. And Harry would never know that he, Edmund, was in love with the girl Harry loved and would obviously make his wife.

"Nothing will happen to Harry if I can help it," he now said. "I have thought of something. If Robert is no longer engaged to you then he cannot call another man out on your account. Give me Robert's ring. I will go to him and make him understand how the land lies. He will have to listen to what I will tell him. It's the only way"

"You really think—" she began.

"Yes," he assured her. "He may not have liked seeing you with Harry, but he cannot pretend he has to kill him. Here, give me the ring!"

"Yes, I can see that," she said. "That would be wonderful!" She was smiling through her tears. "Wait a moment," she said. She turned her back to him, and stooping over, fumbled under her skirt to find the pocket in her petticoat. When she stood up and turned to him, she was holding in her palm, the fabulous jewel, winking, glittering in the candlelight, that expensive bauble, her engagement ring.

Edmund took it, looked at it, and put it in his waistcoat pocket. Then he kissed both her hands, looked into her tear-dimmed face for a moment, felt that contraction of the heart evoked by her seeming fragility, that tremendous desire to protect her—the same, no doubt, that his old friend Harry also felt. Thinking of Harry, he dropped her hands, stepped away from her, and said: "I must go now. But I will be back with good news, I think. Wait up for me a little. I will not be long."

Caroline waited what seemed an interminable time. She paced the drawing room restlessly. Sophia had come down to ask if there were any news, and Caroline could only shake her head. Sophia's whole manner upset her. She seemed almost pleased at all the worrisome things which had befallen Caroline, and her attitude to the idea of a duel betrayed more keen anticipation of its coming off than fear of its taking place. Caroline was struck again with an idea of Sophia she had had before. Sophia was much closer to the débutante ideal than she, Caroline, had been. She loved excitement——even if that excitement gave pain to others——whereas Caroline wanted to live quietly and serenely. How much better for Caroline if she had been like Sophia! Sophia would never give up a Robert de Lisle Devonshire. Not she! Caroline got rid of her as tactfully as she could, telling her that she would give her what news there was to take to Aunt Lucinda when she had news herself, and that could only be when Edmund Browne returned to Wilton Crescent.

Though the time seemed so long to Caroline, Edmund Browne was back in the drawing room within the hour. He looked visibly disturbed as Jerome showed him into the drawing room. "I saw both Harry de Lisle and Devonshire," he said. "But I could persuade neither of them to give up this foolishness. Devonshire is set on the duel. I gather there are a great many old scores to settle between him and his cousin. He talked a lot about honour."

"But Edmund," cried Caroline, "the ring! The ring!"

"Yes," he said, "I made him listen. I told him that you wished me to break your engagement for you."

"Yes, but did you deliver Robert back the ring?"

"Yes," he said. "And Devonshire had a curious reaction to it. He laughed at the idea of your breaking an engagement to him; he didn't believe me, in fact. He put the ring in his pocket and told me that you'd be wearing it proudly by tomorrow afternoon. He seems very sure of himself."

"But you didn't tell Harry——"

"I did my utmost to dissuade Harry," Edmund said. "Remember he means much to me, and I don't want him murdered either. And that's what it will be——murder. I've seen Devonshire discharge a pistol in competition with others. He never misses a target! Robert Devonshire is a bull's-eye man."

"Oh!" said Caroline, looking around her wildly. "To think my headstrongness has brought Harry to this! If only I had told Harry—if only—"

Edmund looked at her sadly. She seemed like a small caged wild animal at hearing his news. Her distress over the impending death of Harry de Lisle was now quite nakedly genuine in her turmoil. He could no longer doubt, he told himself, that she cared deeply for Harry. He paused. He wanted to help her. But he could think of nothing more he could do. Then something did occur to him. One last appeal to reason tomorrow morning at the scene of the duel and then, if that failed . . . ?

"Caro, listen!"

"Yes?" she cried eagerly, anxiously. "You have thought of something?"

"I have thought I will go there myself tomorrow morning. At least I now know that the duel is to take place in that part of Hyde Park known as the Dingle. And the time is a little after five-thirty, when it will be light. I will be there, and I may bring a friend or two to help me. I will not yet give up. Maybe this thing may *yet* be stopped. I will certainly try to stop it."

"I won't be able to sleep," said Caroline. "To think that Harry—"

"You must try to sleep, Caroline. Trust me. Rely on me."

"Edmund! Dear Edmund! I do!"

Edmund turned and left her then. He would do what he could. But whatever he managed, it would still leave him heavy-hearted. He returned to his set of rooms in the Arlington, puzzled at himself, puzzled and pensive.

Chapter 11

Jerome had hardly shut the front door behind Edmund, his hansom cab had barely clattered down the Crescent, when Aunt Lucinda was in the drawing room *en déshabille*, the avid Sophia right behind her, unable to keep away.

"What has happened, Caroline? What has happened? I am dreadfully anxious," said Aunt Lucinda.

"He has not succeeded yet in stopping it. They are to meet in the Dingle in Hyde Park tomorrow morning at five-thirty with their seconds. Neither Harry nor Robert would give up the idea—Robert because of a desire to settle old scores with his cousin, I think, and Harry because he will not be called a coward."

"Then we will be there!" said Aunt Luci firmly, with one of those decisions that she often took in lightning fashion, quite unaware that this time she had not asked any man's advice—not even that of Mr. Trimble. "Maybe," she said, "if I join my voice to the voice of reason—oh, they cannot have thought of the scandal! The risk of you being talked about, Caroline. Perhaps if you too ask Robert one last time, and explain again how mistaken he is with regard to Harry—"

"Is he really mistaken?" asked Sophia innocently.

Aunt Lucinda gave her a look of scorn and impatience. "Of course he was mistaken! Caroline said so!"

"I am coming too," said Sophia.

"Do as you please," said her mother. "I will tell Jerome to get the carriage around at four-thirty tomorrow morning. He will drive us. And now we had best all be off

140

to bed. You look so tired, Caroline, and tomorrow will be another trying day."

Caroline took off her clothes when she got to the guest room and lay down upon her bed. But she did not sleep. She thought, "How strange all this is! A few weeks ago I hardly knew anything about Robert de Lisle Devonshire beyond how he looked and what his name was. Now, whether I like it or not, he is insisting upon my engagement to marry him. I left home because I said my mind in the drawing room that night. I've found out I am an heiress in my own right. And the night all that happened, I was so foolish as to let Harry hold me in his arms. And now he thinks I love him. Do I love anyone?"

She watched the tiny ormolu and onyx clock beside her bed. How slowly the hands moved! They dragged on until they passed midnight; and still Caroline could not sleep. She tossed restlessly, sleeping fitfully at last, but haunted by terrible dreams. At four o'clock in the morning she felt she could not stay lying down any more. She got up and paced about the room.

Sophia had asked to come, too. Caroline supposed it was out of curiosity. She was surprised, therefore, to hear her cousin in her room, moving about, apparently also unable to sleep. Caroline wondered why. Presently, unable to wait any longer, she began to dress. She wore the dress she had run away in, now freshly pressed by the good Rosie, and with its linen cuffs and collar newly washed, starched and ironed. The grey wool, with its sharp white at neck and wrists, suited her. She put on jade earrings and matched them with a little jade brooch. She did these things almost automatically, her mind elsewhere with worry. Then with some notion that she might need her pistol, she checked that it was loaded and put it with her cloak. In the looking glass she noticed her face was white and those grey-green eyes of hers were wide with fear. Edmund *must* get there in time! If he did not, she would have to do something herself. Something desperate—she could not think what.

Taking her cloak, she stepped out of her room just as

Sophia came from hers. Sophia looked haggard and Caroline wondered why.

Aunt Luci joined the girl. "Have you anything warm I could borrow?" Caroline asked her aunt. "It's so cold."

"Why yes," said Aunt Luci. "There's my beaver scarf and muff." Caroline took the furs and tucked her pistol in the muff. She saw Sophia's eyes go big at sight of the little firearm.

"Edmund Browne is coming this morning, Aunt," she now said.

"Oh, thank goodness!" said Aunt Luci. "He is bound to make those men see sense and put off this foolish duel."

The carriage could be heard being brought around from the stable in the Mews. Jerome met them in the front hall. It was obvious that he had something to say. "What is it, Jerome?" asked Aunt Luci. Jerome told her that through the servants' grapevine (a better system for spying could not have been invented, Aunt Luci often thought) he had heard that Major Fortescue was to be one of Harry's seconds, and the other was a Mr. Cavanagh, whom Harry knew from the Jockey Club. Robert's seconds were two young gentlemen of good family whom Caroline had met in Robert's company. They had wealth and no occupation beyond the social round that kept their idleness very busy.

"And the duel is to be in the Dingle, Ma'am: it's a lonely spot."

"Yes, Miss Caroline had told me that," said Aunt Luci.

Jerome went off to get the rugs for the carriage, for it was a raw morning.

"Well, my dear," said Aunt Lucinda, "unless Edmund Browne, or ourselves, can dissuade these young men, one of them will be dead within an hour, and the other labelled a murderer by all right-minded people. . . . Sophia, why are you wearing your new costume?"

Sophia went red. She was dressed in a new tartan skirt and jacket, and carried a golden seal muff to wear with her golden seal jacket. She was dressed as if she were making a call rather than going to a distressful meeting.

Sophia hung her head but made no reply about her clothing, and as Jerome was coming back with the rugs, they were all too busy getting bundled up in the carriage for Aunt Luci to persist in asking her why she was so dressed up.

As Jerome handed the ladies into the carriage he seemed quite as usual. But when he came to whip up the horses, he did it with such fervour that Aunt Luci spoke sharply to him. Turning to her from the driving box, he called down: "I'm sorry, Ma'am, but with all that goes on this morning, I'm that nervous!"

Jerome only expressed what Aunt Lucinda herself felt. It was going to be a difficult morning to get through. They drove around the half circle of Wilton Crescent to get the horses turned neatly and Caroline could not help envying the shut calm houses of their neighbours, the sleeping people unconscious of the drama about to take place if Edmund could not stop it. They drove up from Wilton Crescent to the big gates opening into Hyde Park. Not a soul was in sight in the early hours of that morning, and Caroline felt how queer it was to listen to the horses' hooves in the empty streets, and to reflect that whilst all London lay asleep, secure and cosy, she was going to witness what could easily be a death—unless, that was, Edmund Browne had thought of some way out of the dilemma.

When they arrived just before five in the morning at Hyde Park, the great gates had just been opened by the gate keeper, who had then retreated to breakfast in his little cottage just inside the park gates. The park was deserted and empty. The noise of the carriage wheels seemed unnaturally loud on the gravelled pathway in the beautiful silent park. Caroline remembered Hyde Park only as she had seen it in the Season, in the afternoons, when smart people went walking or riding on horseback, or took drives in their open carriages, to see their friends and to be seen, to take an ice under the trees perhaps with other fashionables, and generally to talk, laugh, and exchange gossip and the news of the day. Now she was seeing the park in another way, a way that might remain in her memory for all time. It was grim. A grey mist was slowly rising and clearing, thin, blanketing wisps like pulled-out shreds of cotton wool. Where the mist had lifted the grass sparkled with diamonds of dew, dew which disappeared as a thin September sun penetrated the damp of the night and showed them the trees, wreathed in the brown leaves of autumn.

They drove straight to the Dingle, a spot which, at first sight, seemed lonelier even than the rest of the Park, for it was hidden from the casual stroller with many trees and shrubs enclosing it.

There they found all four seconds, top hatted and top-coated, already arrived, and each two examining carefully the pistols laid out in their elaborate, satin-lined boxes. All four young men paused in their task and raised their top hats politely to the ladies, but with an air of obvious surprise, stopping their converse and turning to look at the carriage as it came to a halt not far from the duelling ground. The two antagonists kept apart, Harry sitting on a small outcrop of rock, and Robert leaning nonchalantly and gracefully against a tree. Both young men already had their coats off, and Caroline could not help but notice how the white of Robert's frilled shirt suited his dark good looks, whilst Harry merely looked more countrified than ever without his coat. Duels were obviously something to Robert's taste but Harry looked as miserable as if he were negotiating someone's drawing room, clumsy and out of place, even though he was now out of doors. This kind of thing, with all its exquisite politenesses, bowings and scrapings and rules, was not his notion of fighting.

The doctor, Doctor John Dickinson, moved nervously between the two protagonists. He had not attended a duelling affair in more than twenty years, and what had seemed a fairly common thing when he was a young man now seemed to him, in middle age, a little extraordinary and something that really couldn't be happening. Not that he disapproved of it. He had always felt that duelling was perhaps the best way to settle a point of honour. But he would have refused to come if he had given himself a little more time to reflect. However, he had known both young men since they were boys, and on the whole he preferred to be able to face both their families as having done the best he could for whichever one of them was hurt. Of course he had no idea that this was to be a duel to the death. He thought in terms of one man winging the other, because in the last days of duelling, when he was a young man, that was what had happened. At least, in England. Of course, in France! But then the French! Well, the French were an excitable, theatrical lot. You knew that the minute you got off an English boat at Calais.

Now who were these women? Women should not be at duels. This was purely a man's affair. He hoped they would not be allowed to hold up the duelling. Having gone so far he wanted to get it over with, do whatever he would have to do, and get back to the safety of his doctor's office.

Caroline looked around quickly. Where was Edmund Browne? He had said he would be there with a friend, or friends. But where was he? The seconds were measuring out the duelling ground, trying to be sure it was all on even terrain. Edmund Browne would have to arrive in the next few seconds if anything was to be done. But no sign of him. And then it occurred to her that perhaps he was not coming. He had been so sympathetic about her distress over the duel, that she'd quite forgotten she had any reason to be angry with him. She had told him everything, had trusted him completely. When she came to think of it, what reason had she to trust him so utterly? After he had failed to convince either Robert or Harry, why had she imagined that Edmund would manage something at the last minute to stop the matter? Why had she believed he even wanted to stop it? What was it to him? Every time she saw Edmund Browne she let herself be confused into remembering the tutor she had trusted as a child. But he had changed. That horrible editorial! Then, how could she think so well of a man who so obviously thought so little of women? As Edmund Browne did not come, and did not come, she began then to ask herself why she had imagined that the word of such a man could be taken seriously. She thought, supposing he is one of those who always want to please the people they are with? People who do not bother to keep promises once they are out of sight of the person to whom they have promised? He was obviously a man who liked to charm. He had pleased Sir Ernest de Lisle Devonshire and her uncle when he had read that editorial aloud. He had pleased the Editor of *The Times* when he had agreed to write it. And he had pleased her with fine promises when she had seen him. For why not? This way he could find grace and acceptance with everybody. No, he was not coming. And all this thinking would get her nowhere. Edmund Browne had left her here at the duel to take care of matters herself. More probably he had never dreamt that she would arrive at the duelling place herself and so would have been able to concoct some smooth story of how he had arrived too late, or something of that sort. The man was indeed odious! She would not make the same mistake with him again.

Hardly waiting for the carriage to stop, Caroline alighted without the help of Jerome, and gathering her cape about her, rushed to where Robert, startled to see her there, but cool as always, now waited to receive her.

"Robert, you can't go on with this!" she called to him when she was still some paces away from him.

"Why, good morning, Caroline. How well that grey dress becomes you! I am flattered at your coming. But how did you know it was here? It was supposed to be a well-kept secret. Did Harry come looking for sympathy and tell you? I'm very touched by your coming, anyway, but you can't stay. Please get back into your carriage where your aunt and cousin are still sitting. This isn't the place for women—though I shall always remember that you came. But I assure you I'm in no danger."

"Robert, please! Please give up this terrible duel. You will kill your cousin and—people will say you are a murderer!"

"Not the people I care about," he said. "As for killing my cousin—that's exactly what I intend to do. After all, I'm sure I will be right in claiming that he intended to kill me. I had to defend myself: everyone knows Harry's quick temper."

"But there's no reason! I'm not going to marry you! Edmund Browne surely made that clear to you!"

"He made me understand how Harry has been pursuing you. Must have been from what he said. Harry deserves what he's going to get. He's been trying to make love to the girl I'm going to marry. He almost managed a breach of promise between us: But of course I won't have that! Once this morning is over I shall put my ring back upon your finger and I'm sure you'll never be persuaded to give it up again!"

"But it isn't Harry. It isn't Edmund Browne. It's me! I don't want to be engaged. I want to be free. Harry has done nothing—"

"I am the better judge of that! I know what Harry has been up to! Browne merely confirmed my suspicions. Harry has been taking things from me all my life, trying to make me ridiculous. Well, he won't take you!"

"But this is preposterous, Robert. Harry and I—"

"I don't want to hear about Harry and you. Browne told me all I need to know and I refuse to accept it—"

"What on earth has Edmund Browne said to you?" Caroline cried. "It's all wrong, whatever it is! Harry is innocent—"

"I don't want to discuss it," said Robert. "If you want to tell me about it after this duel is over, I suppose I shall have to listen, however distasteful it is. But I already forgive you. I'm sure nobody but Harry was to blame."

"Robert! You're preposterous in what you evidently think."

"Think! I thought it before Browne came. Now I *know* it!"

Caroline did not know what to say. Robert seemed to become more implacable and distant the more she talked. What had Edmund Browne said to him? She could only guess—but that was silly. She had never said in any way that she cared about Harry—other than as a friend. But it was obvious it was no use trying to reason with Robert now. Perhaps Harry could be persuaded to give up this duel before he lost his life in it. She turned from Robert to go to Harry. As she did so, she saw Sophia crossing the grass towards Robert. She was crying!

But Caroline had to be quick if she was to see Harry before the duel began. Already the seconds had paced out the ground. Harry, seeing her coming, put out both his hands to her and without thought, she gave him her hands.

An immediate smile broke upon his plain face. It was obvious that he was glad she had come.

"Caroline, I knew you cared," said Harry with all the plainness of a simple man.

Caroline was surprised by these words but, with a quick look at Harry's ecstatic face, she decided not to disabuse him for the moment, for he continued:

"When you look at me the way you do now, I think I may have a chance to wing Robert before he wings me. Perhaps I can be just that second quicker with my pistol than he thinks I can be. He's so sure of himself. . . . he may be too sure. The fact that you care puts heart into me."

What could she say to him? She hesitated, and at this second Major Fortescue accompanied by a second of Robert's she did not know, a Mr. Clewiston, stepped up to her, removed his beautiful military hat, and said: "Deuced difficult, ma'am, but I must ask you, and the other ladies, to withdraw. We are about to begin and those who are not of the duelling party must stand aside. Allow me, ma'am." He crooked his arm to start her moving away from Harry and Caroline had to accept.

Should she have told Harry that Robert meant not to wing him, but to kill him? She did not know. But her troubled heart prompted her to think that she had said nothing. The more Harry believed that he had a chance and that, in any case, it was merely a matter of one or the other being wounded, the better for him in these, perhaps his last, minutes.

Sophia and her mother now entered the carriage being brought there by one of Harry's seconds, Major Fortescue.

"I did my best," said Aunt Lucinda, "I begged Robert to give up this thing, or merely to wound Harry. He refused to listen."

Sophia, seating herself in the carriage, now said:

"Oh Caroline, isn't Robert splendid! And how can you have been so thoughtless! Robert told me that your lack of dignity—he did *not* say your flirting, but I think he meant it—with that stupid man Harry de Lisle has forced him, as your fiancé, to shoot that worthless cousin of his. And possibly Robert will be tried for murder! Such a brave man, such an honourable man, to be put in such a position by your encouragement of Harry's attentions!"

Sophia collapsed into tears at her own words and their meaning and Caroline looked at her with astonishment. What tarradiddle had Robert managed to tell Sophia?

Mrs. Newcombe looked at her daughter sharply. "Don't show your intimate feelings in public, so! And don't talk like that to Caroline. Sophia, I am ashamed of you!"

"But Robert is no longer Caroline's," said Sophia. "I *heard* what she said to him. I heard ... I mean, I overheard ... Caroline doesn't want him. He is as free as air!" She finished rather lamely, her face suddenly suffused as she realised she should not have admitted to overhearing things not intended for her.

But whatever might have been said to Sophia in response to her outburst was never said because, looking to the duelling ground, all three women saw that both shirtsleeved young men, having been backed up together, were now pacing the allotted distance away from each other to the spot where, on the count, they were entitled to turn and fire.

Again Caroline looked wildly around her. Where was Edmund Browne? Whatever she thought of his character, if he could only turn up now and stop this madness! But there was no sign of him. Caroline felt a fierce flame of hatred towards him in her heart; as fierce a flame of hatred now as she had once, as a child, felt a fierce flame of love.

The two men had reached their distances, had wheeled

around, pistols raised. There were two sharp reports, one upon the other, the second so close it was like an echo of the first. And then a third shot was heard, almost on top of the first two. There was a cry which came from neither Harry nor Robert, though it was only later that this was remarked.

Robert was clutching his forearm, his right forearm, and blood now stained his white shirt sleeve. He dropped his smoking pistol and sank on his knees to the ground. Through the fingers of his left hand blood pumped terribly from the wounded right arm. He was deathly white. There was a second when nobody moved and then the doctor and Robert's two seconds, suddenly no longer languid young men, ran to where Robert now lay in his blood.

Aunt Lucinda had descended from the carriage, Caroline after her. Sophia came last but pushed past her mother and her cousin. She was calling wildly: "Robert! Robert! If you die—" Sophia had thrown all discretion to the winds and now had fought her way through the little group around Robert. Sinking on the grass beside the wounded man, she gathered Robert's head into her arms and pillowed it upon her lap.

Harry stood there stupidly looking across to where his opponent had fallen and eyeing his own pistol with surprise. Presently he walked over to where Robert lay, his seconds with him, and said: "But I can't have hit him. Why—"

"You winged him all right," said one of his seconds.

"And badly," added the doctor, who was busy, his little black bag opened on the grass where he knelt beside the wounded man. "You hit an artery and the bone is shattered. He may never have a really straight arm again!"

"Oh!" moaned Sophia. "Oh, Robert!"

Harry, distressed at the sight of Robert, and puzzled by the weeping Sophia, turned to Caroline. "Caro, you know I only accepted the challenge for you. Now I know you repulsed me at your aunt's because you were afraid of him. I felt sure of it!"

"No, Harry," Caroline said firmly. "I was not putting

you off because of Robert." She felt sorry for Harry as she spoke. He was such a good-hearted man, as puzzled now by love as he was by hatred, especially Robert's hatred. Not to be liked by his cousin, he could understand. But hated!

Now Harry's seconds, seeing that Robert was all right and that they could do nothing for him, turned to look at the coppice in front of which Harry had stood. There was that third shot to explain—and the strange cry. They were of the opinion that the shot had come from Robert's side and the cry from Harry's. Arriving at the coppice, Major Fortescue stooped over something on the ground. When he stood up, he was wiping a bloodied hand on a handkerchief. Robert's seconds now joined Harry's and looked down too. There was a moment's terrible silence between the four young men, then:

"Dead!" said Fortescue simply and clearly. His voice carried on the still morning air. Everyone started up to look where he stood. There at the edge of the copse was what at first sight seemed a heap of ragged clothing, but as the rising sun pencilled beams of light through the young trees, one saw that the heap of rags was all that was left of a human being—a tramp, who now lay with a bullet drilled through his grey head.

"It can't be our man," said Fortescue to Cavanagh. "This corpse is behind de Lisle. It's got to be Devonshire's gun. Yet the sound of two bullets being fired came from de Lisle's side, I'll swear it. And then, deuce take, it Devonshire is too good a shot to shoot this wide of the mark."

"Unless he shot a fraction after the bullet entered his arm. Such a wound as he received would certainly deflect his aim. I think it may have been Devonshire's bullet that found this tramp."

"Maybe. But how could de Lisle fire twice? Each man had but one bullet in his pistol—we checked that with the other seconds. Better go and speak to them now. In any case we need the doctor, though I'm sure this poor fellow's dead."

As though he had heard their request for him, the

elderly doctor came nervously up the slight incline on which the coppice was set. "Good lord!" he exclaimed, seeing the body on the ground. "This will mean the police."

"And I had thought," said the doctor sadly, "that with just a bullet in the arm, the whole duel might have been kept quiet. It's out of the question now."

Whatever brought them no one could at that time imagine, but at this moment a sergeant and two policemen came around the edge of a clump of trees and moved in upon the scene. The group of policemen looked so efficient in their navy blue coats, black shining leather belts and stiff hard helmets, with their truncheons held ready for use. But to some extent they also seemed silly, for they were out of breath and had the air of men who were late for an appointment—a ridiculous idea, for they could not possibly have known of the duel. Their arrival must have been coincidental, thought Caroline.

They promptly took command of the little group, taking names, addresses, particulars of everyone. Caroline heard words "Arresting . . . disturbing the peace . . . duelling in a public place . . ." and then she was being guided by Jerome into the carriage. But the police sergeant stopped Jerome before he could climb to his box. With his hand upon the bridle of one of the two horses, the sergeant said: "Just follow our van to Bow Street Police Station. I won't ask the ladies to ride in the police van, but be sure to be right behind."

"Oh," said Aunt Luci, leaning out the window. "You can't possibly mean it, Sergeant."

"But I do mean it, Ma'am. I'm sorry to incommode you ladies, but the law is the law, and it has been contravened."

"Why can't they at least use simple English," said Aunt Luci, with a characteristic touch of asperity. "If he means the law has been broken, why can't he say so, right out?"

"Maybe because the law has not been broken," ventured Caroline, "just a little torn." She tried to smile as she made her feeble joke, but her heart was heavy. Bow Street Police Station! It was awful! How could she, Caroline, have brought everyone to this pass? She was miserable. She had seen the police march Harry off in the van, and Robert had only kept his freedom because the doctor had expostulated and said his patient must be put to bed, and that quickly. There would be work for a surgeon to do.

Arrived at Bow Street Police Station, Caroline was silent from misery. Aunt Luci was silent too, because Mr. Trimble had long ago explained to her that she was to say nothing at any time (if she had trouble with the police) unless he, her solicitor, were present. But they both had to listen to a tearful Sophia tell how it was all Caroline's fault. The desk sergeant didn't want to hear whose fault it was. He wanted to say there would be an inquest, and they would each be notified to appear. At last they were released, and Jerome handed them back into the carriage.

They had arrived when nearby Covent Garden was still bustling, tidying up after the early hours of work. By the time they were free to go, it was well past ten a.m. and Covent Garden was dead. Only a few wisps of straw and one or two cabbage leaves were blowing into Bow Street to witness its close proximity to the famous vegetable and fruit market.

When Caroline thought of Edmund Browne, and his promise, a hot flood of anger suffused her. But this was drowned again by a feeling of helplessness and regret—helplessness to stop the on-rolling ball of Fate and regret that all these things had happened. Nothing had gone right since she had spoken up in the drawing room. In fact, like it or not, things seemed to be going from bad to worse.

Chapter 12

The carriage had at last nearly reached Wilton Crescent. Sophia sat in her corner in her tartan finery of the morning. Her skirt was now grass-stained, and her face was tear-streaked. But her manner was defiant. This defiance puzzled Caroline because she had realised, when Sophia ran to the wounded Robert, that her cousin was in love with him. If she had been Sophia, she would now be feeling all the shame possible after making such a public demonstration of love to a man still determinedly affianced to herself, Caroline, whether Caroline wanted it so or not. Robert, Caroline was sure, had never even looked at Sophia. Now Caroline felt sorry for the girl who, however defiant her manner, must, she told herself, be feeling shame. Nevertheless she could not but agree with Aunt Lucinda's words to her daughter:

"—making a public spectacle of yourself! It'll be all around the officers' mess by this forenoon. Count on Major Fortescue for that! Whatever your feelings, Sophia (and at your age they can only be imagined feelings), I never thought you would behave so shamelessly in public. Oh dear, at the thought of the way your name will be bandied about now, I vow I could faint! If only I had my *sal volatile* with me!"

Sophia made no answer. She continued to look defiant. Actually her air of defiance was to ward off comments on her behaviour or, worse, questions to make her explain herself. If the truth were known, Sophia did not at all regret her actions. At least Robert now knew how much she cared for him. If he ever agreed to breaking off the engagement—and the way Caroline went on, he might very well do so—then she, Sophia, would be waiting. Sophia had made a bold bid to get what she wanted. If she should somehow succeed in marrying Robert, she knew enough about the fashionable world to be sure that the wagging tongues would quickly turn from criticising her to congratulating Robert and wishing her all happiness. Besides, people could be reminded how young she was: just turned eighteen. Yes, thought Sophia, if things look awkward I can always insist on my youth.

Busy putting herself in Sophia's shoes, Caroline said to herself: "How dreadful it must be to want to marry someone who is very unlikely to marry you." Even if Caroline had stepped aside and Robert came to care for Sophia, Sophia was not going to make a début, nor would she have a dowry. Mrs. Newcombe's Ogilvie blood gave her the right to make a débutante of her daughter, but her means forbade it. Without a début, without a dowry, Lady de Lisle Devonshire would not even know that Sophia was in the world. Oh yes, she had met her here and there, but Lady Devonshire also met horses, dogs and furniture here and there. One didn't really *know* people unless they came "out". Robert might know Sophia but his formidable mother would see to it that he never married a penniless girl. Pity crept into Caroline's heart—pity mixed with a little contempt. Whatever love Caroline might feel for a man, she was certain that she would not be so lacking in pride as Sophia seemed willing to be. She would never act in such a way as practically to *ask* a man to marry her!

Caroline's attention now wandered outside the carriage window. There was a wind rising which gathered up old newsprints and skittered them along the road; in the gutter small leaves flittered together with little eddies of dust. The crossing sweepers were out with twig brooms. How normal, how ordinary everything seemed. Just another London day. Yet Caroline had not had a morning anyone could call ordinary. Nor could she look forward to an ordinary day. She was in deep trouble and had caused others to be in deep trouble—her aunt, Harry, even Robert, for if she had not provoked his instant jealousy—and however unintentionally, she had done so—this duel would never have happened. There would be horrible repercusions from this morning. A man had been killed. When her Aunt Millie heard of it and, worse, when Uncle Ham did . . . ! She did not finish that thought.

Her Aunt Luci now broke the silence, quite as if she had read Caroline's thought: "I must get hold of my solicitor at once. As our names are now with the police, Mr. Trimble must be told immediately what has happened. He will advise me of the best course to pursue. And the newsprints—perhaps Mr. Trimble will know some way of avoiding having our names used."

Caroline thought: the newsprints? No, she could not hope that the affair would not get into the newspapers. Her engagement to Robert de Lisle Devonshire had been a prominent item in the social columns. She could only hope that the printing of the story would be delayed and that they might be able to slip out of London before reporters began to ferret out where she lived. She knew that there might be some delay in getting the facts because neither Harry nor Robert would let a woman's name be dragged into the newspapers if it could be in any way avoided or at least put off. The fact that the police were now involved meant probably that by tomorrow morning it might get into the Press. But at least that would give her a little time to think what she should do, and what Aunt Lucinda could do and say. So she thought. However, when the carriage turned a corner past a number of buildings which were being demolished (some said to build a hospital), to her horror she saw a billboard which read "Stop Press! Duel in Hyde Park." And the newspaper? *The Times*! No! No! It was out of the question. Jerome had slowed the horses to a walk now so they could presently turn into Wilton Crescent. This meant that Caroline could really see the placard plainly. There it stood, the news vendor and his piled up wares beside it, a few copies under his arm. As Caroline stared a man stopped and bought a copy. He immediately turned to the Stop Press item on the back page. "Duel in Hyde Park"! No, she could not quite believe it of him. It was too perfidious. She had turned to him in her distress. He had offered her comfort and help. But who else knew of the duel, who else in the newspaper business, but he? The only person was Edmund Browne. The only person connected with the duel and with *The Times* was Edmund Browne. There was no one else. He had seemed sincere. What of it? All the time he had been thinking of his newspaper and what a good story a duel in Hyde Park would make. He was a knave! An arrant knave! Her uncle had often said of journalists that "no journalist is a gentleman and no gentleman could afford to be a journalist". Everything they learned, he argued, was for sale to the newspaper that employed them. Anger and humiliation possessed her mind. Pain flooded her heart. And following on that pain, a hot flame of rage. Oh, if she ever saw him again what she would tell him! She would make him suffer! But she would never see him again: *that* she could promise herself.

Caroline turned in her pain and rage to draw her aunt's attention to the placard, that evidence out on the street there that proved Edmund Browne's baseness. Oh, *that* was why he had not turned up in Hyde Park to stop the duel as he had practically told her he would. But of course he had not wanted the duel stopped. He had wanted it to happen. For all she knew he had encouraged Robert to go on with it, whilst telling her that he had done the opposite. It gave him a good story for his newspaper. Had he not been willing to make a scurrilous statement about women to please the Editor? Why should he not then sell out his one time little pupil! A mere girl! It gave him a good story for *The Times*. She wondered how much the newspaper would pay him for this betrayal. And he must have had a spy posted to tell him that the duel had actually taken place. She was about to draw all this to the attention of her aunt when she saw how pale Aunt Lucinda was. She was lying back against the carriage cushions now with her eyes closed. She looked tired and Caroline realised that Aunt Luci, for all her active ways, was not so young. She should be spared this last blow—at least for the time being. So Caroline said nothing.

At last they were at No. 70 Wilton Crescent. Jerome flung the reins on the backs of the mild-tempered horses, jumped from the box, opened the carriage door, let down the carriage steps, and was now handing her aunt on to the pavement.

The faithful Rosie must have been waiting inside the door, for no sooner had the carriage come to a halt than the gleaming, black painted door opened, and Rosie in her white morning cap and voluminous white morning apron stood there waiting for them to enter. She looked concerned.

"Oh, Ma'am," she said to Mrs. Newcombe, "Mr. Browne has been here. He had to go to his newspaper, but he says he'll be back. He was in such a state, all upset."

"When he comes," said Aunt Lucinda, "show him right into the drawing room."

"No!" said Caroline quickly. She glanced around the little front hall looking for the morning paper *The Times,* and then saw that Rosie was holding something behind her skirts obviously to conceal it. "Give it to me, Rosie," Caroline said. "It's *The Times* you're hiding, isn't it?"

Rosie reluctantly produced the newspaper folded to the back page and the Stop Press. Her face was full of concern.

"Oh!" exclaimed Aunt Lucinda as she read the Stop Press. "Duel in Hyde Park"! And in the small print it says: "Quarrel over heiress."

"It must be Edmund Browne, Aunt, who told of it to *The Times.* He is the only one connected with the newsprints who knew of the duel. Contemptible man!" she added passionately.

Aunt Lucinda sank on a small hall chair. "I would never have believed such infamy of him! He seemed such a gentleman!"

Caroline thought now of his mocking, sarcastic air in the conservatory. She could quite imagine him looking on the contretemps with Robert with just that same mock-

158

ery—as though he looked at a scene in which he played no part. That was why he had struck her as almost aloof, not the least bit involved himself, deliberately withdrawn, indeed. Here, of course, was the reason for his air of being outside her difficulties with Robert, her concern for Harry. It was undoubtedly the reporter in him which had bidden him take such an impersonal interest in what was going on. He *had* seemed as if some shutter in his mind had been pulled down went she talked with him. He was observing and recording all the time for his paper. It must be the explanation. Oh, how she hated him! What a wicked, cold, calculating heart!

"Let us keep our heads," enjoined Aunt Luci now. "We are all tired. Heavens knows what we will have to put up with before the day is out. Police maybe. Reporters! Oh dear, it's all too much for me! And for you, too, Caroline, I'm sure. You look so white! I suggest a warm bath and breakfast in your room. Sophy, go and take off that grass-stained dress and bathe your face. A little time in bed wouldn't hurt you either. Oh and Jerome, Rosie, we are not at home to Mr. Browne, or indeed to anyone. Naturally, of course, the police. But I shall see Mr. Trimble about that. He will know what to do."

Rose, and the little kitchenmaid, Kate, brought up big ewers of hot water by the backstairs to make the slipper bath in Caroline's room deep and warm. Fresh from the comfort of it and wrapped round in a soft pink bathrobe of her aunt's, a little tight in the shoulders, a little short in the skirt, and a little too ample in the middle, Caroline nibbled on toast and drank hot chocolate. She felt physically less worn out then.

"A bit of sleep, Miss," advised Rosie. "A bit of a lie down is what would do you good." She was tidying up from the bath and removing that article from the bedroom. "Troubles," continued Rosie, "are always worse when you bring a tired mind to think on them."

A tired mind? Yes, Caroline certainly had that, and a heart that pained. She had been deeply hurt by Edmund Browne. Each time she had admitted him to her friendship, he had turned out to be other than he seemed. She had danced with him and sung with him only to find that he could write as though he despised women. She had spent an evening with him at the inn and had subsequently and, she thought, naturally, turned to him for advice about the duel because he had made her think of him as a kindly man, and he had betrayed her. So thinking, she let Rosie draw the curtains against the light and, climbing into bed, slept the uneasy sleep of a tired and weary girl. She had gone to sleep on Rosie's admonitions to do so, she awoke to Rosie's urgent pleas.

"Wake up, Miss Caroline! He's downstairs and he says he just has to see you. The Mistress is out, gone to see Mr. Trimble she said. And he's downstairs, Miss, I mean Mr. Browne, not Mr. Trimble."

"But you and Jerome were told we would not receive him!"

"I know, Miss. But Jerome isn't here. He's out to the wine merchants, to see about your aunt's sherry wine. And Mr. Browne is that persuasive, Miss. Said it was important. Then he kind of pushed past me, quite polite, Miss, but that definite, that masterful. I wish you'd come, Miss."

"But I'm not dressed, Rosie."

"He says he doesn't care, Miss Caroline. He'll wait."

"Tell him I won't see him. I just won't come down."

"Wouldn't be surprised Miss, if he didn't come up!"

"He wouldn't dare!"

"I don't know about daring, Miss. Seems like he's willing to dare anything the way he feels. Wouldn't put anything past him, Miss. Walking up and down the drawing room, he is, like a caged lion."

"Oh!" said Caroline angrily. "Oh! But what can I put on?" she asked. "I will not get dressed. I shall see him, if I do see him—and I suppose I shall have to—for just one minute."

"Well, begging your pardon Miss, but I borrowed this new *peignoir* from Miss Sophia's room. It might be a bit loose, is all." Rose held out a yellow velvet peignoir ruffled at neck and sleeves with tea-rose taffeta, and with a tea-rose taffeta petticoat to go underneath.

Caroline looked at it with distaste. It was so wilfully *coquette*. But she put it on, and saw in a hurried glance in the mirror that it accentuated the black of her curly hair and the creamy colour of her skin. She did not want to look closely at herself in this seductive *robe de chambre,* but if she had bothered to do so she would have seen that it became her well. Rosie quickly put up her tendrilly hair over the rats, pinning it in place with a few well-placed combs of tortoiseshell so that it framed her face and left her small ears, like two pink-white shells, exposed to view. The open neck of the *peignoir* and the dark upswept hair brought out again the delicate look of her slender neck, a fine stem (had she but known it) to carry such an imperious little head. She entered the long drawing room with an expression of hardly controlled fury which made her big eyes brilliant and kept her chin at a level of hauteur he had never seen in her before.

He got up from the plum velvet sofa with that maddening grace that came naturally to him, smiling at her. He held out his hand in greeting but she ignored the formalities—she did not want to even touch his hand—and said:

"What effrontery brings you here?"

"Why, Caroline!" He was shocked. She could not help but notice how the silver grey of his frock coat suited him, how handsome the black cravat was on him, and how much the high, white collar set off the fine olive tone of his skin. He looked what indeed he was, a man of the world, beautifully tailored, beautifully barbered, and for some reason the very fact of his extreme good looks made her all the angrier. His expression was calm but puzzled.

"Don't wear that innocent air!" she said, sweeping down on him. "Don't act as if you are my friend! I remember what you promised and know what you didn't do, and I hate you for all of your lying behaviour."

"But," he said and his voice held a note of astonished bewilderment, "I came to explain, to tell you . . ."

"You have nothing to tell me. There is nothing you can tell I do not already know," she stormed, and as she talked she walked up and down the parquet floor of the drawing room, her yellow velvet train swishing behind her

on the light coloured parquet, the rustle of her taffeta petticoat adding inevitably to her charm, her whole body full
of anger and force, the sort of anger which found some
faint relief in the impatient kick she gave to the train of
the peignoir when she turned angrily at each end of the
long room in her quick walk.

"You took me in entirely," she said. "I *believed* you
when you said you would be there in Hyde Park, that
you'd find some way at least of trying to stop the duel. I
waited for you with such faith—and in vain. And then—
and then—you gave the story to *The Times*. Gave it?
Sold it! For money. How horrible! How can you dare to
come here to face me . . ."

"Because I am innocent," he broke in. "Innocent of all
you impute to me. I guessed you might be thinking these
things; that is why I insisted on seeing you."

"Yes, you are innocent! Innocent, I suppose, too, of
that editorial you took such pride in reading in my uncle's
drawing room and which led to all my trouble!"

"That was an unfortunate moment," he said.

"Unfortunate! That is all you call it? I've tried to forget
what you wrote, but then your behaviour to me makes me
realize that you have very little opinion of women. Oh
yes, I'm just a girl, a country girl, a girl you once taught.
I can be taken in with a little romantic waltzing, a remembered love song, a nice talk on a stormy night in an inn. I
can be fooled and fooled! But there is a point where it is
enough!"

She had clenched her small hands into fists and looked
now as though she could strike him.

He caught those fists before they could reach him, and
held them in his grip. What a girl! Wild, tempestuous,
beautiful, yet with that glint of steel somewhere in her. He
could feel her heaving breast against his, could smell the
perfume of her black hair, could see the cream of her skin
and her grey eyes aglint with green lights. He could feel
the struggle of her small body against the force of his
grasp.

"Stop talking!" he told her. "Shut up!" And then to his
own astonishment he added: "I'm in love with you!" He

shook her now by the arms and held her so that she was forced to look up at him. For a moment she stared unbelieving, then she threw back her head and laughed, a light, gay ripple of laughter ending on a note full of contempt and anger.

"Love?" she said. "What is this? The prelude to an interview. Am I to say I love you too? Is that how you will pry into how I feel and think about this whole terrible duel? I can see the headline: Heiress Tells All!" She was beyond herself now and said anything at all that came into her mind, however silly, so long as it would hurt him. Now she twisted suddenly and was free of his grasp. "Deny," she said, "that you had anything to do with *The Times* printing that story of the duel."

"Unfortunately I can't deny it," he said. "I confirmed to them that it had taken place. I—"

"There!" she said. "I knew it!"

"You don't understand the circumstances," he began.

"I think I do," she said. "You owed it to your editor. After all, it's for that you get paid. You were there at the duel. But as a reporter—concealed somewhere so you could confirm that the duel *The Times* already knew about had actually taken place. Oh, you must be proud of yourself! You have left Harry, that good friend of yours, actually in the hands of the police, Robert wounded and in trouble with the law, too. Some poor wretched man dead. Some innocent. There will be an inquest. We shall all be there, I'm sure. And we had counted on *you* of all people to stop this thing before it began. But for your own ignoble purposes I'm convinced you encouraged the duel. And you have the effrontery now to stand there and try to tell me that you love me—love me . . ."

"I do," he said and, as she had paused in her storming way, turning to take up her angry march again, he reached out and held her now in arms that would not let her go.

"I do love you!" He put a hand beneath her small chin and forced her head back so that she must look into his eyes. "I love you," he said more quietly, and bent and kissed her too quickly for her to twist away. His mouth was hard pressed on hers in a quick, rough kiss and as their lips met she felt a flame of passion run over her, such as she had never experienced before. For a moment she relaxed against him, surprised out of her rage, and then feeling the tears would betray her next, she flung away from him. "Go—get out! Get out, please!" she said. She pulled her hand across her mouth as though to wipe off his kiss. "I want nothing of you—nothing! You stifle the air I breath! No, don't dare touch me again. Go! Just go!"

Then he picked up his silver grey top hat, paused, looked at her, made as if to speak again, and then sighed, an audible, heavy sigh of great sadness, and he left.

Astonishing girl, he thought as he went. Wrapped in mysterious thoughts and totally incalculable. She did not understand what had happened and it seemed to him she did not wish to understand. She flung words about her wantonly, prompted by her own enormous pride, by instinct and by pain. She had been cruel; no girl had ever been so cruel to him as her words. But, of course, she thought she had been betrayed. She did not understand the workings of newspapers, and that much that happened would not be by his decision. But even as he began to make these excuses for her, he began to be angry with her too. Why could she not let him explain?

No, she was not fair. If this is what came of loving a woman with a temper and a mind of her own, then he would prefer to love any of the silly creatures he met constantly at dinner parties. But that was not right either. Horribly apparent, the truth pressed cruelly in on him. It was she whom he loved. No other. And as that knowledge smote him, that he had not just been telling her he loved her, but actually did, whether he liked it or not, a feeling of utter loss came to him. All his life he had dealt with difficulties. He had always felt he could master anything that was wrong and put it right. But here was a difficulty he could not manage. Damn the girl! Damn her? He loved her to distraction!

He writhed, remembering how he had run like any messenger boy here and there for her. And like a messenger boy she had treated him. This was torment. He hated her for the pain. He loved her, wanted her. Surely this was understandable? Amongst women she was unique.

He arrived at the Arlington. He was proud of the set of rooms he had achieved there. He was rightly pleased with the success he had had in Fleet Street which had caused him to be invited to live in this exclusive building. It was a building only for bachelors: no woman had ever been seen there. Now suddenly the building full of bachelors like himself seemed remote and lonely. He had always been happy to live alone. Now he no longer wanted to.

Caroline was alone in the drawing room. After all her sound and fury, and audible silence had descended. An empty silence. He had said he loved her. She threw herself down on the plum coloured sofa, and she wept. Her weeping was as wild as her temper had been wild. Her tears fell upon the innumerable stiff, indifferent little cushions and she clutched them in her grief, her whole body a thing of agony.

She remembered his kiss and her response. The touch of his lips still lingered on hers, sweet, and dreadful with self-knowledge at the same time. She cared about him! That horrible man! Oh, why did she care? Why could it not have been Robert—or even Harry? Anyone but Edmund! But it was Edmund she wanted, with all the passion Robert had sought from her and had not found. What was she to do? She loved Edmund with every scrap of her being and, as the knowledge grew in her of how passionately she cared, how she longed to be in his arms again, longed for another and another embrace, longed to return those embraces, she struck the little, prim cushions so unconcerned with her suffering, using her clenched fists. She said aloud: "I'll never see him again. I'll never consent to be alone with him. Never! Oh, Heaven help me!"

Chapter 13

Aunt Lucinda was distressed.

"Yes," she said unhappily. "Mr. Trimble says that, as I suspected, we may not all be called as witnesses at the inquest, but we will all have to go. And you, Caroline, will certainly be called to testify, he thinks."

"Oh, Aunt Luci, I am so sorry to have dragged you into this!" said Caroline.

"Why, child, you didn't plan it," said Aunt Luci kindly. "But I am wondering if after all we can escape reporters. There have been none yet."

"There was one, Mr. Browne," said Caroline, grimly. "I got rid of him." Her face was set and pale, but her voice was firm again. Before her Aunt's return from Mr. Trimble's, Caroline had taken herself in hand. She was now dressed in her paisley dress again. She had bathed her face, so puffed up with tears, in rose water and she hoped that, since her aunt did not see so well without her glasses, and Sophia was out shopping with little Katie in attendance, she would suffer no comment about her tear-ravaged face.

"Mr. Browne?" repeated Aunt Lucinda. "I do find it hard to believe that he is mixed up in this to our greater distress when he had offered to help us. I had every confidence in him. I'm sure there must be some explanation—"

"There is," said Caroline, grimacing. "We must remember that Mr. Browne is a newspaper man. His first duty is to his newspaper. I think from his point of view, he fancies that he is merley doing his job. Remember the editorial against women? Apparently it was not his wish to write that, but his duty to his editor, I gather. He may

166

even have come to Hyde Park as he had promised he would do. But if he did, he was hidden so he could report that the duel had actually taken place and *The Times* could print that news. Who sent the police? It must have been he. Remember no one else knew of the duel—that is, no one who was connected with newsprints, excepting Mr. Brown. When he was here, I asked him to deny that he was responsible for the story. He told me, he actually had the effrontery to tell me, that it was he who confirmed it. It's unpleasant to know that he was never our friend, but we have to look facts in the face."

"Confirmed the duel!" said Aunt Lucinda in horror. "Then he is a terrible man. And no gentleman. I must say the duel was noted only in *The Times*. Mr. Trimble had *The Globe, The Herald,* and *The Morning Post* in his office and none of them mentioned the duel at all. How horrible," said Aunt Lucinda. "And we trusted him!"

There was a gentle knock at the door. Jerome entered. He carried a silver salver with a letter upon it. It was a letter for Caroline from her aunt. Caroline's heart contracted at the sight of the sharply sloping handwriting of her Aunt Millie. Her eyes blurred with fresh tears as she tore open the letter to read:

". . . miss you so much. So distressing that you felt you had to leave home . . . Your uncle very angry but has agreed to wait to hear from you: he would prefer you to come home willingly. We will fetch you when you say. You must marry Robert and quickly so as to hush up any scandal your leaving your home may cause . . . Your heart-broken but loving Aunt Millie."

"I have brought the people I love most nothing but trouble," Caroline moaned to herself. "Trouble to both my aunts. After all, even Uncle Ham doesn't quite deserve to have his name in the newspapers. They will all hate it. What can happen that will be good now?"

The afternoon stretched in front of her. A long, grey afternoon of loneliness and of worry. What could she settle to? She would have liked to go out and see Mrs. Erskine at *The Englishwoman's Review*. It would be nice to tell her all that had happened to her, perhaps get some advice from her. No, she would not tell her of Edmund and her feelings for that wretch of a man. She could not bear to tell anyone of that. She really did not wish even to speak his name. It was impossible not to mention his name to Aunt Lucinda, because her aunt had to be made to realise that Edmund Browne was a dangerous man—an enemy who fought not with tactics you could counter in the open, but with masculine charm and even, the last time, with declarations of love. She did not believe he loved her. He had betrayed her to the newspaper he worked on. For money! But she loved him. "Oh my God!" she prayed silently. "Let me stop loving him!" She tried to think of Robert. He was hurt and she should, from common decency, visit him and see how he was doing. Perhaps in the end she would marry him. After all, if she was never to have the man she really loved, why not do as everyone wanted her to do, marry Robert? After all, it was pretty clear that marriage was the only career for women. Aunt Lucinda, she felt, for all her own air of independence, would agree to that idea. From one or two remarks that she had dropped Caroline understood her aunt to believe that her coolness with Robert was but temporary. It was obvious that Robert, on his side, had no intention of breaking off their engagement. Perhaps he did love her? If he did, it would help so much towards her own willingness to try to become as fond of him as is possible for a girl hopelessly in love with another man. The practical side to her nature told her that she did not wish to become a spinster. And if she did not accept Robert, it would be quite easy to find herself still single at thirty. Girls who dropped out of the débutante circle had no means of meeting men. No, she must try and think of Robert and of her engagement very coolly. But that would take a few days. She wished she could step away from the daily events of her present life, from the excitement of it too, so that she could face the idea of marriage to Robert more with her head than with her heart. It was what Aunt Lucinda, Uncle Ham would have counselled her if they had been able to see into her heart and mind.

The door opened and Sophia came in. She was very angry.

"I can't get to my own door unmolested," she protested.

"What *do* you mean?" Aunt Lucinda asked.

"Look out on to the pavement," said Sophia bitterly.

Caroline walked quickly towards the windows on the street. "You'd better stay well behind the heavy curtains," Sophia called to her, "or they'll see you." Caroline touched the velour of the curtains at the side and peeped out. "There is a group of men on the pavement," she told Aunt Luci. "They seem to be in front of this house."

"Yes, they *are* in front of this house!" snapped Sophia. "They're newspaper reporters. They stopped me. Wanted me to go to a studio at one of the newspapers and sit for my portrait to be made with a camera. There's a man from every newspaper in London out there, I'd judge, by the numbers of them. For a few moments they thought I was you."

"Well, thank Heaven they didn't know you were *you*," said Aunt Lucinda sharply. "After your behaviour in the park this morning—"

"Yes, I was wrong," said Sophia bitterly. "I thought with all that blood on his shirt that Robert had been killed."

"Even if you thought he was quite dead that was no way for my daughter to behave," said Aunt Lucinda angrily. "Robert Devonshire is engaged to your cousin—not to you."

Sophia hung her head. A wisp of fair hair fell over her plump doll's face. "I couldn't help my feelings," she said defensively.

Caroline looked at her pityingly. She could feel for Sophia. Now she herself knew what it was to love where that love would be no use. Caroline got up and went to Sophy and put an arm about her. "I'm sorry you feel so badly," she said.

"I wish you wouldn't—bother me!" said Sophia crossly.

"You are the one he is going to marry and you don't want him. But I don't want your pity, please!"

Whatever Aunt Lucinda or Caroline might have said to this was never said for with a light, quick tap on the door, and not waiting for an answering "Come in," Jerome entered. He was agitated.

"There are reporters everywhere, Ma'am," he said to Aunt Lucinda, speaking directly to her. "They're asking to see Miss Caroline. I said she wasn't here—that she'd gone to the country. But they said that one of them had seen you enter this morning, and now they've seen Miss Sophia and they want to come in and see anyone who will talk to them. Say they won't go away until they've seen someone in this house."

"Can't you call the police?"

"I could, Ma'am. But they couldn't do anything. These men are just doing their jobs—least that's the way they look at it. And I daresay the police would look at it that way, too. Their editors sent them to get a story and after all that's the way they make their money—bothering people in the news."

"But they're molesting us!"

"No, Ma'am, they're not. They can stay all night outside the house on the pavement if they want to, and they say they will keep a twenty-four-hour watch. It does mean no one can go in or out without being pestered."

"Whatever can we do?" asked Aunt Lucinda. "They're threatening."

"No, Ma'am, they're not. They are not threatening. They're just waiting. They have to do that: they work for their newspapers."

"Well, we're beginning to know what that means," said Caroline bitterly. "Working for a newspaper seems to take all the decency out of people!"

There was a silence. Then Jerome coughed discreetly and said:

"Begging your pardon, Ma'am, but I think I see a way to get rid of them."

"And what's that?" asked Aunt Lucinda.

"Well, Ma'am, if Miss Caroline truly wasn't here—"

"But she *is* here."

"Yes, Ma'am, but maybe she could be spirited away. I mean if I were to tell those reporters that the young lady will see them directly. I could put them all in the morning room and whilst they're in there, Miss Caroline and I could slip out the back way and Miss Sophia and yourself could see these people. Miss Sophia needn't answer any of their questions. She's under age, you are her legal guardian and she can say she can't talk without your permission. You can tell them what you choose to tell them and no more. They'll be disappointed not to see Miss Caroline. But we can tell them that we thought it was Miss Sophia that they wished to see. And like I already said to them, Miss Caroline has gone out of London to the country somewhere."

"But won't they pester Miss Sophia, Jerome, on some other day when we are not here to protect her?"

"No, Ma'am, not a bit. They don't seem to realise even that she was there in Hyde Park. They don't seem to rightly know who was there, beyond the duelling party itself. They'd love to know but you know, Ma'am, you're more than a match for them." Jerome's eyes sparkled with such good humour at the thought of Aunt Lucinda tackling the Press that Aunt Luci herself began to smile. Then she said:

"But if Miss Caroline is going out the back way, why should we need to have reporters in the house at all?"

"Unless they're safely in the house they will see us coming up the Mews. Those reporters are crawling all over the place. They're even watching the back door. But if we get them in here, they'll all come. Miss Caroline and me can leave by the Mews and get a four-wheeler at the corner to wherever Miss Caroline will spend the night. A couple of nights of her being elsewhere should do it."

"Yes, I see. But I wish Mr. Trimble were here. The thought of the house being full of reporters and you absent . . . I don't like not having a man in the house."

"Nothing easier, Ma'am. Rose can go and fetch Mr. Trimble in a cab. They've nothing to say to Rosie and any way they'll soon find out from her she isn't the talking kind. I'd be happier myself, Ma'am, to know Mr. Trimble was with you when I can't be there myself."

"And where will you take Miss Caroline, Jerome?"

"Ah, there's the rub. Ma'am. I can't think of any place. Maybe Miss Caroline could think of somewhere? Do you know anyone, Miss, who'd give you a bed for a night or two?"

Everyone waited for Caroline to come up with a name. Caroline thought of the friends of her débutante days. No, none of them would do. They would all be agog with her tale of reporters, and they would drive her wild wanting to know the details of the Hyde Park duel, the very details she was determined no one would learn from her—how the duel came about and, yes, how she felt about Robert. Anyway, they would judge her quite mad to run away from home, to leave comfort and security, to question her engagement, to risk a life maybe spent by herself. They would find her out of her senses not to marry Robert whilst she still had the chance to do so. Robert Devonshire, with the money and position the Devonshires had? And now her own fortune to add to his. Together she and Robert would be millionaires and more. No, there was no one she could go to on the spur of the moment like that, and no questions asked. If only Mrs. Erskine were in London. Again Caroline wished for that friend.

"Isn't there really anyone who could give you a bed just for a day or two until something else happens in the world and those newspaper men cool off a little and get interested in something else?" Jerome almost pleaded.

"I wish I could help you," said Aunt Luci. "But I can't. My friends are middle-aged like myself and would be fearful of getting tied up in scandal. I don't feel I could ask any of them."

"Of course not," said Caroline. She began to feel a little desperate at the thought that she knew no one intimately enough to ask them to take her in without needing to know every detail of why she needed a bed. Then she thought of someone. Stroud, Elizabeth Stroud, the dressmaker at the Sign of the Geranium, in Beak Street, Soho.

If only Stroud could be persuaded! She was sure she had been let go immediately for her uncle would never pay a dressmaker, or anyone else, who no longer could be of service to him. But Caroline had written her a note asking her to continue with her trousseau and telling her she would be paid. It was worth asking Elizabeth Stroud, anyway. She could only say "no". And somehow Caroline felt she would not.

"My dressmaker," she now said to her aunt. "She's known me since I was sixteen and she came to turn down my dresses. I see her for a few weeks every year. She lives here in London."

"Your dressmaker?" said Aunt Lucinda, looking doubtful.

"Why not?" interjected Jerome. "No one will look for her there."

"I'll have to tell Stroud," Caroline thought. "I can't let her take me in unless she knows about the duel and the reporters. It wouldn't do if I didn't. If she refuses to have me then I'll just have to come back here after dark."

"How soon can you be ready, Miss?" asked Jerome. "And may I suggest Rosie lends you her oldest cape? She has one with a hood she hardly ever wears now. You take the shopping basket on your arm, and if we come out the back way and anyone stops us we'll say it's only the maid and me going to do some household shopping. Can I know where you're going, Miss?" Caroline gave him the address.

And so it was that Caroline arrived in a four wheeler and in the company of Jerome at the Sign of the Geranium in Beak Street, Soho, where she found a neatly lettered piece of cardboard which read "E Stroud, top floor, front."

Elizabeth Stroud was at home. Caroline had guessed rightly. The moment Mr. Hamilton had realised that his niece was not there he had dismissed the dressmaker, paying exactly for the hours she had worked and not a penny more. But she had had Caroline's letter and so she had continued with the silk petticoats and nightclothes which had already been planned.

"For Heaven's sake!" exclaimed Stroud on sight of Caroline at her door. And then: "Come in, Miss. What can I do for you?"

Caroline quickly told her.

"Oh Miss, I couldn't!" said Stroud.

"That's all right," said Caroline, hiding her dissapointment, "it's a lot to ask."

"Oh no, Miss. It isn't that it would be trouble," said Elizabeth Stroud. "It's just that it isn't fine enough here for a lady of your sort to stay."

"A lady of what sort?" asked Jerome.

"Well, a *lady*," emphasized Stroud. "This isn't any place for a lady."

"And how's about it being a place for a girl?" asked Jerome. "I never noticed Miss Caroline put on any airs. Now, if it were our Miss Sophy—" he stopped, embarrassed. "Well, as I say, you can give Miss Caroline any kind of a shakedown and she'll be grateful."

"Oh, you mustn't *give* me anything," said Caroline. "I can well afford to pay—"

"I wasn't meaning that, Miss," said Stroud. "Although I won't refuse your money for I don't have too much myself. But to sleep *here,* you that's used to the best?"

"I'd be extremely thankful," said Caroline.

"Why don't you let Miss Caroline look into the next room?" asked Jerome suddenly, "and me and you, Miss Eliza, can have a bit of a talk. I don't think you know half the trouble Miss Caroline is in."

"Well the second room isn't any more comfortable than this," said Stroud. "But step this way, Miss Caroline."

Caroline entered the second room and pretended to survey it. Frankly, Stroud's rooms shocked her. The two little attic rooms, sparsely furnished with cast-off furniture, neat and clean as Stroud herself but bespeaking endless small endeavours to save pennies at the price of all comfort. Darns and patches held furniture covers together, there was a threadbare carpet, patched in more than one place with another piece of unrelated carpet, and the whole tacked to the bare, unpainted floor boards. Over all was the harsh smell of laundry soap testifying to

Stroud's efforts to rid the place of London's grime. But Caroline's eyes opened wide on the sagging bed, the spotted mirror, the fire grate that had fallen backwards and could not be used, the sagging floorboards, some of them even missing in corners, the immaculate table cloth folded to one side of the stained table, the air of crushing poverty the whole place held. Caroline's heart contracted. Poor Stroud! Caroline had had no idea she lived like this. But Stroud was a success in her own view. She kept herself. What was it like for people who had less work than Stroud? What was it like for people who had to resort to burning the wooden banisters to keep themselves warm? And Uncle Ham had let her live on the income from property like that; had even boasted that he had made profits to add to her fortune! And he had felt quite sure he was doing right to make her a good income. She did not understand something, she felt. Uncle Ham went to church: he prided himself on being a moral man.

Caroline shivered a little. Wasn't marriage, any marriage, better than coming so close to harsh realities? Maybe it was better to let Uncle Ham look after her properties and then hand them on to Robert. But it was clear Uncle Ham gave no thought to the tenants. Neither would Robert. Had she, Caroline, the hardness of heart to take her profit where she could, no matter what the conditions endured by the people who gave her those profits? No, she had to look into things at least. If her income was to come from slum property, she had to know the conditions under which it was derived. If only she were indifferent to suffering! She longed briefly for that wonderful moment on the staircase at the ball when Robert had come towards her with an outstretched hand, when she had realised that all she had to do was to say "yes" to his offer of marriage and she could live the rest of her life in that golden world of wealth where the hardships of the people would be no concern of hers, where a little polite visiting of the poor and the sick would be all that was expected of a great lady. But no, she was not made for that.

Stroud interrupted her reverie by coming into the room.

"If you want to, then, Miss," she offered, "you can stay here with me for now."

And so it was arranged. Caroline would stay two nights; at the most, three. Meanwhile the reporters would surely lose interest. Jerome, provided by Caroline with the necessary guineas, went out into the street and presently returned with a mattress, carried by two small boys, all ears and eyes and snuffling noses. Jerome got rid of them with the princely sum of two pence each and then proceeded to undo the bundle he himself was carrying: sheets, a pillow, two blankets.

"Lord love you! Spending all that money! I could have managed," chided Stroud, looking at Jerome.

"Yes," said Jerome. "I know your sort, Eliza Stroud, I know how you'd manage. You'd have given Miss Caroline your bed and sworn you had an extra something in here you could take out of the air at night. You'd have slept in the armchair over there. You'd have gone to bed after Miss Caroline and got yourself up before she could so she'd never have known how you slept. I know your kind!" Jerome sounded angry and gruff. But Elizabeth Stroud smiled at him. The smile changed her face and Jerome's manner became a little less stiff. He excused himself and was back in twenty minutes with a basket full of groceries. "Miss Caroline told me to do it," he lied to Stroud, hating to be found doing a good deed.

"Still and all it was thoughtful of you to buy them yourself. You could have told me to do it."

"You've got enough to do with the work you've got." Jerome's gruff tone was still there but now he smiled. "Now you live your life same as always," he told Elizabeth. "Miss Caroline isn't the kind that gets in your way. She knows you have your bread to make."

"Well," said Stroud, after Jerome had descended the steep little stairs for the third time and was gone. "I've got a guest. Me that never had a guest in the whole of my life. Not even when my father was alive. He felt we couldn't afford it. And I have a young lady of quality!"

"Don't talk like that," said Caroline. "You're as

much a lady as I am. You make a living: I don't know how to, that's all the difference."

"This is for you," said Caroline later that afternoon, and put two guineas in gold on Stroud's stained table. "Now it's not too much. I don't want you to go without anything because I'm here. Whether you know it or not, you're doing for me what no friend would do: sheltering me. You said I could pay, Stroud. Now, please let me or I'll have to spend the night in the streets! There! And thank you."

Chapter 14

Caroline awoke in Beak Street and had a moment when she could not think where she was. Then she found her eyes upon the figure of Elizabeth Stroud at her work table, engaged in her endless sewing. "I have been stitching since first light," she told Caroline cheerfully, and laughed at the girl's expression of shock.

"I know you chose sewing rather than governessing, but how did you ever begin to get needlework?" Caroline now asked Elizabeth with curiosity.

"If you'll eat some breakfast now," said Elizabeth, "I'll tell you whatever you like to know. There's some milk and bread. It's what I usually have. I'll get it."

"No, please don't wait on me, Elizabeth," said Caroline. "There's no reason why I shouldn't look after myself."

"All right then. You'll find the milk in a jug on the sill outside. It's covered with a cloth to keep the soot out. The bread I keep in that old biscuit box. I don't eat butter—can you manage it dry?"

Caroline nodded. She had never, in all her life, eaten

dry bread as an oridnary meal; it was always a punishment from her uncle. Now here this woman Elizabeth Stroud ate it as a matter of course, with milk so skimmed it was almost like blue water. She began to realise the truth behind what her aunt had said and Lady de Lisle Devonshire had repeated: that the only career for women is marriage. But what about all the poor women like Elizabeth Stroud who never married? Anger at the mocking editorial in *The Times* touched her again.

Suddenly Caroline was really curious about Elizabeth Stroud. "How did you begin to get sewing work?" She repeated her question.

"I began poorly, as most girls do," Elizabeth said cheerfully.

"How do you mean, poorly?" Caroline insisted.

"Oh, a job with a dressmaker, picking up and counting pins. Pins were even more expensive in those days than they are now, for each pin was made by hand."

"But the sewing?"

"Well, I could already handle a needle, so I was put to work tacking and basting cut-out garments, sewing endless pieces of cloth I never saw made up into the whole garment."

"Then how did you ever learn to make a dress?"

"Having to make one, one day!"

"Did that happen quickly?"

"Oh, no! I was working eighteen hours a day doing every sort of odd job. I slept over the shop in a small attic with four other girls. These rooms are a palace compared to *that*. Then I began to get to know the work."

"And then?"

"Well, I still wasn't paid money for my work—only my keep. I could count the coins I had that were my own in those days. Then they had a rush job for Mr. Worth of Paris, some ball gowns that had to be finished in a hurry for a girl's coming out party. They'd got behind with the work so they had us girls working in relays around the clock, sixteen hours on, eight off."

"Elizabeth, how did you *manage?*"

"Better than most," laughed Elizabeth, never ceasing

her sewing. "I had good health still, and so could work and be fresh longer than the others. After that, Mr. Worth would ask for me, so I began to earn real wages."

"Did you move out of the dormitory attic then?"

"Yes, first to a tiny attic room, but it was my own. Then I saved money to afford this place. I had to be sure of my rent for a month before I could move in. You never know when the work may slacken and you will be sacked with the others. This place may not seem much but it means home to me. I treasure everything in it." And Elizabeth Stroud looked around the poor furniture with pride.

But what Caroline saw, following Elizabeth's eyes, were the sagging floorboards, the broken grate, the dusty, flaking plaster, the spots of damp in the ceiling. Being Caroline, she was forthright.

"Who is your landlord?" she asked.

"How would I know?" asked Elizabeth. "He never comes here. The rent man comes by with a little book with my name on it, and takes my rent every week. He doesn't like talking. He has never told me who he works for, and I have never asked."

"But don't you think you ought to know? Shouldn't your landlord look at his premises, replace floorboards, put back the plaster, see why there is damp in parts of the ceiling?"

Elizabeth laughed, quite a girlish sound. "Excuse me, Miss Caroline," she said, "but it's clear you are from the country. Nobody ever bothers about premises here—not rooms let to the poor. My rooms are *good*. I pay two shillings a week for them. That's dear. You should see some of the others!"

"You mean it's general to neglect tenants?"

Elizabeth shrugged in reply. "Of course!" she said. "We're lucky to get places to sleep. Rooms like these," she added proudly, "often contain a whole family. A man, his wife, and maybe eight children—or ten. They have to take turns sleeping. Two rooms for one person—that's luxury! It's my only luxury and I love it. I hope I can always keep it. I'm the only one I know that has two rooms all to myself, and not many slates missing. There's a barrel of rain water that's in good repair in the yard, and in *this* house we all keep, excuse me, Miss, but there's no other way to tell you, the privy clean. It only serves twenty people, and the people from the restaurant, of course. We have a good house here—comparing, that is."

Caroline was silent. She had properties. She wondered in what condition they were. That banister her uncle had spoken of—what sort of a lodging house did that story come from?

Suddenly Caroline made up her mind. Today was Friday. Why wait to hear from Mr. Joachim? The nervous energy which plagued her caused her to feel she could not sit still. She had said she would look at her properties and repair them. It was better to do that than to sit in Elizabeth's rooms, thinking of all that had happened since she had left home: of her quarrel with Robert, of the ring which she had sent back to him, of Edmund Browne's behaviour, and of the awful consequences of the duel itself.

Better to be busy. She began to dress hurriedly.

"I am going to look at the buildings I own," she told Elizabeth.

Elizabeth paused for a moment. "From what you told me of those properties you can't go alone, or even with me. You'd be injured, even killed."

"I know," said Caroline quietly. "I'll stop at my solicitor's office and see if he can get me that man he told me of, right away."

"If he can't get him, wait until he can. I'm used to London and I wouldn't go to a place like that without a protector."

Mr. Joachim received Caroline with a little surprise. "Well," he said, "you certainly are a young lady who can't wait."

"No," said Caroline truthfully, "I hate waiting for anything. Can you get that Mr. Louis Brady now?"

"He was supposed to come here this afternoon. But—" Mr. Joachim shrugged his black broadcloth-covered shoulders, and threw up his hands in a gesture of hopelessness. But the face he raised to Caroline from his littered desk was smiling, and there was a youthful twinkle in his eyes.

"It's a wonderful thing to be young," he said. "Young and impulsive. You shall see your properties right away if I can get hold of Brady. Let me see if Donald can't roust him out, even if Brady will feel it is a bit early in the morning."

Donald, the twelve-year-old, was dispatched and took off at a run, rattling noisily down the wooden stairs, delighted to be off a stool if only for a few minutes. And soon Mr. Brady was toiling up the selfsame stairs, and came into the room with an easy rolling gait.

"At your service, Sir, Ma'am," was the greeting of this portly fellow, who looked more like a shepherd, a carter or a coal heaver than anyone remotely connected with the Law. He was short and thick, with wide, powerful shoulders and short, sturdy legs. He was dressed in leather breeches and a thick corduroy cutaway coat, leather leggings and stout boots, the whole surmounted by a tall, very much worn, but carefully brushed beaver hat. With a flourish of that heavy hat he took Caroline under his bow as a big merchant ship might take a small rowboat. They were soon in a cab to Marble Arch.

Once in the cab Mr. Brady swept off his hat again and seemingly deliberately dropped it on the wooden floor of the cab, crown downwards. The crown made a dull metallic clang against the floor. Caroline looked startled and Mr. Brady smiled:

"Sounds like metal, don't it? Well, it is!" He put the beaver hat back on his head, giving it a sharp tap to keep it in place with the stout stick he carried slung from thonging of leather passed twice around his wrist.

"People sees a beaver 'at," Mr. Brady confided to Caroline. "And a beaver 'at it is. A beaver 'at ain't nothing to be afraid of. But they taps me on it and my skull don't crush. And then if I lose Brown Betty 'ere," he indicated his cudgel, "I can allus crush the other fellow's skull with the top of me beaver 'at."

Caroline shuddered.

"I hope there won't be anything like that," she said. "I just want to look around today."

They alighted halfway down Oxford Street. After Mr. Brady had looked around for a few moments he walked her over to the north side of that street and then down a little alley in which an opening squared out into a well of houses, three sides of buildings surrounding a central Court. Leg Iron Court. Caroline's heart sank. The Court was so dark that she felt afraid to enter it.

"Well, 'ere it is!" said Brady. "If we're going in we'd better get started. This ain't no neighbour'ood to loiter about in."

Taking Caroline by the elbow he moved her in. The stink of rotting refuse met Caroline's nostrils, mixed with that of human excrement and the sweetish stench of the bodies of some cats or dogs tossed somewhere. The smell of filthy water, dripping from some broken pipe could be discerned as a separate horror. Children were everywhere, very young children, wearing cast-off clothing not good enough for the most ragged grown-up, though it was clearly grown-up clothing not cut down to size, but merely rolled up in leg and trouser or chopped off roughly in the skirt. Round each front door were shoes and boots in terrible states of disrepair. The shoes and boots stood there as mute evidence of poverty, for the children and the women had to take them off whilst they were in the Court. They could not afford any further wear on their wretched footwear. Two goats, tied to doorknobs, bleated their woes whilst the children, ragged and emaciated though they were, indulged in some sort of play. Here, some had taken up a few of the red bricks of the Court's floor and were trying to pile them into a column of sorts; there, some children tried to skip with a dirty bit of rope, but it was too small for the skipping so they cried at each other and at the rope, endlessly frustrated. It was still morning, yet already figures sprawled in doorways, clearly dead drunk.

"Red biddy," explained Mr. Brady. "Methylated spirits mixed with the dregs of red wine. It usually means a man will one day wake up dead." Caroline pressed closer to

Mr. Brady and looked about her some more. She looked at the small grey babies held in the arms of little girls, little girls with sullen, un-childish faces. At every door and window women crowded, riveted by the appearance of a lady in their terrible Leg Iron Court. A few men sat in hopeless despair, looking at nothing, not even at the appearance of Caroline: she was just part of a world in which they no longer wished to take part. Lines of washing, the clothes grey and torn, stretched across the Court from just above the people's heads. The sight of this washing, the sight of the worn-out shoes, still too valuable to wear at home, the sight of the children trying to play in that evil place, all smote Caroline. She must do something. She must do something, and most definitely at once.

Caroline looked at the paper Mr. Joachim had given her and quickly back at the half-obliterated numbers on the sagging front doors. Yes, every building in that Court was one she owned.

"I want to enter one of these houses," she told Brady. "Ask permission."

"Permission? You don't 'ave to ask permission, Missis. It's all your'n."

"Yes, I do have to ask permission," said Caroline. "These people pay rent. I am asking to enter their homes. So please ask permission of the woman in that doorway." She pointed to number thirty-three, where stood a woman who seemed more cleanly dressed than most others. Brady, after a grunt of disapproval, inquired of the woman if the lady could look at her room, as she was a charity visitor and wished to help.

Overhearing him, Caroline asked him in a low tone: "Why don't you say I am the landlord?"

"Because I don't want to 'ave to use this, Miss," he said, indicating Brown Betty. "Some of these people could be violent if they thought you were the landlord. Landlords ain't popular around 'ere."

Caroline was silent and indeed a little fearful as she followed the silent woman into the dark house. The woman took her down some dingy steps, damp and sleazy with dripping water, and into the cellar. In the room she stepped aside so Caroline could see it had been built to hold coal. Hardly any light came into it. The window reached partway above the pavement, so that you could see the feet of the people outside, but every pane of glass was gone but one and the holes had been stuffed up with rags and paper to keep out the worst of the cold. The furniture consisted of a wretched, sagging bed, a table missing a leg which was propped up on a box and a chair missing its back.

When Caroline came upstairs to the dark Court it looked light to her by comparison.

"This is terrible," she said, more to herself than to Brady. Then she turned to the woman whose cellar "home" she had seen, and said quietly: "All this is going to be repaired and cleaned up. What rent do you pay?"

The woman's expression did not change at the idea of repairs. She quite clearly did not believe what Caroline had said. But she answered the question about her rent. "One shilling," she said. "I'm not behind with the rent. But I can't pay more."

"How many people are here in this Court now, do you think?" she asked Brady. Brady gave a shrewd look around the Court.

"Somethink over a 'undred and fifty," he said.

"And how many would you think *live* here?"

"Well, say three or so to a room and mebbe twelve rooms to each 'ouse, and as there are eleven houses in all, I'd say about four 'undred people, but they ain't all 'ere now because this is day time and they're gone out about Lunnon to see what they can pick up—scraps, thieving, work if they can get it and whatever else is to be got. Some of the people 'ere may even 'ave steady jobs, but they can't afford to move from where they do 'ave a place, even if that place ain't so wonderful."

Mr. Brady stopped. Speeches were not in his line and he was astonished that, asked a question, he could say so much.

"I want to see more," said Caroline firmly. She saw more—roofs without slates, the grey sky scudding past above; attic rooms holding whole families; unmarried girls managing in a corner of a room re-rented from the man and his wife who had originally rented the room but couldn't pay for it all by themselves. Their ragged children slept in turns on the bare floor covered with torn and dirty quilts. She saw rooms where the plaster had long since left the walls, where the ceiling sagged threateningly and the walls showed such a multitude of stains that it was hard to decide what the colour of the wall had originally been. Wet fell down many a wall in a continuous clammy excrescence. Mould grew everywhere. Rotten wooden boards and battens greeted her eyes on every side. Stone steps leading to cellar homes had often been worn into shallow basins and each of these basins held a saucerful of—what?

"Sewage, by your leave, Miss," supplied Mr. Brady.

People stood aside for her, silently. They watched her with a sort of animal indifference. They had seen charity visitors before. None of them ever came back to Leg Iron Court. But Caroline saw more perhaps than most charity visitors. She saw all the pathetic attempts of women to make homes for their families. That was washing on the lines, those worn boots were carefully arranged against the doorways, there was the smell of meatless stews being cooked, the little photograph tucked up on a nail above a bed, of a soldier serving the Queen, and looking so smart in a uniform which must seem wonderful to his mother. Worn brushes and combs, a holy picture, a little bit of ribbon carefully folded on a shelf. These things moved Caroline to anger at her uncle's neglect of these people, and to action.

She came back to Mr. Joachim's office, her sense of shock and outrage replaced by a calm determination. Such buildings must be put into repair at once. Mr. Joachim was not surprised at her attitude, but he seemed pleased with her air of decision.

"How soon can I use my money?" she asked.

"You can do better than use your capital," he told her. "You can get a loan against the buildings, put them in repair and with the same money you now collect in rents, pay back the interest on the loan. There may be rooms in those buildings in such bad shape they are not even used. Repair them and you'll soon be able to begin to pay back the loan. Meanwhile you are making those buildings worth a great deal more than at present. You'll have to choose your tenants. Not all of them deserve sympathy, but a great many do deserve better housing. I know a young builder, a carpenter, he'll give you good advice. I can arrange . . ."

Mr. Joachim forgot his other work. His voice waxed on, full of sound planning. He had often thought of doing some sort of work like this, but he himself was always too busy with his legal work. He had imagined that one day he might find a man who would do the work and let him take an interest in it. He had never thought of a girl. But why not a girl? Why not especially this girl? She hadn't fainted or drawn back from Leg Iron Court. Mr. Brady had winked at him over her head when they had first returned to Mr. Joachim's rooms. When Mr. Brady winked, it meant that the client was what Mr. Brady called, in understatement, "a bit of orl right."

Chapter 15

Nobody had ever before seen such a pair of spanking bay horses as pulled Lady de Lisle Devonshire's victoria. That is, nobody in Beak Street, Soho. At the Sign of the Geranium the carriage stopped, one of the grooms jumped down, Lady Devonshire put her marvellously grey-gloved hand to rest on the liveried sleeve of her groom and so assisted, stepped down into the small street. A crowd of small, ragged urchins sprang up around the carriage from nowhere, windows opened on either side of the street, and slatternly housewives looked down from upper windows at the wonderful equipage and the even more wonderful figure of Lady Devonshire herself. Men stopped serving drinks in the little bars and came to the doors of their drink shops to gape at all the grandeur. The proprietors of tiny shops left their counters and their customers and draped themselves in their doorways to have a look. Indeed, everyone in the small street came to a stop whilst they all examined the remarkable visitor.

The driver of the bay horses and the groom now bearing Lady de Lisle Devonshire on his arm both looked coldly above the heads of the people just as if they were not there at all. Lady de Lisle Devonshire seemed also oblivious of stares, laughter and comment. To emphasise her oblivion she had taken out her gold and mother-of-pearl handled lorgnettes and now gazed through them at the small building facing her as though she would get it by heart—the exact size, shape and colour of every ageing brick. The creaking sign above her head had not only the title she sought, but the blurred outline of what could once have been an artist's rendition of a red geranium. Lady de Lisle Devonshire, disdaining the entrance to the restaurant of that name, and the invitation of its aproned, bowing, napkin-whisking owner to step in and be waited upon, coolly turned her attention to the narrow pine staircase that led up to the rooms above the restaurant.

Her quick eyes had soon read the legend "E. Stroud, top floor, front," printed on a white piece of cardboard in faded purplish ink, and tacked to the lintel of the street door. Lady Devonshire proceeded upstairs at a stately gait and, when she reached the top landing and there was nothing over her head but a skylight, she perused the names on the two little doors facing her on that landing and found another card which declared "E. Stroud, dressmaker". She dismissed her groom with a wave of an imperious hand and, folding her lorgnettes with a snap, rapped hard on the wooden door. She had to rap twice before Stroud opened it cautiously, afraid, maybe, that newspaper reporters were waiting outside. But when she saw the grand lady on her doorstep, a lady dressed in the very height of the latest fashion, Paris-made *Alexandre tournure* and all, she flung the door wide open and said to the marvellous grey dress and the marvellous sables and the quite too marvellous hat, "Oh do come in, ma'am. You must be looking for Miss Caroline."

Caroline was standing in the living room of the two rooms with her back to the little table on which Stroud's sewing lay. The furniture had been somewhat displaced to make room for a mattress.

"Why, good morning!" said Caroline brightly. Fanny de Lisle Devonshire did not permit herself to reply to this greeting, but gazed around the room exactly as she might have done if she had still been holding her lorgnettes. She obviously could not quite believe what she saw. Her eyes coming back to the mattress, she said in tones of shock: "Am I to believe that someone *sleeps* on that?"

"Oh, I tried to make Miss Caroline take my bed when I saw what she had brought to sleep on. But I couldn't persuade her," said Stroud.

"Of course not," said Caroline. "Why should you give up your bed? You work. I don't. Not yet, anyway."

"Work?" said Lady de Lisle Devonshire, in the same tone that she might have said "drink". "Work! What *are* you talking of, Caroline? And what are you doing here?"

"Shall I go, ma'am?" Stroud offered.

"No," said her ladyship graciously. "You will please stay. As I gather you are Miss Caroline's only companion, it is possible you will be able to talk a little sense into her."

"How did you know I was here?" asked Caroline.

"I prevailed upon your dear cousin, Miss Newcombe, whom I found at home in place of your aunt—"

"Sophia told?"

"Oh come, Caroline! Is this a conspiracy? That's exactly what that elderly maid at your aunt's said when I left a message for Mrs. Newcombe to say I was coming here." She mimicked Rosie perfectly: " 'Miss Sophia told?' But what on earth is wrong with my knowing? I will not tell the newsprints, or necessarily your uncle. I am a better friend to you, Caroline, than you imagine," she went on. "I *want* you to have a little time to yourself."

"You do?"

"Why yes, to come to your senses. You are engaged to marry my son, and—"

"But I'm *not*!" said Caroline firmly. "I returned his ring."

"In a moment of girlish petulance, I'll be bound," said her visitor. "You are publicly engaged to my son. The announcement has hardly appeared in the Social Columns of the newspapers when you hand your ring to another man and ask *him* to break off the engagement. Robert has now loudly told the world he understands your motives were of the highest: you were sacrificing yourself and your married state to try to prevent a duel between him and his cousin Harry, who has so violently fallen in love with you and embarrassed you greatly with his declarations."

"But that's not true!"

"Come! Come! You are not going to tell me that you are interested in Harry?"

"No. Of course not. But I have done my best to break off with Robert because I do not love him."

It was out. Caroline had said it. She experienced a sense of relief, as though she had been carrying a heavy burden about with her and was now, at length, permitted to put it down. But her sense of relief was soon dispelled.

"Yes. Robert told me that you have declared you do not care for him. But, as I showed him, you were distraught at the time. Come now, I saw your aunt and uncle before I came to London. Your uncle was for setting off after you at once, but I persuaded him to let me try and be peacemaker. Your uncle admits that he was perhaps a little harsh with you from time to time, in his anxiety to see that you did not ruin your life. He is very anxious for this marriage to come off. I am here with his full approbation, and that of your aunt—"

"How is Aunt Millie?"

"Very distressed, I'm afraid. Anxious that you return home, and without delay."

Caroline was silent for a moment. Her poor aunt, always trying to pacify her husband and to make her niece as happy as she could—that very niece whom she so little understood! But this time the disagreement was not over a request for a new pair of gloves, or the company of someone of whom Uncle Ham did not approve. This time it was a matter of the whole of Caroline's life and her happiness in it. So Caroline steeled herself against the instant wish to run home just to put her arms about her aunt and assure her that all would yet be well with her headstrong niece.

"It would be quite fitting now if you came to stay with us at our house," said Lady Devonshire with apparent kindness. "Certainly you should do so until all these wretched rumours about the duel and the reason for it die down. It's what Robert wants and it's what I want."

"And Sir Ernest? What about Sir Ernest? Doesn't he want an abject apology from me?"

"Come, come! What a foolish girl you are! Sir Ernest will do as I say. He was very upset with you the other night. But when he sees that the happiness of his son, his only son, is at stake. . . ."

Caroline was startled. She had not thought of Robert as capable of feeling. She said a little stupidly: "Robert unhappy?"

"And why would he not be? The girl he loves, the girl whom he has asked to be his bride, the girl for whose honour he fought a duel—"

"Robert exaggerates. He has had a quarrel with Harry for years. Harry knocked him down, and naturally he wants revenge. My honour was not in question."

"That matter of honour, surely, was for Robert to decide, as your affianced, your natural protector. —As I was saying, the girl he is engaged to marry, the girl he loves, now seems to spurn him."

"But I do not love your son, Lady Devonshire."

"Oh come, Caroline, I know you have been brought up in the country, but you can't possibly talk like a lady novelist! Such books are for day-dreaming. The best marriages are founded on mutual interests."

"And what mutual interest would I have with Robert?"

"My dear child, do not tell me than an old title is not of some consideration? And Robert intends to go into Parliament. He will be Lord de Lisle Devonshire one day. With his connections and your inheritance—" Lady Devonshire broke off. No, no! That was the wrong thing to say to this country ninny—she would never understand. So Lady Devonshire added: "And of course Robert adores you—"

"But *I* do not adore *him!*"

"Is there someone else?" asked Lady Devonshire shrewdly. "Surely not Harry de Lisle? No, of course not. There—you need not tell me who it is. Whoever he is cannot have asked you to marry him or you would be telling me a very different story today. So you will not be marrying *him*, whoever he is. But you love him!" Caroline flushed. "There, there! Your secret is out, but it shall go no further, I promise you!"

There was a silence.

After bearing with the silence as long as her natural lack of patience could stand, Lady Devonshire said: "And what of my poor son? He lies there in bed with a useless arm and a high fever. Don't you wish to see him, to let him know that you regret the pain you have caused him, to let him see you wearing his ring again?"

"I can't see him," said Caroline.

"Why not? Because of this mysterious Other? Reflect, Caroline, a married woman has a great deal more liberty than an unmarried one. Providing you are discreet, no-one, least of all myself, will expect you to live without a little dalliance."

Lady Devonshire's voice trailed off as she watched Caroline's face. Caroline was evidently struggling between shame and fury.

"Now, now!" said Fanny Devonshire, "there is no need to get upset. I can see that you have been quite distressed by recent events. But when the shock of it all wears off, you may find yourself pleased to be still engaged to Robert. You may then begin to see that one has to be practical about life. Marriage for women is the only practical way to live. It is the only way you will get your own way with things, and a little freedom. You must start with the thought that no marriage is perfect—not even one with my son."

Caroline made to interrupt. But Lady Devonshire insisted: "No, no, listen to me, Caroline. What is the alternative to marriage? You will be alone in the world. I gather you may take an interest in your properties, but that is no life for a woman."

Lady de Lisle Devonshire looked round the room carelessly, glancing quickly at each little knick-knack—the china dog, the glass vase, the fly-blown pictures—and said: "Don't imagine that the property you'll inherit would be even as possible as this slum."

"If you please, m'lady," said Stroud with dignity, "I am proud of what I have here. This my home."

"Hmm!" said Lady Devonshire, and then ignored Stroud. She turned to Caroline and said. "Unless you agree to the marriage that your uncle and I have been at some trouble to arrange for you, Caroline, I fear your uncle will disown you. *You* are strong-willed. *He* is strong-willed himself. He does not wish to be publicly flouted by you. I don't know if you have seen the newsprints, but your story is being touted by every vendor in town." Lady de Lisle Devonshire reached into her huge sable muff and her hand came out with a cheap broadside, the *Town Crier*, a scandal sheet. She put it on the table next to Caroline and Caroline shrank. In crude lettering she read: "Débutante and Duel. Miss Caroline Hamilton engaged to two men . . . two brothers . . . rich in her own right . . . spoiled only child of millionaire . . . money from slum properties. 'She aimed too high socially,' says friend." Caroline turned her head away from the sheet and Lady Devonshire said on a note of triumph: "Ah, I thought so! It's not so pleasant when they pillory you. The *only* thing to do now is to marry Robert, and to do it at once. It will give the lie to everything and to everybody. I am here as much on the part of your uncle as I am here on account of my son. We want you to decide before the newspapers find you here, we want to get you out of this—this slum!"

There was silence. Lady de Lisle Devonshire waited for Caroline to say something. Elizabeth Stroud looked anxious, even afraid. Caroline saw this and put an arm about her. "I like it here," she said firmly. "I'm staying at least for now. I'm grateful that Miss Stroud took me in."

"Very well," said Fanny Devonshire. "I'm putting the ring on this table here. Think hard about all that I have said. And you, my good woman, help her to think hard. She does not know what the world, outside of marriage, is for women, the world of endeavour. Perhaps, Stroud, as you do know something about the unprotected life, you can help to give weight to her uncle's wishes and my words." She fished in her meshed gold purse and came up with half a sovereign for Stroud.

"Oh no, Milady!" said Stroud, backing away.

"You know the value of money, Stroud. Take it when you can get it." She put the money firmly down on the table next the ring, as though to emphasise the difference between the scrap of gold given as a tip to Stroud and the magnificent ring, the splendid ring, with the magnificent, splendid life, the safe life, that went with it. With one last meaningful glance at Caroline, Lady Devonshire swept from the room, majesty and power in every line of her stately carriage. She felt she had done a good day's work. The Hamilton riches and Caroline's own quite considerable fortune were surely as close to her now as they had ever been. But she meant to make them not only close but certain. Caroline would give in yet.

There was a little silence as the door closed behind the great lady. Caroline said softly to Stroud: "I'm awfully sorry: you take me in and all you get is a horrid scene and insults."

"Well, at least I have this," said Elizabeth, trying to smile. She reached out to take the golden half-guinea and put it in the thin, worn purse she fetched from her pocket.

"You're not going to accept it!" said Caroline. "What about your pride?"

"Oh," she said, "the poor can't afford pride. Pride is for rich people. I learned early on that you can't eat pride, wear pride nor sleep on it. No, you have to have money and a secure place in the world before you can afford pride."

"But aren't you angry with that woman?"

"Why no, Miss. And I think she is right. She meant for me to tell you that and she knew I would. You've got a clear choice between that ring and living your own life. What a young lady of quality, even one with money, can do alone in a great city like this, I cannot imagine. Married women or elderly spinsters with money can take up charitable work."

"Suppose I choose to look after whatever my father left me? There are properties let to the poor—"

"That's easier said than done, Miss. Lady Devonshire called this a slum; she has no idea what a slum really is. You've been to see your buildings and you think you could manage that property. But you can't. You'll never be able to work with that kind of tenant. Maybe if you were a hardened spinster, had spent your life in slum work—but I wouldn't envy you. If I were you, I'd look hard at this ring even if you don't love the gentleman that goes with it. You think of the safety his name, with a title and all, will give you. He'll take on the management of your affairs and you won't know worry about money or want of it, nor will you know what it is to be so lonely you could talk to the wall! There! That's a real speech for me. But I got it all said. And if you still choose to go on your own way it won't be because I didn't tell you!"

"Dear Elizabeth!" said Caroline gently. She thought for a moment of the real reason why she could no longer marry Robert—her love for Edmund Browne. But to speak of that was an agony; even to think of it was to press into her own heart a steely point of pain. If she gave in to that pain she would render herself helpless, paralysed. She must make every effort to put Edmund, not out of her mind (that was impossible), but to the farthermost reaches of it.

As the evening drew on and they prepared for bed (Stroud, to save candles or oil for her lamp, had formed the habit of going to bed when the light of the day went, and of arising when the sun came back) Caroline began to feel the presence of the ring in the room. Even in the dark its jewels seemed to wink and glow and torment; and the wheels of the train began to return to her memory, the wheels of that train she had used to run away to London, and their message now was: "Take the ring. Take the ring. He doesn't love you. He doesn't love you. Take the ring or be alone. Alone. Alone. Alone!" And then she was asleep. But even in her sleep the ring winked at her, leered at her from the table. "Take me and Robert Devonshire," it seemed to say, "or be lonely, lonely, lonely. . . ."

The first thing she noticed when she awoke in the morning was that ring. It lay on the table where Lady de Lisle Devonshire had laid it, all the rich stones winking with the rays of the sunlight streaming through the attic window. She turned her face away. There *was* something menacing in the ring, there *was* something almost evil about it. She would not keep it here—in any case, if it were stolen, it would be dreadful—so when she had dressed, she put it back into the pocket it had been in before, and pinned that petticoat pocket close. Again the heavy ring hit her slender knee like a large stone when she walked. But now she found she really resented it. It symbolised a trap—a trap she could so easily fall into if she were weak; and one could be weak if one were lonely. She must get busy. Only if she were fully occupied could she resist the easy path to Robert Devonshire's arms. So she bethought herself of Aunt Lucinda and her house. Yes, that was the thing to do. She would take the ring to Aunt Lucinda and ask her to look after it.

She walked out into Soho wearing Rosie's old cape. In Shaftesbury Avenue she picked up a four-wheeler which took her through the whirl of Piccadilly Circus, along Piccadilly itself, past Buckingham Palace, to Wilton Crescent. She noticed with relief that there was no one—no reporters—waiting on the pavement in front of No. 70. The newsmen must have given up on finding that she really was not there. She kept the four-wheeler waiting, but was glad when Jerome answered the bell quickly.

She said: "Oh, Jerome, can I go straight up to Aunt Luci's?"

She meant to Aunt Luci's bedroom, but Jerome said: "Though your aunt is not yet dressed, Miss, she is up and is in the drawing room, writing letters, I think. It is nice to see you this morning: you see the ruse worked, and we got rid of the gentlemen callers?" He glanced at the empty pavement behind her. "So I suppose we'll have you back here right away?"

"I don't know yet, Jerome," she told him smiling. "I think it might be as well to stay away for a day or so."

She ran upstairs to the second floor drawing room. There sat Aunt Luci in a mauve and écru lace taffeta wrapper, with her hair in a matching mob cap of taffeta. She was at the escritoire and her white quill pen was scratching busily.

"Oh, Caroline!" she exclaimed. "How lovely to see you!"

"My apologies for being so early," said Caroline. "But I have something that cannot wait. Indeed I have a favour to ask of you. Can you keep Robert's ring safely for me?"

"Robert's ring? But I thought he had it!"

Caroline quickly explained what had happened.

"What an odious woman!" exclaimed Aunt Lucinda of Fanny Devonshire and her visit. "But I'm afraid she's right, dear Caro. I really feel that a good marriage—"

"Yes, dear Aunt. But I think I must give myself a little time. Meanwhile, the ring?"

"Oh dear, yes!" said Aunt Lucinda. "I can well imagine that there's no safe place at your present lodging. Jerome told me what it was like. Wouldn't you like to come back here?"

"Yes, I would," said Caroline. "But in a day or two. I am learning a great deal where I am—things I might never know otherwise. Perhaps in a few days? Meanwhile, here is the ring."

"It is a handsome thing!" said Aunt Lucinda. "It shows that it was made a long time ago. Such stones! Such a setting!"

"Yes. It's beautiful. Where can we put it so that it will be safe?"

The squeak of the door, which needed oiling, announced Sophia's ill-humoured face.

"Oh, *you* here?" she said ungraciously to Caroline.

"Yes, Sophy, but only for a moment." For a second Caroline thought of asking Sophia why she had told Lady Devonshire where she was, and then she decided it wasn't worth it.

Aunt Luci was saying: "Now, let me see, where can we put this ring? We really ought to have a safe, I suppose. I could give it to Mr. Trimble to put with my own valuables. But then he'd ask so many questions! No, I've got a better idea. I shall put it in the secret drawer here in my *escritoire*. Oh dear, it's stuck! Ask Rose to come and open it. Oh, there it is! It's working now." Mrs. Newcombe having pulled out a drawer, and having pushed upon a piece of carving, touched the back of the receptacle left by the missing drawer and a little door opened, showing a small space behind. She now wrapped the ring in her tiny lace-edged handkerchief and put it in the secret space. Pressing the drawer back in, she pushed the piece of carving another way, and then breathed a sigh of relief as the escritoire presented its usual innocent look. "There!" said Mrs. Newcombe happily. "Now, no burglar will ever get it!"

"Thank you," said Caroline with a sigh of relief. "Now I've got to go. I have a four-wheeler waiting."

"Oh dear! All this time! How extravagant of you!" Aunt Lucinda rose and hurried from the room, Caroline following her.

As Caroline watched the mauve taffeta billowing down the stairs in front of her, a flutter of femininity, she was smiling.

Arrived in the front hall Aunt Luci said: "Oh, I almost forgot. There's a letter for you on the hall table here. A very official looking letter."

She handed Caroline a long, thick, folded-over paper with a wax seal holding it close. It was inscribed in perfect script, a very clerkly hand.

"Mr. Joachim. The lawyer!" said Caroline excitedly.

The message was simple:

My dear Miss Hamilton:
    I will await you at my office at your convenience.

The only part of the letter which was indecipherable was the signature. But Caroline made out a big 'J' at its beginning.

Caroline went back to Beak Street. She was very glad to be rid of the ring. The coming of Mr. Joachim's letter seemed a good portent. Maybe she could manage her properties—Mr. Joachim seemed to think so—and if she could, maybe she could make friends in time and a life of her own. A life of her own! She squeezed down her rebellious heart which told her: "Edmund! Edmund!"

As Caroline's cab had turned out of Wilton Crescent, Mrs. Newcombe delayed in her own hall to give Jerome a few household directions. The squeak of the door above her head told her that her daughter was only now leaving the drawing room. Mrs. Newcombe called out to her: "Come and have some breakfast with me, dear?"

"Oh, no thank you, mother," said Sophia. She was trembling as she turned towards the door of her own room. She entered her room and then quickly closed and locked the door. Then she opened her plump hand. Nestling in its palm was the winking, glittering heirloom ring. Robert's ring. The Devonshire engagement ring that Lady de Lisle Devonshire thought was safe with Caroline.

"They can't blame me for just borrowing you!" she said to the ring, and then slipped it on her own engagement finger. It was a little tight. But she held out her hand and admired the ring upon it. It looked very well. "Oh, Robert!" Sophia said as she looked at it. How tall, dark and handsome he was! She loved the—the saturnine look about his face. She shivered, thinking of it, and then laughed delightedly. She had "his" ring! She put out her hand to admire it again, and then she brought it to her lips and kissed it. Darling Robert! She pirouetted, smiling, up to her cheval mirror and there looked at her excited face in the glass. "Engaged to Robert de Lisle Devonshire!" she whispered. "Oh, if only I could bring it off!"

Chapter 16

As Caroline entered the room at Bow Street Police Station where the inquest was to be held, her attention was riveted by a shaft of sunlight coming from a window high up in one wall. This finger of light pointed directly at the raised table behind which sat Dr. Charles Cholmondeley, Chairman of the Enquiry.

Caroline felt very tense. Looking around the packed room, she knew that all the people there were present because of her. Yet she had never meant to cause disruption in anyone's life, nor to cause pain and anxiety. It was extraordinary how, without ever intending to, she had set in motion a number of actions which those few honest words of hers in her uncle's drawing room had not been meant to bring about. It was not yet a month since she had run away from home. And now two men had fought a duel over her and another man—some poor, unknown wretch—lay dead. And here all these people were to answer the questions put to them and to try to find out how this man had met his death.

Nearly every person in that room was personally known to her, but of them all Caroline was really only conscious of one man, Edmund Browne. He was the man she loved, and, in the same breath as she admitted that to herself, she knew she hated him. There he sat with the "gentlemen" of the Press. Gentlemen? Edmund Browne was no gentleman. Here he was for no other reason than ghoulishly to observe what went on and in particular, she was sure, her reactions to it. Although she had been at pains to avoid reading the newsprints, she had been unable to escape headlines in the streets as she went about, her face concealed by Rosie's old cape, which Rosie insisted on her keeping for the moment for just that purpose.

Her portrait, the one made for the announcement of her engagement, stared back at her from banners such as "The Woman in the Case." or "Miss Hamilton avoids Press". She tried not to look now in Edmund's direction, but her whole being was attracted to him as by a magnet. Why did he have to look so distinguished? He was wearing a dark bottle-green, French wool frock coat, with darker green satin lapels, a dark green satin waistcoat lapelled with the bottle-green wool, and light coloured trousers. Anyone else would have looked a dandy dressed thus, but Edmund was too masculine for that. The coat set off his tall, slim, yet finely muscled build. His dark brown moustache and beard set off the black-lashed, intensely blue eyes that could sparkle with laughter and yet be at times so clear and grave. Before her mind could stop it, her wayward heart had told her that for her he was the handsomest man alive. But she despised him. She could accept with resignation that the story of the duel, which had died down a little now in the Press, would be all over the front pages again. But that Edmund Browne, who had once called himself her friend, should personally report on the enquiry disgusted her. Surely this kind of reporting was no part of a leader writer's job? Now he was looking grave as he talked to an older man beside him. Another reporter from *The Times*? But why would they have two reporters?

Then Caroline saw her aunt and uncle. She was moved that they had come. She guessed what an effort it must have been for Mr. Hamilton to come and to sit in that court with her. She knew it would have been difficult for Mrs. Hamilton to stay away. Caro made a tiny motion of her right hand and smiled to her aunt by way of greeting. But it was her uncle who made a motion back, and Caroline found the quick tears starting to her eyes. Perhaps she had misjudged her guardian all these years. He was proud and obstinate and unyielding, but there he was now with the family solicitor, brought, Caroline was sure, to protect her if he could. She could not do as he wished and marry Robert Devonshire, but Caroline was glad that there could be some *rapprochement* after the inquest was over.

Caroline could not greet anyone else for at this moment, Dr. Cholmondeley remarked to the room: "May I have silence, please? Silence and your attention. As I am wont to say on these occasions, I have time to spend but not to waste. Would everyone please be seated?"

As Caroline sat down with Elizabeth Stroud beside her, she saw that her aunt had reached for her uncle's hand and they were surreptitiously holding hands now. How little Caroline felt she knew about people and their relationships.

As the room came to order with much shuffling of feet, scraping of chairs and last-minute coughing, Caroline raised her head. Harry de Lisle was looking at her. He sat across the room flanked by his solicitor and gazed humbly, adoringly, and somewhat beggingly at her. He had spent a few unpleasant days in jail because, despite his solicitor's admonitions when attempting to post bail, Harry was apt to find himself in a *mêlée* with any policeman who as much as laid a finger on him. He was a simple man and an upright man. The police were a somewhat new body in London, meant to deal with the real criminals that infested the streets. Harry had never thought to have anything to do with them.

Caroline had not written to Harry or been in touch with him. But then she had not been in touch with Robert. And for the same reason. She had wished to encourage neither of them. Lady de Lisle Devonshire had not been back to see Caroline, and Caroline supposed that she was keeping her word and giving her time to think. She was not in the court now, nor was Robert. Caroline had been surprised when she noted this but also relieved. She did not yet know what she could possibly say, any more than she had already said, to either of them.

Dr. Cholmondeley, who had just tidied the papers in front of him, now shot his cuffs, clasped his long, lean hands in front of him and made to speak. At this moment a considerable disturbance was heard at the back of the

201

room. A murmur arose from the public, and even the seven jurymen turned to look. Lady de Lisle Devonshire was making an entrance. She swept in regally, sable-muffed and furred for the cold weather which would soon be upon them, and all dressed in a black silk velvet costume and matching bonnet, the whole lined with a delicious shade of lime green. She looked, as usual, magnificent, and one began to see why the new fashion, the bustle, would conquer the fashion world. Worn as Lady de Lisle Devonshire wore it, it added height and dignity. She turned and held the large doors wide open, standing aside so that attention was focused on the stretcher on which lay Robert Devonshire—thinner but handsomer than ever, his dark good looks accentutated by the romantic pallor of his skin and an air of illness bravely borne. For a split second there was a silence of astonishment in the room and then Dr. Cholmondeley, half rising from his chair, peered over his table through his steel-shafted half-glasses. "And what, pray, have we here?" he demanded.

Lady de Lisle Devonshire advanced her imposing person towards him, hand outstretched, and with a gracious smile said: "Fanny de Lisle Devonshire and her injured son." Dr. Cholmondeley ignored the proffered hand. "Damn these rich important women," he thought, and then he went on: "I meant *that*," he said, pointing to the stretcher. "What is the meaning of *that*?" Dr. John Dickinson, fancying the gruff question was addressed to him as the attendant physician said, the fingers of each hand in his waistcoat pockets, his voice pretentious: "Complicated fracture of the humerus."

"Yes, yes," said Dr. Cholmondeley. "I know he was shot in the arm and not in the leg. So why can't he stand, or rather, sit, like other people?"

"Post haemorrhagic anaemia," said Dr. Dickinson with immense gravity.

"My poor son often feels faint," Lady de Lisle Devonshire offered in a charmingly helpful voice. "Yes?" said Dr. Cholmondeley dryly, looking at her over his steel-rimmed half-glasses, and added brusquely: "Bring a chair!"

Lady de Lisle Devenshire's smile froze. She sat down, furious. When Robert was given a chair Caroline realised that he was looking directly at her. She inclined her head stiffly, but along the row of chairs another bonnet moved forward. Sophia, in her second best costume, a dusty rose-pink wool with a blue velvet cravat that matched her blue velvet bonnet and above all her china blue eyes, bent her lambent gaze upon the handsome sufferer. Her doll-like features were contorted into an expression of concern, and Caroline could not help but notice that Robert responded to Sophia's attention. He looked at her with his fine brave eyes, enduring, but anguished. "Poor man!" Sophia was heard to murmur under her breath. "Be quiet!" whispered Mrs. Newcombe firmly.

"Are we now all present?" asked Dr. Cholmondeley and without waiting for an answer to this sardonic question, he began: "Now let us begin at the beginning. This is an inquest upon the body of one Donald Cheever, of fourteen Leadenhall Street, in the City of London. The deceased was found in that part of Hyde Park known as the Dingle on the morning of the twentieth of October, killed by a person, or persons, unknown. No weapon was found near the corpse. The victim had received a ball in the head from a pistol. This was judged by Dr. Smyth, the doctor known and employed by the police in such matters, to be the cause of death. The victim was dressed in the rags of a tramp but, on enquiry, it developed that Donald Cheever was not a tramp but a *bona fide* reporter for the *Morning Star*. He was disguised as a tramp so as to observe the duel undetected and report to the newspaper employing him that it had taken place."

At the mention of Donald Cheever's real identity, there was a commotion in the room. Everybody looked at everybody else. This was the first time that any of them had known that the dead man was not a tramp.

Caroline looked at Elizabeth Stroud, startled. A reporter for the *Morning Star*? What could this mean? Could it mean that it had not been Edmund who had reported the duel to *The Times*! But the *Morning Star* had no connection with *The Times*. Of that she was sure. And Donald Cheever had been dead before he could report anything of the duel. No, it had to be Edmund!

The commotion in the court had become louder. Dr. Cholmondeley rapped on the table in front of him and said: "Quiet in the courtroom, please! This is not a beer garden, but an inquest!"

"Quiet, please!" echoed Dr. Dickinson. Dr. Cholmondeley turned and looked at him slowly. "Thank you," he said. "But when I need help I shall ask for it. You are a doctor with medical experience only, I take it? I thought so. Well, I am a medical man with legal qualifications, and the *only* person in charge here." At that, Dr. Dickinson went scarlet, tucked his chin within his wing collar as though for protection and closed his mouth tightly.

The jury of seven men together at an adjacent table tittered. "This is not a place where jokes are made," said Dr. Cholmondeley, looking hard at the group. "Sorry, Mr. Coroner," said the chief juror.

Dr. Cholmondeley took a deep breath, and in a voice clearly tired of repetition of something he often had to say, said: "And let us get that straight. I am not a "Coroner". I do not care for that new-fangled corruption of an old title. I am a Crowner. I represent the Crown."

There was complete silence in the room. "Now," said Dr. Cholmondeley, "let us get on with it." He glanced at some notes in front of him and said:

"Robert de Lisle Devonshire, you are my first witness. Yes, Yes. Bring your chair."

Robert, on being sworn and then questioned, gave evidence that he had had a metting with his cousin Harry de Lisle to "settle an affair of honour" in Hyde Park at dawn of 20 October.

"And what was this affair of honour?" demanded Dr. Cholmondeley.

"It concerns a lady, sir," said Robert stiffly.

"Which lady?" demanded Dr. Cholmondeley without ceremony. "Come on, please. We have not got all day!"

"My fiancée, Miss Caroline Hamilton, sir."

"And what was the story?" Dr. Cholmondeley continued to pry. "Tell the story from the beginning—in your own words, just as you remember it."

And so Robert, disliking every minute of this public interrogation, was forced to recount the scene in the conservatory and then the later one in Mrs. Newcombe's drawing-room. A murmur arose from the public seats—a murmur of amused interest. Caroline felt the blood staining her face. She could feel people pointing her out to each other. How awful to have her whole private life thrust into public view like this!

"That is enough noise back there!" said Dr. Cholmondeley firmly. "If there is any more talking excepting that which I and the witnesses before me do, I shall have this room cleared of everyone but the immediate parties to the inquest."

Robert continued with his story and Caroline would have like to flee the room. Told aloud, as Robert was reluctantly having to tell it, it sounded either as if she were a heartless flirt, or Harry an out and out rogue. Robert obviously preferred the latter version, as it did not suggest that any woman could prefer another man to him.

Harry de Lisle was next sworn and gave his account of the duel. When it came to speaking of Caroline, he said: "Since Miss Hamilton was afraid of her fiancé, I was about to undertake to tell him that the engagement was off, as Miss Hamilton was marrying *me*."

"Oh, the idiot!" thought Caroline. "I never gave him any such idea!" But had she, unconsciously, had she?

"That will be enough!" said Dr. Cholmondeley to Harry, who was getting ploughed under by his own unaccustomed verbosity and tending to repeat himself. "Is Miss Hamilton present?"

Mr. Trimble got to his feet.

"Yes, Dr. Cholmondeley," he said. But the name came out "Chol-mon-dilly"; he was obviously having difficulty with a name that wasn't so usual.

"And who may you be? You don't *look* like a young lady!"

"Lor' no!" answered Mr. Trimble with an uncertain

laugh, confused at the idea. "My name is Trimble. I represent, Dr. Cholmondilly, the young lady and—"

"My name may be spelt C-H-O-L-M-O-N-D-E-L-E-Y" said Dr. Cholmondeley with obvious forbearance, "but it is pronounced 'Chumly'. And since you are clearly not Miss Hamilton herself, would you please be seated?"

At this moment a round-headed, bald-pated, rosy-cheeked, stout little man with a white fringe of beard, who was sitting next to George Hamilton, rose to his feet.

"If it please you, Mr. Crowner, sir, a question. I represent Miss Caroline Hamilton, and my name is Bumbry—B-U-M-B-R-Y." The Court tittered. "—Ethelbert Bumbry."

"Yes, yes!" said Dr. Cholmondeley. "Nobody has any difficulty in spelling *your* name, or pronouncing it. Sit down. If you *are* a solicitor, as I presume you are claiming to be, you should have learned long since that you may give your client such advice as you have but you are not to speak aloud at this proceeding." Mr. Bumbry sat down abruptly.

Dr. Cholmondeley surveyed the room severely and said: "Let us have a clearer understanding. As I have said before, this is an inquest. I am the inquisitor here. That means *I* shall ask questions, and persons shall reply to them in their own words, *not* in the words of their solicitors. If Miss Caroline Hamilton is present, would she kindly arise and come forward?"

Caroline came forward and was sworn. She felt terrible standing there, every eye upon her. She felt alone and afraid. Was her behaviour alone responsible for Mr. Cheever's death?

Dr. Cholmondeley took off his half-glasses. "Begin at the beginning," he said. "Where did it all begin?"

"My fiancé, as he has explained, presumed that he had need to defend my honour."

"Was there any truth in his feeling? Come now, Miss Hamilton, you are under oath. Was there an understanding between you and Mr. de Lisle?"

"Harry? Oh, no!"

Caroline felt herself go scarlet. Dr. Cholmondeley was

looking at her shrewdly. "Then you are in love with another man?" Reluctantly, Caroline nodded.

"And are you planning to marry *him*?" Caroline managed an almost inaudible "No."

"But he has told you he loves you?"

"Yes," she said.

"Did you feel menaced by your fiancé's refusal to free you of your engagement to him?"

Caroline hesitated, then: "Yes," she said.

"You may return to your seat. But remember you are still sworn. I may wish to question you again."

Caroline, still aware that the humiliating blush had not yet left her face, returned, her head bent low, to her seat. She could have died. She had broken her engagement in open court and in open court, too, had told Edmund Browne that she loved him. She felt his eyes upon her but although she felt an intense desire to look at him, she firmly turned her eyes away from him. Up to this time he could have had no idea what she felt for him, and she had meant to keep it that way.

Caroline sat down miserably, her eyes upon the ground in front of her.

Chapter 17

The seconds were sworn and gave evidence on the priming of two pistols, and the single bullet identical in each; and on the sound of the two—or, as now seemed definite, three—shots.

The sergeant of police was sworn. He said that he had searched the trees in the Dingle when it had come to his attention that there had probably been three shots. He had dug a bullet from a tree facing Harry de Lisle's position, behind where Robert Devonshire had stood.

"And this bullet—was it different from that found in the deceased?" asked Dr. Cholmondeley.

"No, sir. It was identical."

"And the bullet probed from Robert Devonshire's arm?"

"That was another kind of bullet entirely."

Sensation in court.

"Then we can presume that de Lisle did not wing his cousin as he claims, but that someone else shot Mr. Devonshire. Someone concealed and facing Robert Devonshire," said Dr. Cholmondeley. "It is clear that Devonshire's arm was pierced just as he took aim, and so his own bullet was deflected and found Mr. Cheever."

Dr. John Dickinson gave his evidence in a hurt tone. He was still suffering from the slight the Crowner had dealt him earlier.

"And why did you consent to officate as a medical man at a duel in these enlightened days when duelling is frowned upon?"

"I had known both young men since boyhood, and I feared they would find no one else at such short notice. Besides, a duel does not seem so wrong. I remember when Prime Minister Pitt called out Tierney—"

"And I remember when Canning called out Castlereagh," remarked the Crowner tartly, "but that doesn't mean—"

"And I remember," Aunt Lucinda's bell-like tones were heard from the back of the room, "I remember when the Duke of Wellington called out Lord Winchelsea." Aunt Lucinda was so glad that the atmosphere was taking on a more friendly and social character. "The Duke of Wellington was old-fashioned and—"

"Madam," said the Crowner, "whoever you are, please note that we are not at a ladies' tea-party. That'll be enough about memories. This is an inquest—I would like the jury to pay attention to me now, please. I will give you a summation of the facts. A man is dead. He was dressed as a tramp but was in fact a newspaper reporter, one Donald Cheever. He was shot during a duel between two men over a woman. The duellists intended to exchange two shots. But three shots were fired. Who shot the third bullet? It could not have been intended for Mr. Cheever, for it was aimed at Mr. Devonshire and subsequently removed from his arm. Did the concealed person, under cover of a duel, intend to kill Devonshire? If so, what could have been the motive of taking Mr. Devonshire's life? Who was the party who would benefit from the death of Robert Devonshire?

"You have heard Miss Hamilton say that she was trying to break her engagemeent to Robert Devonshire. She had more than once tried to get him to agree to break the engagement. She has admitted that Mr. Devonshire's refusal caused her to feel menaced. She has now told the court that she does not intend to marry Robert Devonshire. She has indicated, further, that there is another man, and it is possible that he was present during the duelling, maybe concealed. Could this man have been trying to get rid of Mr. Devonshire so that he could come forward and claim Miss Hamilton? Or could some other party, unknown, perhaps unconnected with the duellists—" The voice droned on.

Caroline thought what a terrible man the Crowner was! She dreaded his searching vision which seemed to see into minds. Suddenly the macabre atmosphere of the inquest reached her. Dr. Cholmondeley would pry into anything if he thought he could find a clue as to why a man lay dead. He wanted to know whether this had indeed been an accident or whether something deeper lay there and a crime had been committed. Maybe there had not been murder, but had there been attempted murder? Someone shooting to kill not Mr. Cheever but possibly another of the party? Caroline felt that Dr. Cholmondeley despised her. But then, why not? Because of her thoughtless behaviour she had set in motion events which had caused the death of a fellow human being. And now the question of attempted murder, too, overhung the court.

"Could this bullet be from a little pistol?" A young voice pierced the pause the Crowner had made. The voice sounded beguilingly innocent. It was Sophia who had spoken.

"You are not supposed to interrupt my summing-up," said Dr. Cholmondeley. "This is most irregular. But if you have information which is not in the record I had better have it. Whoever you are there, come forward and be sworn."

Sophia, with a triumphant, secret smile and an air of pleasure at the notice she was getting from the room, came forward eagerly. She swept a triumphant glance at Caroline, and a warm, sweet, womanly look softened her features as her eyes found Robert's face.

Sophia was sworn. "Well," said Dr. Cholmondeley, "what do you have to say? What little gun were you speaking of?"

"A pistol belonging to my cousin Caroline Hamilton. She can shoot it, too. When we were younger I saw her do it. I heard her say just before the duel "I could kill Robert! Shoot him, I think!" She left our carriage at the last minute that morning at the Dingle. I believe she was concealing something in her muff. She had asked my mother for a muff at the last moment—"

"Oh!" said Caroline. "Oh!"

"I think Miss Caroline Hamilton had better tell her own version of this story. You may sit down, Miss Newcombe."

Caroline got anxiously to her feet. This was terrifying. The spiteful Sophia was accusing her of trying to murder Robert. She was coming forward when a masculine voice was heard.

"I'm afraid I must speak!" said Edmund Browne decisively.

Dr. Cholmondeley for the first time that morning looked startled. "What is this?" he asked. "What is it?"

"May I be sworn?" asked Edmund firmly.

He went forward, past Caroline, touching her arm briefly in passing. She, aware of her declaration of love for him, shrank back.

"If you have something to say, why did you not come forward earlier, Mr. Browne?"

"I believed the inquest was not an enquiry into how Mr. Devonshire was wounded but rather how Mr. Donald Cheever met his death. However, now that Miss Hamilton has been so unjustly accused . . ."

"Go on, Mr. Browne."

"I felt that if I did speak it would only give rise to further news stories, and Miss Hamilton has already been noticed in the Press to an extent that must have made her very unhappy. I felt I should not add fuel to that fire. I consulted Counsel, and was told that I need not speak since the inquest was about the death of Mr. Cheever, and the conclusion was bound to be misadventure . . ."

"The jury will ignore that remark," the Crowner said. "They are here to draw their own conclusions. Now, Mr. Browne, continue."

"Well, now that Miss Hamilton is being accused . . . Mr. Devonshire's wound was caused by me. I, not Miss Hamilton shot him."

The Crowner's eyebrows almost reached his hairline in astonishment at these words. He looked at Edmund Browne standing there facing him, his head thrown up, one slender hand on his hip holding back his opened coat, the other hand on the table as he leant forward, intense and proud.

Dr. Cholmondeley looked from Edmund Browne to the bewildered face of Harry de Lisle and then on to the face of Robert, red now with mortification as he realised how he had been shot. He turned back to Edmund.

"And how did you conceal yourself, Mr. Browne, so that you were not observed?"

"I came before the duelling party and concealed myself in a thicket."

"And why would you take such a risk, shooting at a man? Surely you, a well-known figure, would realise that you were risking some unpleasant publicity."

"I had promised Miss Hamilton that I would prevent the possible killing of Harry de Lisle by his cousin. I knew Robert de Lisle Devonshire was a deadly shot and that he was incensed against Mr. de Lisle. I believed then that Miss Hamilton was sentimentally interested in my old friend Harry de Lisle, and that their affection was mutual. I had tried to dissuade each cousin from the duel. I could not. I did the next best thing—saw to it that no terrible harm could come to Harry."

"And you did all this to protect Miss Hamilton?"

"Yes. I wished very much to see that Miss Hamilton came to no harm—she is a lady whose happiness I greatly desire."

The Crowner looked at Caroline.

"Humph!" he said. "Three men! All interested in one young woman! What a wild young thing you've got there, Mr. Hamilton. I don't know whether to congratulate you, or to be sorry for you!"

The Court was now too fascinated by the story they had heard unfold even to titter.

"Was it you, then, who called the police?" the Crowner went on. "They received a message from a small boy who did not know who had given it to him."

"Yes. It was I. I hoped that they would come in time to stop the duel. Then I would not have had to take action. But they came too late."

Caroline was astonished and ashamed. And he *had* told her he would be there, that he would help, because he really did love her. Or *had* loved her at that time. Did he love her still? She realised with a sickening lurch of her heart that he might no longer love her. How badly she had treated him! But the story in *The Times*? How to explain that?

Dr. Cholmondeley levelled a wintry smile at Edmund Browne. *The Times* was, after all, *The Times*. "You have of course, witnesses who could corroborate your story?" he asked.

"Yes, I do. My colleague here, Mr. Croft of *The Times* news desk."

"Mr. Croft, please be sworn."

Caroline saw that Mr. Croft was the older reporter to whom Edmund had been talking at the beginning of the inquest. Mr. Croft said: "I was on the news desk the night before the duel. Mr. Robert Devonshire's groom had come by with a story of the duel which he wished to sell for money. But I could get no confirmation of the story until the duel took place. I had heard that Mr. Browne knew these people and I asked him to confirm the story. He told me he had just come back from Hyde Park, but begged me to kill the story. So Browne authenticated it, though unintentionally. I have a friendship for Mr. Browne, but we had nothing of interest for the Stop Press news. I felt I had a duty to *The Times,* and I printed it. None of the other newspapers had it. Mr. Browne went out to Miss Hamilton's very upset that the story had been printed."

Caroline listened to Mr. Croft's evidence with mounting distress. It was clear that Edmund had not done her the least harm. She felt worse and worse about the way she had treated him.

Mr. Croft was still speaking:

"I can only presume that the *Morning Star* was tipped off in the same way we were, by a servant of one of the parties looking for financial gain. The *Star* sent Donald Cheever to investigate. I venture to say he was disguised and in hiding so he could report the duel without being found there. And he died by a bullet not intended for him."

"Thank you, Mr. Croft. As you will appreciate, you are not here to reach conclusions: that will be for the jury to do when I have finished my summing up—"

A voice from somewhere in the room now spoke up.

" 'Ere, I've got summat to say!"

"Who is that?" called out the Crowner angrily. "Step forward. You are not supposed to interrupt this court!"

"You won't say that when you 'ear wot I 'ave to say!"

"Who are you? Come here. State your name and address and be sworn."

The whole room was murmuring at this yet further interruption. A man, a total stranger to everyone, walked up to the inquest table.

"Silence!" demanded the Crowner. "Silence, I say!"

A total stranger? Caroline had a premonition that something quite dreadful was going to happen. She had seen this man before. A man all jowls and eyes, a man who liked to indulge in roguish smiles and broad winks. The landlord of the Fox and Hounds. Good heavens—he was not going to—? But he was!

Chapter 18

The landlord tossed his rolling head and glanced with a pair of roguish eyes around the room. "Seed these people afore," he said confidentially to the Crowner, but in a voice that carried to every corner of the court. "They was together in 'is rooms one night at my inn," he continued, pointing to Edmund Browne. "Went for a walk, 'e did, 'e said. Just ran into 'er, says 'e, under a 'edge. Run into 'er? They'd arranged to meet o'course. I wasn't born yesterday, your worship."

"Sir, that will be enough," said Dr. Cholmondeley acidly. "What are you meaning to tell us?"

"It was a love night. 'E practically ate 'er with 'is eyes. And 'er . . ." The landlord went off into a coarse, droll laugh.

"Be quiet!" Edmund said fiercely. "It wasn't like that at all!"

"Not like that at all!" Caroline echoed in a whisper, her shocked hand at her mouth.

"No, you was both two innocent little children," he said. "She looked pretty with nothing on but 'is shirt!" The public guffawed and the jurymen had trouble hiding their smiles. The seconds were also hiding laughter. Caroline, crimson to her eyes, was appalled. She cast a wild look at her aunt and uncle. Her aunt was collapsed over a great handkerchief of her uncle's and was quietly weeping. They no longer held hands. Her uncle's stern face

214

was washed clean of all human expression. He sat bolt upright, a stern, outraged man. Caroline trembled.

"Get to the point," said the Crowner.

"The point being that o'course 'e'd 'ave killed for 'er. 'E'd 'ave killed the young woman's future 'usband to get 'im out of the way. She was gorn off in the morning. I seed her stealing off, and it scarcely dawn. Gorn to the other chap, I'd say. 'E was jumping all over my place with jealousy when 'e found out. 'E'd kill for 'er all right."

"That is a conjecture," said the Crowner sharply to the jury. "Kindly take no notice of it. You will deduce from consideration of the facts, not from the conjecture of others."

The innkeeper went on: "When I seed it in the newspapers I said, I knows 'em, and I knows my duty. I came right up to Lunnon—"

"Yes, yes," said Dr. Cholmondeley. "But this is most irregular; you should have made yourself known to the authorities and given evidence in the proper way when called upon to do so."

The landlord looked a little crestfallen. "I was just waiting for 'im or 'er to catch theirselves—"

"That's enough," said the Crowner. "Thank you for your evidence. You may go and sit down. Mr. Browne, do you deny what this man has said?"

"No," began Edmund, "but—"

"And Miss Hamilton? You may reply from where you are. Just stand up."

Horrified, Caroline got to her feet.

"True or not true?" asked the Crowner in an unemotional voice.

"True—but—"

"That is all. Thank you, Miss Hamilton. Sit down, please."

As Caroline hesitated, searching for the words to say that Edmund had spent the night at the inn downstairs in a chair, the Crowner added sharply, "I told you that was enough—"

"But it isn't enough," interrupted Edmund Browne. "I

215

must insist on saying that I spent the night in a chair in one of the public rooms of the inn."

From where he sat, the landlord laughed unpleasantly, and called out loudly, "I'd know. Why, the place was so deserted, the fire went out."

"That will do," said the Crowner coldly. "All this has nothing to do with the inquest. No, Mr. Browne, you've said everything you can to help the young lady. I must get on with the business here."

Edmund hesitated, and then sat down with an air of helplessness.

"How chivalrous," said Sophia, quite loudly.

Caroline shrank. From then on, words came to her as from a distance. She dimly understood that the Crowner was finishing his interrupted summing up. She heard him explain patiently to the jury that the bullet found in the tree was the one shot by Harry de Lisle. He spoke again of Robert Devonshire's bullet, and explained how it must have been deflected to find the unfortunate head of Mr. Cheever. In the course of the enquiry, he continued, it had developed that a third shot was fired. Mr. Browne had admitted to firing that shot, and had stated that his intention in aiming at Robert Devonshire had been to wound Mr. Devonshire in such a way as to prevent *his* wounding Mr. de Lisle, or gravely injuring him. The jury had met to enquire about the death of Donald Cheever. It would be safe, said the Crowner, to conclude that this was a death by misadventure. But it was the duty of the jury now to consider whether a second crime—an attempted murder—had been uncovered by the enquiry. Mr. Browne had admitted an interest in Miss Hamilton—a passionate interest; and it appeared that Miss Hamilton returned his affection. Miss Hamilton could not free herself of her engagement to Mr. Devonshire. Could it be that Mr. Browne had planned to take the life of Robert Devonshire, under cover of the duel, in order to free Miss Hamilton for himself? Was Mr. Browne's story, then, as he presented it—a romantic and gallant one? Or was it a sordid attempt to murder a man in cold blood?

The jury then went out, but returned almost immediately. They found that Mr. Cheever's death was accidental, and they were inclined to believe Mr. Browne's statement as to his reasons for wounding Mr. Devonshire. Edmund was not to be held for attempted murder.

This made the Court break into pandemonium. Caroline saw that Edmund was surrounded by well-wishers, admirers and reporters. All the commotion in the room centred on him. His story had caught everyone's imagination, and now Caroline would be merely a part of the Edmund Browne story. She was aware that the Court ordeal was over. The room was emptying. But her personal ordeal was just about to begin. People stared at her as they came near to her, and then looked away as they went by.

Caroline saw her uncle coming towards her. His face remained frozen. Her Aunt Millie stood just behind him. She looked at Caroline, but oh, so mournfully, and she was still quietly weeping. Then Mr. Hamilton came and stood in front of his niece and regarded her silently.

"You will now have your own money," he said from his frozen face. "My advice is, find some older female to live with you. I shall not wish to see you in Wiltshire. Your aunt and I will have all this to live down. I thought you wayward but—not this."

For the second time that day Caroline lowered her eyes. She felt tears of mortification and of hurt prick her eyelids. She could see the *Wiltshire Gazette* in her mind's eye. If they could build up all that about the murder of a governess, they would have an enjoyable time with Miss Caroline Hamilton of The Grange. "Uncle," she tried. "I'm so terribly sorr—" Her uncle turned and walked away from her as she spoke. His face remained set. Aunt Millie, with a look of pure anguish at Caroline, would have liked to speak to her, but dared not, and followed her husband. "Oh, please!" Caroline called out after her. But the slight figure of Mrs. Hamilton did not stop. Her husband, at the sound of Caroline's plea, had turned his head to give a short, sharp signal over his shoulder to his wife that she was not to stop, but was to follow him out of court. Caroline was in total disgrace with the only world she knew. From now on she would have no friends, not even her old friends. She would be ostracised.

Mrs. Erskine was standing before Caroline, her face full of compassion.

"I've been sitting in a corner of the room," she said. "I only came to London last night. I came here today because I had a feeling you might need me." Caroline burst into tears in her arms. Mrs. Erskine patted her shoulder. Then she said: "Come, Caroline, courage! The day will yet dawn when a woman's private life will not be a matter for public scandal."

"But I never—"

"What you did or did not do is not important. The world will be perfectly happy again when Edmund Browne marries you."

"Marries me? But—"

"Well, of course he must! A man with such a sense of honour as Edmund Browne will not hesitate to give you his name and protection. And all will yet be well when the marriage takes place."

"But Edmund must not—"

"He cannot leave you with your good name dishonoured. He compromised you. He must give you the protection of his name now, and I am sure he will."

"But I could never accept such a thing!"

"Well, it is the usual thing. And you said in court that you loved him. Once the story of the night at the inn came out—a great indiscretion on your part, my dear—everyone knew who the man you had referred to earlier in the questioning must be."

"But if he feels forced—No!"

"My dear girl—I do admire your spirit. But an offer of marriage is at least what you can expect."

At this moment Robert de Lisle Devonshire chose to come by. He looked at her with his dark look. "Well, Caroline," he said, attempting raillery, "it wasn't very nice being jilted in open court—and I don't believe that Edmund Browne would have found any joys in your company *I* could not have uncovered. However—he's bound to offer to marry you now. I'm glad. But I won't want to come to the wedding!"

He laughed a little self-consciously.

"Poor boy," said Sophia distinctly. "It's a dreadful shame. If *I* had been Caroline—" She stopped and flushed scarlet. Robert looked at her with interest.

Then Lady de Lisle Devonshire arrived. "Well," she said looking at Caroline through her lorgnette. "So the name of the man in your life has come out! Really, Miss Hamilton, I would never have believed that you could go so far—and whilst engaged to my poor, dear son who loved you! I don't believe there will be any necessity for us to meet again. Come, Robert!"

"In a moment, Mother." Robert demurred for the first time in his life. Lady Devonshire looked surprised. She did not like to be told "in a moment", when she was used to "right away, Mother".

Robert bowed elaborately to Caroline, a picture of total, handsome, masculine grace. But his eyes were on Sophia, who returned his looks with a blush and a tremble. He turned and left. And Lady de Lisle Devonshire turned away from Caroline and swept past her, her nose in the air.

"Well," said Mrs. Erskine. "Now perhaps you see why it would be better for you to marry Mr. Browne, and without delay. Surely *now* you will be woman of the world enough to recognise your only way out of this dreadful mess."

"Oh," said Caroline. "But it is all so horrible!"

Mrs. Erskine patted her shoulder, nodded kindly and affirmatively at her and said: "I'm sure he'll ask you. He will have to after all this publicity. We must meet again soon, my dear. I shall be in touch."

"Let's go home." Elizabeth Stroud pulled at her sleeve. "Of course you did nothing wrong. I know that. But none of them want to believe you."

Aunt Lucinda moved forward now and said: "It is kind of Miss Stroud to ask you back to her rooms, but I think you should come home with me, Caroline. *I* have every confidence in you, and if George Hamilton had a little sense—at least *this* branch of the family believes in you, however black things look."

"Then I'll say goodbye for now," said Elizabeth Stroud.

"No," said Caroline quickly. "You've been a true friend. I don't want you to go home alone. Aunt, if I come with you, may I bring Elizabeth for tea?"

As Aunt Lucinda was nodding, Harry de Lisle came over.

"I'm sorry you are in such trouble," he said to Caroline, and added with great simplicity, "I think I got you into some of it. But I didn't mean to. I thought you needed rescuing from Robert."

"Yes, I know, Harry," said Caroline. "And thank you for—" She almost said "speaking to me kindly when noone else does," but instead finished, "always being so kind."

But Harry lingered.

"Is it true?" he asked unhappily. "I mean, do you love Edmund? Edmund is like a brother to me. Tell me, Caroline, please?"

There was something so unsophisticated in the question that Caroline impulsively gave him her hand, as she had turned to him in the conservatory on that night which now seemed so long ago. "Yes, it's true, Harry," she said. "I didn't realise until the duel and then it was too late to tell you and Robert. And besides Edmund had not spoken."

"But the night at the inn?" asked Harry simply.

"That was innocent," said Caroline with equal simplicity. "Edmund took pity on a runaway girl, soaked with rain."

"You will marry him, then, and I hope you will be happy. I know you will."

Caroline did not say that to Harry she would *not* marry Edmund. What would be the point of telling him how she now felt—that she could not allow what the world would see as her dishonour to be covered in such a way?

"Well, I wish it could have been me," Harry smiled. "God bless, Caro." He bowed over her hand and so took his leave of her.

"Shall we go?" she said to her aunt.

"Yes, yes indeed," said Aunt Luci.

A subdued group arrived in the carriage at No. 70; even Sophia was quiet. She knew now that she was unlikely to see Robert again. Aunt Luci had not once looked at her on the way home, and Sophia guessed that her mother was still too angry to trust herself to speak to her. She should not have accused Caroline like that in court. But the opportunity had been there, and for the life of her she could not have resisted it. She had only now begun to realise the gravity of her suggestion, and what dreadful consequences it might have had for Caroline. At the time she had thought only of making Caroline uncomfortable— Caroline, who had made *her* so unhappy by her engagement to Robert Devonshire—an engagement Caroline did not care for, and which she, Sophia, would have given her life to have.

Chapter 19

Caroline was out of the dark, chill room of the inquest, that room with all its probings, its touched-upon passions, hates, fears, ambitions and loves, its terrible inquietude. Caroline was back in the familiar hall of No. 70 Wilton Crescent. But she was not back in a familiar world. She was in a world where she avoided Jerome's face, Rosie's eyes. She did not wish to read in them any doubt of her decency, or even any sympathy with her in her public shame.

Aunt Lucinda obviously had something urgent to say to Caroline. Caroline could tell that from her nervous and restless attitude. The difficulty for Aunt Lucinda in speaking of what was on her mind had to do with Elizabeth

Stroud's presence. Aunt Lucinda was glad that Caroline had not abandoned Stroud to go to her lodgings alone; she would have been disappointed in Caroline had she done that; but on the other hand, what to do with Elizabeth Stroud now that Aunt Luci wanted to talk to Caroline about something personal?

It was the engagement ring which was on Aunt Luci's mind. In view of the public renunciation of Caroline's engagement, Mrs. Newcombe knew that the proper thing to do was to return the ring at once. But she felt she could not quite discuss that in front of Miss Stroud.

She need not have worried.

Elizabeth had been standing in the hall quietly whilst the family took off their wraps, wondering just what she should do. That extra sense of hers which told her when she was *de trop* was prompting her now. Jerome, guessing her problem, said in a quick whisper: "I know you have been used to better company, Miss Stroud, but maybe this is the moment to have a cup of tea with Rosie and me in our sitting room below stairs." Elizabeth flashed such a grateful smile at him that Jerome noticed how pretty and young she could look, and ventured a further step: "It has occurred to me, since we met, that you and I might become acquaintances?"

"Why not?" Elizabeth answered. "Even friends, Mr. Jerome."

"Well," said Jerome, and then astonished himself by abruptly asking something he had thought but had never meant to put into words, and certainly never expected to say to her: "Why have you never married?" He broke off, shocked at his lack of restraint. To make a personal, and such a very personal, remark!

But Elizabeth laughed and said easily, "It's not a long story, Mr. Jerome. Nobody ever asked me." Her tired face was lit up with human warmth.

"Will you step this way, Miss. Miss Eliza. And the name is Jim. I could see you home presently if you like."

"I would like," said Elizabeth, smiling.

Aunt Lucinda, quite unaware that her servant might have an interest of his own, merely blessed Jerome for the tact with which he had removed that nice Elizabeth Stroud from what was possibly going to be an unpleasant scene between her and her daughter. But first, the ring.

She motioned both girls upstairs and into the withdrawing room. Once there, she closed the door firmly, and without even taking off her bonnet, went immediately to her desk, pulled open the little drawer, pressed the secret spring and felt in the open space thus revealed.

There was nothing.

Lucinda glanced in shock at Caroline, and then bent down so that she could look into the little secret place, saying in horrified tones: "It's gone! The ring has gone!"

"It can't be," said Caroline. "Let me look."

She too bent and searched, but there was nothing to be found. As she was about to speak, Caroline's gaze fell on Sophia's face. Guilt was clearly written on it.

"Sophy!" Caroline asked, "What do *you* know about it?"

For answer Sophia, putting both her hands over her face, sank upon a chair and burst into tears. "I took it!" she wailed. "I took it!"

The pink colour in Aunt Lucinda's face deserted her now, leaving her light sprinkling of freckles floating on a skin grey with fear. "Sophia, you are many things, but surely not a thief!"

There was a terrible silence.

"Where is the ring, Sophia?" asked Mrs. Newcombe presently, in a voice almost drained of feeling.

Sophia removed a hand from her tear-streaked face and put it deep into a pocket in her skirt. She came out with a little, embroidered handkerchief, its four corners knotted together. She held the little bundle out towards Caroline.

"I took it," she said, "because it made him nearer to me. You didn't want it. You didn't want him. I thought I'd put it back, and nobody would ever know. Oh!" she finished, on a fresh wail, "I wish I had never seen him!"

Caroline looked at Sophia in amazement. To care for Robert Devonshire like that! As much, apparently, as she cared for Edmund. But Robert was so different from Edmund. Robert was a vain, selfish, jealous, possessive man. But, to be fair, Caroline thought, it is *I* who see him as vain and selfish. Perhaps to Sophia he is neither. Perhaps she likes his being jealous and possessive. I see Edmund as maybe others do not see him. But Caroline turned away from that thought. The thought of Edmund, any thought, was too painful to her.

Caroline went to Sophia, and put an arm around her. The girl's shoulders were shaking, and Sophia, quite forgetting all the injury she had done her cousin, leaned gratefully against her, glad of the sympathy.

"Aunt Lucinda," said Caroline, "I think your daughter is very much in love with Robert de Lisle Devonshire."

"But she's scarcely out of the schoolroom!" said Mrs. Newcombe.

"She's nearly eighteen!" Caroline reminded her. "Old enough to get married."

"Married?"

"Why not? The de Lisle Devonshires are a good family. I suppose the best in Wiltshire."

"My dear girl, Sophia and I hardly move in the same circles as the de Lisle Devonshires."

"That has little to do with the case," said Caroline, managing a smile. "I have an idea that Robert is in his own way just as strong-willed as his mother. I have no doubt that he will marry whom he pleases." Caroline remembered Robert's saying to her, on a night that now seemed long ago: "My wife and I will do and say as *I* say." Yes, she thought, such an attitude would be just what Sophia would like—in fact, just what Sophia needed —someone who would tell her what to do and see that she obeyed.

Now Sophia was crying. "And I shall never see him again now. Never!"

"If you would use your head a little," said Caroline, feeling horribly grown up and wise, "you may well be seeing him for the rest of your life."

"What do you mean?" Sophia stopped crying.

"Well," said Caroline, but she addressed herself to Mrs. Newcombe now, "what were you proposing I do with the ring when I had it?"

"Return it, of course," said Aunt Lucinda, "Return it with a nice, dignified note. I would send Jerome in a hansom to take it back so that no harm could come to such a valuable heirloom."

"Wouldn't it be nicer if my cousin Sophia, whom Robert knows, were to return the ring? Jerome could go with her for her protection. I will write a note, but Sophia can be there, and she will be better than any note of mine to bridge the gap between the families. You would, of course, insist on seeing Robert yourself, Sophia," she added, turning to her. "You would not be expected to hand my ring to any of the Devonshire servants. Do you think you could manage all that, Sophia, and do it satisfactorily?"

"Oh, yes," said Sophia, the tears drying magically on her face and her eyes beginning to shine. "I'm *sure* I could!"

Caroline smiled at her: "Well, go and put on your tartan costume—the one you wore for the duel which becomes you so well."

Aunt Lucinda said: "I'm not sure I approve of this. And what if Lady Devonshire should see Sophia and insist on receiving the ring herself? Might not that be embarrassing?"

"But I wouldn't give the ring to her. I couldn't. You gave it to me to hand to Robert only!"

"You'll do all right," said Caroline drily.

Sophia jumped up and held out her hand for the handkerchief containing the ring. The tiny scrap of linen unfolded and Caroline placed the ring itself in Sophia's small, cupped hand.

In Sophia's small, plump palm, the ring looked quite different. It seemed to nestle closely to Sophie's pink and white skin. Caroline had always seen it as gleaming and evil. The great stones were now only beautiful, and the heavy setting looked magnificent against a hand so small, round and feminine. Sophia stood with a dignity new to her, looking down at the ring in her hand. She looked as if she already owned it. Caroline could see a new Lady de Lisle Devonshire, a girl after the present

Lady de Lisle Devonshire's heart (once she had recovered from having lost her chance at the Hamilton money), a girl who would exactly copy Lady Devonshire herself, and love the moulding into a great lady of the world that Fanny Devonshire would give her.

Now Sophia tried to apologise. "Caroline, I've been horrid! Really, a beast! I was just so unhappy. I never really meant to—I didn't realise—"

Caroline shushed her. Best not to remember. She thought, with a stab at the heart, of her own cruelty to Edmund in that very room. How horrible love could make one! How near was hate to love; or should she say, how near was love to hate. How dreadful what pride could do to a relationship! Her own pride had made a relationship with Edmund impossible. Well, Caroline thought, now she would pay for all her tempestuous spirit—pay for it in loneliness and longing for what she could not have. She was arranging Sophia's life, but could she now ever arrange her own? Yes, of course she could work and might even like working; but what of Edmund, the man she loved?

Chapter 20

Sophia had no sooner left upon her eager way, than Jerome entered to announce that Mr. Edmund Browne was in the morning room. Though he was a well-trained servant, he had been with the family so long that, try as he might, he could not quite conceal the satisfaction—yes, and relief—he felt in making this announcement. Caroline noticed this and began to feel vaguely annoyed. Aunt Luci did not even try to conceal her delight that Edmund was there.

"Thank goodness," she said. "I was beginning to fear that being a journalist—well!"

"Well what?" asked Caroline, accurately guessing that what Aunt Lucinda had feared was that Edmund Browne might not present himself to marry Caroline at all. She had been feeling remorse at the way she had mistrusted and ill-treated Edmund when he was last in Aunt Lucinda's house, but now the sense that everyone was expecting him to propose to her and was certain that she would immediately accept, took away some of her remorse and most of her gladness that he was now there wanting to see her.

"Yes, Aunt, please, *what* were you beginning to fear?" Caroline insisted out of her irritation.

Aunt Luci would have preferred to remain silent, but seeing Caroline was put out with her replied honestly: "I only meant to say that I am glad he has the instincts of a gentleman. Some of the journalists—and indeed quite a few of these gentlemen I talk of—are beginning to be a little cavalier with women. But there! It is all resolved. Mr. Browne has arrived to offer you the protection of his name."

"But I did nothing wrong, Aunt Luci, nothing that could cause me to have to be the object of his protection."

"Hush, child! Of course *I* believe that. I'm sure you did nothing. But the world will choose to believe otherwise. Thank goodness Mr. Browne recognises the world for what it is and will make all the amends he can—"

"But he does not owe me amends!"

"All the effort, then, to restore your good name. To see that gossip is stilled. But run along, my dear. This is not the moment to keep Mr. Browne waiting. We don't want him to change his mind. Oh dear, I didn't mean to say anything as bald as that. It is just that all this—all this upset has made me nervous."

Caroline went down the stairs to the morning room in a tizzy of jumbled feelings. Mrs. Erskine's voice in the court-room that morning came back to her. "The least he can do is to offer you his name"—and her own reply: "I could never accept him in such circumstances." Didn't *anyone* think he might be in love with her?

Her heart and head as she descended the stairs to the morning room told her that neither the one nor the other was quite clear about her feelings. She was longing to see Edmund, yet she resented seeing him in circumstances where he must feel obliged to offer her his heart and hand. She resented the idea that he had come to save her from the results of her own folly in running away and then having no roof to run to. She had compromised herself. He had not compromised her. She remembered now the sight of him sitting up in the armchair before the cold fire in the big main room of the inn, the dog asleep at his feet. He had behaved as the soul of honour then. He had behaved wonderfully again about the duel. He had come to her rescue yet again in court today, and now here he was, preparing to do what? To sacrifice himself once more for her.

No. She would not accept charity from him again just to save her good name. If he really loved her—but did he? When he had given evidence in court, he had spoken of his wish to take care of her. Was his feeling for her just the affection of a tutor, a man older than herself, for a girl who seemed to be in endless difficulties and who had appealed to him for help? Or did he love her as she loved him? Well, she would soon know. With head held high, Caroline put her small hand on the heavily chased brass door handle of the morning room, turned it and entered.

Edmund Browne stood near the window looking out on the small garden. He had thrown off his ulster, but still held his hat in hands that appeared to be nervous. He started at her entry and then, putting the hat down upon a table, walked over to her.

"Caroline!" He had put out both hands to her and she gave him her hands, but managed to step back a little so that he could not imagine she was rushing into his arms. At the same time her heart, which had been hurrying from the moment that Jerome spoke Edmund Browne's name, now began to thud unbearably.

"I came to see you as soon as I could. I had to satisfy the journalists first."

"Oh, of course," said Caroline, her voice cool and haughty as she had not quite meant it to be. And before she could control her pride, she had added: "Of course, you had to look after your newspaper interests before you could come to me."

"Oh Caroline, that is not worthy of you! You would not have wanted me to have reporters tag me here!"

"Of course not," she said, "I'm sorry. I suppose I'm too tired. I say what I don't mean to say."

"Well, I will say what I have to say," he said, "and leave you to get rest. I have come here, as I suppose you've guessed, for your sake."

"For *my* sake?"

"Well, of course. To offer marriage to you."

"Is *that* what you are doing?"

"Yes, and I can see I am doing it clumsily. I feel terrible about what happened in court—your being exposed to that horrible story told by the landlord. But the scandal will be over soon as they know you are going to have my name. When you are Mrs. Edmund Browne nobody will dare to whisper—"

"But supposing I don't want to be Mrs. Edmund Browne?"

"Come! You can't refuse!"

"Why not?" she said coolly.

"Because of all the gossip, the scandal—as I have said."

"But you haven't asked me if I love you."

"I know you do. You said as much in Court this morning, and I—"

"I admitted I loved you. Loved. Please note that loved is the past tense of love—"

"Caroline, what is this nonsense? Are you telling me you did love me but that you don't now? That's ridiculous."

"Oh, is it? Are you telling me that you love me, Edmund? I have not heard a word about love from you in all this."

"But, good heavens, I'm offering you my name!"

"That's very handsome of you. But then that's the least the public can expect of Mr. Browne. Mr. Browne is a gallant fellow who shoots Robert to save his friend Harry. Or was it to help the little heiress Miss Hamilton that you shot her fiancé? Anyway, you stole away without telling anyone, leaving the rest of us to suffer, Harry to go to prison and me to feel I had been betrayed—"

"But I didn't steal away! I went to try and keep your name out of the newsprints and then I came here, yes, to this very house to offer you my heart and hand. I'm trying to do the same now."

It was true. All true. But the more truth he spoke, the more justified he was in reproaching her for her unkindness, the more unkind she seemed to get. He was so absolutely in the right and she was so absolutely in the wrong. She tried to pull herself together, to be more reasonable. But now he was put out.

"I don't understand you," he said. "You put yourself in a compromising position because of your childishness in running away from your home—"

"Childishness!"

"What else was it? To climb out of a window on a night of storm showed a childish flouting of the conventions and a flighty, ungovernable temper which was bound to end in disaster—".

"Well, it's my disaster. Thank you for pointing out to me that it *is* mine. And now, if you please, will you go away and leave me to deal with my own disasters. I assure you I don't need your help."

"Don't be silly, Caroline, and—yes, childish again! What will you do if you don't marry me?" Now he was angry.

"Manage my properties," she told him.

"Fiddlesticks!" he replied. "No girl—no woman, indeed—can manage London properties."

"I can."

"Not in the London slums. I understand from Joachim that that is the sort of property you have inherited."

"I can manage it," she told him, "and make a better life for the tenants than Uncle Ham ever did."

"You'll lose your fortune."

"That remains to be seen."

"Then there is no more for me to say!"

"No, there isn't. You've said too much already."

"Thank you, Caroline. You *are* gracious." They were both breathing hard, facing each other like two contestants rather than two lovers. What had gone wrong?

"I don't understand you," he said again. "I thought you would be glad if the scandalmongering was stopped."

"Why? What does that matter to you? Oh, I see, you would like people to know that, journalist or not, you *are* a gentleman and would certainly offer to marry the girl you had ruined. . . ."

"*I* didn't ruin you!"

"Then who did?"

"Perhaps your own strong-minded impetuousness. . . ."

"Is that wrong?"

"Look where it has got you. . . ."

"I'm free and independent. What's wrong with that?"

"Because people might imagine I did not offer to marry you."

"Ah, there! It's out!"

He tried again:

"Caroline, get hold of yourself! Marry me! It's the only way to save your good name!"

Anger rose in her, almost choking her. Maybe he meant well, but "the only way to save her good name"?

How self-confident he was. He seemed so sure she'd accept.

"Oh, no!" she told him. "There are other ways. If I must have a loveless marriage, I'd sooner go to Australia on one of your famous boats—"

At this he reached for his ulster and his hat. "I can only suppose," he said, very much on his dignity, "that there is nothing else I can say?"

"Nothing!" she flashed.

He bowed stiffly to her. she saw his strong, well-made hand go out to touch the brass door knob. He opened the

231

door, went through it and closed it quietly behind him. Only when she heard his feet retreating on Aunt Lucinda's staircase, steps growing fainter and fainter and then the shutting of the heavy front door, did what she had done come over her. But of course she did not, she could not, go running in the street after him. And even if she could have done that, she could not now urge him to forget her angry words, beg him to marry her on any terms so long as he was hers and she was his. She sat on the settee in the morning room a long, long time. But this time she could not weep her misery out. Misery sat enthroned in her soul; tears would only deepen her knowledge of misery's enormity and undermine her self-control, so that calming herself would become even more difficult. In a word, she suffered, and now discovered that whilst happiness may be shared, suffering is done alone.

What a mess she had made of everything! She had run away from the only family she had ever known. She had broken her engagement in such a public manner that anyone she might have known from débutante days would now avoid her as a jilt. She had turned down, and for the second time, the only man she could ever love.

She sat still. If only she could have cried, for the skin of her face felt taut with unshed tears. To her came the knowledge that she had now said goodbye to her unthinking youth. The person who presently patted one or two stray locks into smooth order on her head, and put the tumbled cushions back into their accustomed places on the settee was, if not quite a woman yet, not a child and no longer a girl. She felt for the first time the full meaning of her acts; they were no longer merely wilful demonstrations of protest, but her conscious acts, her decisions. She shivered, and then, controlling her tremors, stood up and straightened her shoulders. It was up to her now, and herself alone, to conduct her life.

As for Edmund, he had left, hurt and angry, thinking that at least he had learnt his lesson. He had loved her and would love no other, but he would never ask her to marry him again. He would marry, of course, one day; he was not an idiot who would tragically choose to live his life alone, but he would not now marry the girl he loved. He took himself to his Arlington Chambers. The porters greeted him pleasantly: he was glad that at least they never permitted women here.

Chapter 21

"Where to begin?" said Mr. Sapperstone, surveying Leg Iron Court with a sigh. He was a very tall, thin, gangly fellow who used his narrow building ladder as a movable wall, leaning against the side of the rungs, a hand and arm through the holes between the steps. His prominent, pale blue eyes looked out knowingly from between their red-rimmed lids, and the red tops of his large ears flopped out to support his deerstalker cap. His thick, straight, flaxen hair shot down beneath the peak of the deerstalker in front and made a duck's tail of hair, answering the peak of the deerstalker in back. He wore a carpenter's apron with a wall of tools imprisoned in the oblong pocket across it, and he savoured a nail rolled between his teeth as if it were a succulent drumstick. Occasionally he took out the nail and looked at it as he talked with an air of surprise that made you think he felt it should be a chicken leg, but then he always put the nail back and sucked it again. Besides the interesting assortment of tools across his apron, he carried a cylindrical carpet bag. He had made this himself from two circular bits of wood with a roll of carpet tacked between. His "mate", a lad of fifteen or so, all large feet, large hands and large adenoids, stood with his mouth agape from surprise and a little fear. His round brown eyes roved around Leg Iron Court and then roved back to the carpenter as though seeking guidance on his behaviour. Meanwhile the carpenter's "horses" which he held, and a long narrow table top, both used in making up a carpenter's work bench, seemed to explain in a moment to any onlooker the word "impedimenta".

Caroline stood beside the two backed up by Mr. Brady, whose watchful eyes turned quickly in his head, noting every movement in the tenants who lounged against walls, sat on door steps, crowded around the only water pump, or leaned out of top story windows. They had all come to look at Caroline, and Mr. Brady wanted them to know he had come to look at them all.

"Where to *begin,* Miss?" repeated Mr. Sapperstone.

"How about looking at the foundations?" asked Mr. Brady.

"Yes, the foundations," said Caroline, flashing Mr. Brady a grateful look.

"Hah!" Mr. Sapperstone removed the nail, contemplated first Mr. Brady, then Caroline, and said: "You mean begin with the foundations and maybe finish with the roof?"

"Well, I'd say the foundations, the walls and *then* the roofs," Mr. Brady suggested amiably.

"*You* in the building business?" asked Mr. Sapperstone sharply.

"Nope. 'Course I'm not!" said Brady. "But I know a thing or two about places like this. You want to know where to begin? Miss H. here I'm sure agrees with me: foundations, *then* walls, and lastly, roofs."

Mr. Sapperstone eyed Mr. Brady as though contemplating which of several remarks he might choose to make would best convey to Mr. Brady that the building business was a little more complicated than that. To avoid any unpleasantness between her two escorts, Caroline said hastily:

"And then there's the doors back and front, and the missing windows, and I suppose we'll have to find out if that pump works—if there's washing and drinking water enough."

"Don't mind if I do start with the foundations," said Mr. Sapperstone graciously, after this hasty speech by

Caroline. " 'Ave to begin somewheres. Foundations, it is, then walls as I like, and roofs to please everyone. I'll start on that very 'ouse there at the middle of the back of this 'ere Court." Mr. Sapperstone regarded the house he had in mind thoughtfully. "Looks like the oldest one to me," he said, "though, suffering saints, none of 'em is exactly young. These Courts is dark and black and the 'ouses is so black with age they make it blacker."

Mr. Sapperstone now indicated that Caroline and Mr. Brady should go on towards the middle house. The little groups of tenants, as though at a previously agreed moment, moved in towards the house Caroline was making for. Mr. Sapperstone paused in the walking of his ladder forwards to the house, put it down and leant upon it.

"Seems to me like those tenants want to talk somethink over."

"Go and ask them?" Caroline prompted Mr. Brady.

Mr. Brady settled his beaver hat more firmly on his head, clutched his stout cudgel and descended upon the knot of people, to whom he made a terse statement:

"This 'ere is Miss 'Amilton," he said. "She just come into this property. She visited it the other day. Some of you must've seen her. Seems like she wants to mend it up a bit, put it together proper. That's her carpenter and his boy. We're wanting to get into that middle 'ouse there to begin work. Now, 'ow's about moving over a bit and letting the lady by?"

"Don't want anything mended," a dirty man with an old stove pipe hat on his head said loudly. "Tell 'er to get on 'er way. We don't need 'er kind in 'ere."

" 'Taint what you need, it's what yer going to get!" said Mr. Brady sharply. "She owns these 'ouses, see, and she can do what she likes."

"Just let 'er try!" said the dark man, not moving a muscle. A roar of agreement went up from the group:

"We like things as they are!"

"We don't need no ladies 'ere!"

"Thanks for the charity, but no thanks!"

"Tell 'er to get out of this 'ere whilst she can! Tell 'er to skidaddle quick before we makes her." This last from a

235

big, stout woman with hair that hung in a tangled mass about a sour and evil face.

"A mudlark!" said Mr. Sapperstone, under his breath.

Caroline had heard of mudlarks—people who climbed into the filthy mud of the Thames River when the water was at low tide to search in the odorous mud for any trifles of bone or household implement which might have been cast into the river, which was used as an open sewer for the deposit of every bit of household refuse. They sold such things, Caroline could not imagine to whom. But they sold them. For all she was determined not to show fear, Caroline felt like shrinking back from this woman, and indeed from the whole ragged, threatening group.

"We ain't going to pay 'er any more rent," a slatternly girl of about fifteen volunteered. "So we don't want no interference 'ere, see?"

Caroline rallied herself bravely. These people were not so different from herself.

"Mr. Brady," she called from behind him. "Please tell them there will be no increase in the rents."

"Let 'er get out of 'ere and leave us alone," a voice called from the back of the crowd, a young man's voice. The knot of people had grown appreciably larger: new tenants seemed to join the group almost from nowhere— they seemed literally to rise up from the ground. The crowd began to move forward, or rather to shuffle forward, in a silence that was worse than any words that could be tossed at Caroline. Mr. Brady raised his stick. He was going to have to do his best to ward off the front men. In their hands he saw now broken knives, bits of sharpened wood, broken shards of bottles. It looked nasty.

Mr. Sapperstone, suddenly a young man from whom all inertia had departed, signalled silently to his "mate" and the boy, following his hand signals, quickly put down the carpenter's "horses" and placed the flat top across them, forming a carpenter's workbench.

Without ceremony, the lanky builder reached forward and grabbed Caroline. He pushed her behind the barrier made by his workbench, stood behind it himself, and now, in each hand, he held one of his hammers. His boy was equipped with an awl and a heavy pair of pincers.

Caroline realised the danger, but what else was there to do but try and reason with these people. She called out to Mr. Brady: "Ask what they would like to have done in this Court." But Mr. Brady took no notice of her instruction. As the crowd stealthily and silently advanced upon them, Mr. Brady as quickly and noiselessly moved backwards, trying to join Mr. Sapperstone behind the small protection of the carpenter's table.

"Tell them—" Caroline began again.

"Ain't no use, Miss," Mr. Brady called over his shoulder. An ugly murmur arose from the crowd. Any minute now, Mr. Brady knew, that crowd was going to close in on him, Mr. Sapperstone, the boy and Caroline Hamilton, and when that crowd was through, Lord knew what would be left of the four.

Suddenly Caroline knew what she must do. She looked around for something to stand on, something which would make her conspicuous. Mr. Sapperstone seemed to guess her intention. Without really thinking it though, but just feeling that maybe it would work—after all, what else was there to do—he touched his deerstalker hat quickly to be sure it was there, thrust his hammers at his boy (who grabbed with awkward hands because his fists were full of his own weapons) and, placing both hands around Caroline's small waist, quickly swung her on to his carpenter's bench. Then he reclaimed his hammers for each hand and stood near Caroline, ready for whatever came next. Mr. Brady joined him now, behind the carpenter's table and the other side of Caroline. If he had had his way he would have taken Caroline down, but it was too late.

Caroline's sudden appearance on the carpenter's bench had caught the people by surprise, and gave her that minute in which, the crowd being momentarily checked in their purpose, she felt she could speak.

Caroline heard her own voice as though it were the voice of someone else.

". . . give me a chance! Light, clean . . . Paint and paper . . . drinking water . . . window panes . . ."

"Who are you, anyway?" the man with the stovepipe hat yelled jeeringly. He seemed to be some sort of a leader.

"Your landlord," replied Caroline stoutly. "Your new landlord." She could feel her knees trembling as she looked down into those dirty, ravaged, angry faces. But she managed to keep her voice firm.

"No, you ain't our landlord. Our landlord is an old geezer, squeezing the last penny out of us. Never repaired anythink in his life!"

"I know," said Caroline. "He *was* your landlord. But I am in control of this property now and I do want to repair it."

"Go home! Yer too young to be out. Yer daddy will warm yer backside when 'e 'ears you were 'ere," shouted a draggled woman to whose tattered skirts two thin, grey-faced, wide-eyed children hung, fingers in mouths, solemn eyes peering up fearfully from under unkempt hair.

There was a general laugh.

She was interrupted by the sound of a stone crashing into one of the few remaining panes of glass in a nearby house. The boy who had thrown the stone stood there smiling whilst he proudly hefted another, making sure that Caroline saw him before he would throw his missile.

To his surprise Caroline asked him his name. By way of reply the boy threw the jagged stone. It narrowly missed Caroline. At that Mr. Brady stepped forward from behind the carpenter's bench to the front. He was swinging his cudgel menacingly so that other children who had stooped for stones, eyeing Mr. Brady and Mr. Brady's stick and Mr. Brady's face, dropped the stones and watched Mr. Brady's club instead.

"Anyone throw anything more at this little Missis," Mr. Brady called loudly, "an' he'll know he has a skull as soft as a chicken's shell." There was an uneasy silence now and a shuffling of feet. Caroline could hear Mr. Sapperstone's adenoidal boy breathing heavily behind her.

"Look," she said. "If you don't want the houses repaired, all right, you don't. But the houses are mine; they need repair and they will be repaired."

Silence greeted her, but the crowd had not yet begun to move again.

Caroline said quickly:

"Those who want to live here in decent rooms will be expected to keep those rooms as they get them from me—decent. If they don't they can find places to live elsewhere. I heard the banisters in one building were burnt for firewood. That is not to happen again. You can buy firewood from me at the very cheapest prices. But no burning of banisters. Do you hear?"

She stopped to get her breath. The woman with the tattered skirts began to push back the unkempt locks of one of her little girls with a work-worn hand. "Us 'as need of firewood. Can't keep no one and nothink clean with cold water."

There was a murmur of agreement here.

"Well, let's see what she does?" a man called out, sneeringly.

"Fair enough!" Mr. Sapperstone called back loudly and firmly. And then to Caroline he said in a lower tone: "They've got to be shown Miss. That'll be the ticket: showing 'em."

"No more to pay in rent?" someone called.

"Not a penny more: I promise," said Caroline.

"Then wot are you after?" an untidy girl of fifteen or so with a child snuggled beneath her ragged shawl called out. "If you don't want more rent out of us why are you trying to mend these 'ere 'ouses?"

"Because they're not fit to live in," said Caroline honestly.

There was total silence. The men, women and children stared unbelievingly up at her. She looked down at them, grey shapes, sullen grey shapes, in wretched, torn and patched clothing, fourth- and fifth-hand. "Have I won or lost?" Caroline wondered, trying to read the expressions on the upturned faces. "And even if I win today, will I win tomorrow? How can one control people like these?"

239

"They can't believe their luck," offered Mr. Brady. "They don't trust anyone." Out loud he called to them: "Now you've 'eard. Move back there and make way for the little lady."

Caroline turned to Mr. Sapperstone and he reached up and swung her to the ground.

The crowd began imperceptibly to thin. One or two dropped the implements of wood and glass they had carried and they fell on the foul pavement, so dirty it was hard to realise that underneath was red brick. The crowd drifted away as quickly as it had come together, and apparently by the same common unspoken consent. The middle house at the back of the Court was now open to Caroline's view. As Mr. Sapperstone knocked, the door was opened cautiously by a hunch-backed girl, with beautiful large dark eyes full of fear, and a dead white unhealthy face. "Come in, Miss," said this poor cripple. "There's lots of us 'ere will be glad to welcome you. Not everybody stays out in the Court. Not that they mean so badly, Miss. They just don't know no better, that's all."

"I'm Caroline Hamilton," said Caroline impulsively, putting out her hand. The girl hesitated a moment and then shyly produced her own hand from behind her hunched back. "I'm Isobel," she said. "Isobel Creuse. I do plain and fancy sewing—when I get the work." She smiled and held the door wide. Caroline went in.

Chapter 22

The grey street stretched before Caroline, unwinding like a ball of string, tired string. The early morning mist white as strands of cottonwool, the mist from the River Thames, was shredded into thin wisps as the sun sent shining knives of light to cut athwart the night's lingering scraps of damp.

The roar of the traffic came to Caroline as from a distance, though it was actually all about her. She saw the moving vehicles, the packed streets, heard the cries of the carters as they whipped their horses by, caught the sounds hawkers made calling their wares, was pushed by the bustle and jostle of the crowd and leant her slender frame to push herself and so make her way in the rough streets. She seemed aware and walked purposefully but her mind, as she negotiated the traffic on the way to Leg Iron Court and the overseeing of the work on her properties, was far away. She moved in a world of her own, a world in which the shouts of drivers to omnibus horses, the shrieks of small boys and the calling voices of housewives as they shouted to each other from house to house, leaning out from upper story windows, the clatter of horsemen coming down the street, the barking of itinerant dogs, the noise of flower girls, street musicians, the business of persons throwing household refuse from wooden buckets into the gutter, all merely proved the existence of that shell of silence in which Caroline moved. She felt herself now alone in the world; nobody was intimately concerned with what she thought or felt. And she was miserable.

Caroline had kept her room at Aunt Lucinda's. To find some place of her own meant engaging a duenna. She did not wish to do this and finally, Aunt Luci had accepted a sum for Caroline's keep. And now that Robert Devonshire was openly courting Sophia, her cousin was a changed person—a dear, sweet, friendly girl who could not now do enough for Caroline, the same Caroline she had once longed to destroy. But there was still an air of condescension about her sweetness which made it difficult to accept.

Sophia had reason to be friendly. Uncle Ham, seeing that Robert was now courting Sophia, had wakened up to the knowledge that, although related to him only by marriage, Sophia could nevertheless be said to be his niece. And nieces who married title had a warm regard in Uncle Ham's mind. Sophia had had little or no dowry; but now there was a dowry. This niece was so much more after his own heart than Caroline had ever been. A dowry from his purse put that hospital wing by which he had planned to commemorate his memory in some small jeopardy. But he could not enjoy a flowery inscription when he was dead, whilst a niece who was more than willing to accept him as a new-found father could bring him into Society whilst he was living, an enjoyable notion. The sum Mr. McLeod Hamilton settled on Sophia had smoothed out the frown that troubled Lady de Lisle Devonshire's fine brow as she watched Robert pursue a penniless miss. Sophia understood Lady Devonshire's attitude to life, and she also understood Uncle Hamilton's, for the attitudes of these two people merely mirrored her own. So there was a purring satisfaction to be felt around Sophia and a growing satisfaction in Lady de Lisle Devonshire, matched by Uncle Ham's feeling that all was well when opportunity was pounced upon and made to work in his favour. "Luck is only good when brought to heel," was one of Uncle Hamilton's treasured sayings. He had always brought good luck and made it come to heel.

Caroline and Uncle Hamilton had not seen each other since the inquest. It was not that one could say either of them avoided the other; it was more that they did not try to meet. Uncle Hamilton came to London when Caroline was at her property. By the time she returned to Aunt Lucinda's house in the evenings, he would be dining elsewhere. Lucinda Newcombe felt she should make the effort to bring the man nearer to his real niece, but that niece seemed reluctant, and her own daughter Sophia was violently opposed. Uncle Ham belonged to her now. Aunt Luci sighed and thought: "Time will heal—"

Caroline had now been nearly twelve weeks directing the repairs at Leg Iron Court. She had been challenged by the work, and grateful for it. It kept her from thinking continually of Edmund, for she was determined not to fail in her project. She was proud to feel that now she was accepted by the people in her Court, not as a young miss, but as a landlord who was helping them to have better homes. The people who lived there greeted her with a smile now, and she had more hands to help with the work tan Mr. Sapperstone had ever dreamed possible. Some of the tenants had had to be ejected, but they were willing enough. For these people, clean rooms that they would have to keep clean were only a nuisance. And so the rooms they vacated were the first to be done over. When they had had the plaster put back, roofs mended, fireplaces made to work, floors and ceilings made sound and the whole papered or painted, then lodgers could be moved from their broken rooms and these rooms tackled in their turn.

Caroline had provided new water butts, one to each house, which was an unheard-of luxury. She had provided also a rubbish bin for each house, and saw they had well-fitting lids. The dogs and cats who had roamed the Court nosing through household refuse, now took themselves off to better pickings elsewhere. She had built new privies in an obscure corner of the Court. Lastly, she had managed to get a woman in each house to oversee the cleaning of public stairs and passageways. For this she paid them money, but when they did not do the work, or the work was badly done, then she refused payment. They had come to know that she meant what she said and did exactly what she promised, and so they had respect for her.

From these overseeing cleaning women she had formed a sort of committee for the houses. They met in what had once been a disused stable, but which, the dirt having been cleaned out of it, was destined as soon as possible to become a wash house where each family could have its turn on different days of the month with a schedule of hours. She did not want the people to feel they merely received charity, and that was why she made them oversee the cleaning of the property themselves. She went to those meetings but said little. The problems of daily life remained problems for the families living there, but they now had the chance to solve the problems in their own way and with a minimum of guidance.

She was achieving something. And if she needed to be sure of it she only had to look at Mrs. Erskine's face when she came to see the improvements. She no longer treated

Caroline as a little girl, but as a grown-up who had to be reckoned with. Mrs. Erskine had written an article in the *Englishwoman's Review* about Caroline's work in the Court.

Mrs. Erskine also now approved of Caroline's having turned down Edmund Browne.

"After all," she said, "we, you and I, are in the struggle to make women free in their own right."

"But not wholly free," thought Caroline. "I don't want to live my life alone—without a husband in it. That would be terrible." But she did not tell Mrs. Erskine this. If Mrs. Erskine knew how she felt she would, Caroline was sure, immediately guess her secret: that she still loved Edmund. She could not, in any case, speak of Edmund. The wound was too new and, as yet, too sore. In the newsprints, the gossip had now died down. The Empress of all the Russias had been newly delivered of a child, there was talk of a Married Women's Property Act; agricultural labourers were flocking into London and making disturbances in their search for some sort of work. The semi-socialist, John Stuart Mill, was writing more and more of the need to redistribute wealth, an idea that shocked everyone. The world of London news had long forgotten Caroline Hamilton. But Caroline knew that unfashionable Wiltshire would still be turning over the toothsome story of Caroline Hamilton's night at the inn with a man. In polite Society, or out of it, that story would be there to hurt her if she ever wanted to marry.

Also she could not forget her Wiltshire home. Painful memories of it sped through her mind at times, especially at night. She missed her big bedroom, with the mismatched but familiar furniture, and Sarah coming in in the mornings with her cheerful, kindly smile. Aunt Millie's constant care for Caroline's well-being, the sense of belonging and being looked after. Yes, even the "looking after" with which Uncle Ham's presence had daily furnished her. But even if she wanted to go back home, even if her aunt and uncle had wanted her to, she could no longer return. There was no more going back.

One day when Caroline was overlooking the installation

of wash-tubs in the remodelled stable, a man's shape darkened the doorway. She instinctively put up her hand to smooth back the scraps of curly hair which fell so easily from the hairpins. She wondered who the visitor was even whilst she recalled that there was a streak of dirt on her nose, and her once-new sacking apron had paint flecks upon it. She must look a fright. And so she spoke harshly.

"Who are you, please?" He did not immediately answer so she said more sharply: "What do you want?" The silhouette of the man moved inwards to the stable even as he removed his top hat in greeting. The light from the stable window now struck the figure and she recognised it for Uncle Hamilton. He had come, as of course such a man was bound to, all unannounced. He had come suspiciously, like a sniffing hound, scenting the air, expecting trouble, but not finding it.

Uncle Hamilton grumbled some word acknowledging her presence then stared at the whitewashed stable, at the wash-tubs, at the lines already arranged for drying clothes. He looked at her sacking apron, turned around to view the houses behind him with a critical, almost offended air. He mumbled some indistinguishable words and turned narrowed eyes on the clean, new concrete beneath his feet and then on the painted door of the stable, the painted, sound-looking window, all its panes intact. He seemed almost irritated to find a Court which had once been festering with rotting buildings and noxious smells, now clean and cheerful.

Then he said aloud suddenly, with a brighter air: "Can't be making a penny!" He clasped his hands behind him with an air of grim relief. Everything cost money, and money wasn't something that you spent unless you could see that its expenditure would make more money. He had been getting the maximum rent out of these tenants: there was not another penny to be had. Of course some of the rooms, cellars and attics, had been un-rentable, even to the scruffy people who came looking. Cellars full of water and attics with practically no roofing at all. But no one could do anything with those. It would cost too much.

"Caroline!" He addressed his niece in the old peremptory manner. "I suppose, by what extravagances I see here, that you have spent a great deal of the sum I so carefully saved for you. Well, don't expect charity from me when it's all gone."

"Hardly," said Caroline cheerfully. "I'm paying interest on a mortgage, I haven't raised rents and still I'm covering my costs. Mr. Joachim says I will soon make a profit with the extra empty rooms that used not to be let. I have repaired them."

"Profit! Profit!" he said. "Interest? Mortgage rates? Where did you learn all that?"

"From Mr. Joachim, my solicitor," she said.

He sniffed. "Hm," he said. "I'd like to see something that would prove it possible to make profits on what you've laid out here. D'ye keep books?"

"Yes," said Caroline. "Or Mr. Joachim does. I hand him the bills when I've gone through them and he pays them."

"Well, I'd like to see those books," said Mr. Hamilton a little belligerently.

"Any time," said Caroline lightly. "Mr. Joachim keeps them at his office. I employ his bookkeeper on an hourly charge. Everything is in order, I'm sure."

"Hm," said Uncle Hamilton again. "Well, I may just want to see how those books look. Meanwhile, my girl, I'd like to see everything here. I'm sure you've done a lot of work that was quite unnecessary."

From cellars to attics, Uncle Hamilton roamed, testing new floor boards by jumping on them, banging window panes neatly in place with light taps from the signet ring on his little finger, giving a shake to the banisters, sniffing at the painted doors and the fresh wallpaper, looking at the tenants with his head cocked to one side, his cane ready to thrust them off, suspicion in every line of him. Uncle Hamilton did not trust the poor, and he was too much a man of his own mind to change his opinions overnight. But they did look more hopeful; the children and women seemed cleaner to his searching eye, brighter too, if no less noisy. There were no men around! What, could they have gone off to work? Not a mudlark in sight. Where were the people who used to lurk in the doorways dead drunk on red biddy in the early mornings?

"Changed a lot of your tenants," he grumbled to Caroline.

"Yes," said Caroline. "I changed those who couldn't or wouldn't change themselves. A lot of others only needed the chance to make things better for themselves. I got all the churches nearby and somlcsome charitable institutions to give the better sort work."

"You'll have your fine new banisters chopped up for firewood one of these days," he told her.

"We don't think so," said Caroline. "We're almost at the end of January, most of the cold season is behind us and anyway no one needs to chop banisters. We sell them wood at cost prices. We buy a great deal of wood at one time and that brings the price down very much for each family."

"Who is this 'we'?" asked Uncle Hamilton. "You always say 'we'."

"Oh, Mr. Joachim; his accountant I told you of; Mr. Sapperstone, who is doing over a Court for someone else now; Mr. Brady, who isn't here today because I don't need protection, but will always come if I do have trouble with anyone—most likely a wanderer from some other buildings. Oh, there is Mr. Brady now."

Uncle Hamilton slewed his head around sharply to take a look at Mr. Brady, who had just entered the Court. That worthy raised his hat to Caroline and bowed a little in the direction of Mr. Hamilton. Mr. Hamilton stared at the stout figure of Brady and Louis Brady, who had no idea who the gentleman was, stared back, giving Uncle Ham a look quite equal to the one he got himself. Uncle Ham shrugged and gave up his side of the staring match. Now he looked at Caroline in a different way. There was a touch of appreciation in his face now, not unmixed with an annoyed kind of astonishment. Then he said suddenly:

"Well, you must get your business head from me. And a business head in a female, that's a rare thing! Your

Aunt Millie can't keep even her household accounts straight!"

Uncle Ham stopped speaking as abruptly as he had begun. He looked around the Court once more, looked at Caroline again and said: "You must come down and see your Aunt Millie some time. She misses you."

Caroline had the impression that her uncle liked her no better than he ever had, but now, at least, he respected her as he had never been known to respect any woman. She made sense: business sense.

"Well," he said finally, putting back his top hat, straightening his shoulders in a gesture reminiscent of Caroline herself, and getting ready to leave. "Looks as if you're doing good work here. I didn't believe these buildings could stand up much longer, but now I imagine they'll serve you and your tenants for years."

"Thank you, Uncle Ham," she said mildly.

"Don't thank me," he snorted. "Thank your obstinate, strong-minded self! You were probably right: too much of the man in you to waste yourself playing at 'wife' in a marriage. You've got a lot of commonsense. Well, good day to you! Remember we'd like to see you in Wiltshire one of these days. I'll let the gossips know that they've got something more to say about you now than some stupid story of you in an inn! Write us a little ahead and we'll meet you at the train." And he was gone.

Too much of a man about her? She stared after him as he left Leg Iron Court, hailing a lumbering four-wheeler and hoisting himself into it. Uncle Ham had meant to pay her a compliment when he indicated she would be wasted in marriage. But he had hit upon a painful subject. She loved her work, but she did not want to go unmarried. She wanted to get married, and to a particular person—to Edmund Browne.

She had not wanted to think of Edmund and, for a time, when she first took on the work in the Court, she had managed for hours at a time to put him out of her head. But as the work progressed she began to think of him again, indeed she began to be unable to stop thinking of him. His image came back to her and now persisted in

248

her mind with ever greater clarity. Every moment she had been with him, every gesture he had made, every tone of voice he had used, unrolled before her as though she were in a theatre, concealed in a box somewhere, and down there, before her on the stage, herself a shadowy player too, he talked and moved, frowned and laughed. She tried to throw herself into the remaining work at the Court with new ardour so that she could banish him from her memory and imagination, but in the thick of the work, when she was fresh or when she was tired, he came back to her. Her worst moments were before she went to sleep at night in the little tartan room she still occupied at Aunt Luci's home. She would coax herself to sleep with a hot drink before she slept, a book good enough to take her attention, but it was all to little purpose. She spent many a wakeful night. And the work at the Court would soon be over. She began to wonder what she would do with her time then.

She could buy more property, Mr. Joachim suggested, and at advantageous prices, and do again what she was just completing. She was not against doing this, for she liked the work and it was work that needed doing all over the slums of London, but it was not work at which she wished to pass her whole life. She needed dreadfully to be wanted by someone special to her, to be married to him, to have a home they shared. But the only one she could imagine marrying was Edmund. Life, in fact, without Edmund, was hollow. She bitterly regretted turning him down. What an idiot she had been twice to repulse him! And every time she thought that he had twice proposed marriage and twice she had said "no", Mrs. Erskine's congratulations on her refusal of Edmund rang more and more hollow to her. What was pride without love? What was anything without the love of the man she wished now to marry! Oh, it was terrible. They were in the same town, within a few streets of each other, breathing the same air, under the same sky. But she might as well have been in Timbuctoo, or some other far-off place.

"I'd write to him if I were you," said Sophia.

"I—I can't," she said. "Supposing he already has another girl?"

"Well, he certainly won't stay unmarried for ever," said Aunt Luci, meaning to be helpful, certainly not intending to hurt. "He will certainly find another girl one day. I hope so for his sake. After all!"

Another girl? The thought horrified her. But of course he would not stay unmarried for ever. There could not already be someone else; his was not a quickly changeable nature. But in the future there would be someone else. One day there would be another girl. She often now put up her hand to her breast as though that simple gesture would stifle her heart's bitter pain.

She could not go on like this. It was telling on her health, on her nervous system. The sleepless nights, the burden of her heart. But was there anything she could do? Her sense of frustration and loss was overwhelming, her sense of needing love and having it to give, was with her every day. But she could do nothing about it, she thought. When it came to making any move, convention held her. It was up to the man in these matters to come forward. She was, after all, a girl.

Stroud could not understand her. "Love and pride," she said, "they don't mix." And she added: "Here I am, being courted by your aunt's butler. I feel for him and I am more than willing to let him know it, if he doesn't get courage enough to ask me to marry him! Yes, I can keep my pride and my silence and be lonely the rest of my life. My father would turn in his grave, I'm sure. But no, I want to be happy. If Jerome doesn't ask me—I shall ask him!"

Chapter 23

Edmund had not been home very long, but long enough to take off his coat and put on his dressing gown over his fine cambric shirt sleeves, preparatory to working at his desk before dinner would be served him, when his valet came to him in a state of upset.

"There is a—a person to see you, sir," he said. "The front hall porter has called me and is, of course, very upset."

"Why should the porter be upset?"

"Because, because, sir, the person—is a woman."

"Who is this woman?"

"She will not give her name, sir, and it is impossible to guess even her age, or station. She is wearing an old grey cloak—a dolman—and is heavily veiled. You know that women are not permitted in the Arlington."

"Yes," said Edmund. "Whoever she is—has that not been explained to her? That women cannot come here?"

"Yes, sir. But she insists. She is a very insistent woman."

Edmund's heart began to hammer. An insistent woman! It could be. . . . It had to be. . . . But it couldn't be. . . ! He thought. "You had better tell the porter to make an exception and show her up," he said.

Edmund waited in great perturbation whilst the servant went away. It could not possibly be Caroline. But, on the other hand, who else could it be? Everyone knew that women were not permitted in the Arlington. Only such a woman as Caroline would ignore that ruling and present herself. What could she want to see him about? He did not want to see her. And as he said this to himself his heart was hammering unpleasantly. Not see her? Was that really true? Well, it was true that this time he would say little to her, he would listen and let her speak. Yet he felt an almost unbearable anxiety to have her in his gaze.

Suddenly the discreet, silent valet had opened the double doors of his sitting room and there she was—a small figure very erect, her head and face covered in heavy black veiling, the cloak concealing her shape. He pushed forward a chair. Without speaking, she sat down in it, and only then released the frogging on her cape, and let the garment fall on the floor about her. Slowly she unwound the veil, and then they were looking at each other, she sitting, he standing in the silk dressing gown she remembered so well from the inn. The sight of it, so familiar to her, smote her with regret. They had been friends that evening. Her thinness hurt him. She looked as if she had suffered; but then, so had he.

"You shouldn't come here, Caroline," he said.

She smiled faintly. "There are a great many things I shouldn't do, and that is one among them," she answered. "But I do what I must."

He shook his brown head with its crisp, thick hair at this. Doing what she must had brought a great many problems to a great many people. "Now that you are here, what can I do for you?" he asked coldly.

"You can—you can—" she began, and then she stopped. She had come to him on an impulse; being with him, she realised how hopeless it was to speak. She could hardly tell him, "You can love me as you used to do. I need your love." And she had forgotten how handsome he was.

"What did you want of me?" he asked again.

"After all, nothing!" she told him. He frowned in bewilderment. "As you will agree, I force you again to compromise me by coming here. I was foolish to come. I'll go."

She reached for her black veiling, but as she did he noticed her hand tremble. Surely those were tears in her eyes? He could not bear to see her cry, not Caroline, with all her spirit. But what touched him most were the hands with which she wound the veil around her head. The little hands looked work-worn, the nails cracked. Why the sight of those work-worn nails should have touched him he did not know, but suddenly he knew he had something to say before she left.

"Well, before you go, I'd like to tell you something. I was wrong. You *have* repaired the houses you inherited and made the tenants happier for it. You have proved that a landlord can be kindly, do well by tenants and *still* make a profit—"

"How do you know about that?" She stopped winding the black veil and raised her face, all a-strain, to look at him.

"A letter. I have a letter," he said.

"But who on earth would write you about me? Sophia! That terrible, interfering Sophia!"

"Well, in fact, no," he said. "Not Sophia. Someone quite other. I'd say a friend, though on the surface a bit of a rough-seeming friend." Edmund picked up a letter from his desk and handed it to Caroline. It was Uncle Ham's expensive letter paper, used exclusively by him.

"Uncle *Ham*?" she exclaimed. "Why would *he* write?" He took the letter from her and read aloud:

" '. . . so my niece has done what I would of course eventually have done myself, and I suggest that a visit from one of your young men could give *The Times* a paragraph or two to show that slum properties *can* be well-managed for the poor and yet give the owner a well-earned profit. . . .' "

"As a matter of fact," Edmund told her, watching her face, "when the editor gave me this from your Uncle Ham with a request that I suggest one of our reporters to do the assignment, I had it in mind to go myself. I thought I would write an editorial on it."

"An editorial? Making fun, I suppose, of a woman's efforts?"

"Oh, Caroline, no. That is unworthy of you. It's a long time ago that I wrote the editorial you always have in mind. I don't have to write anything these days, unless I want to. But if I had to do it again, I'd still write that unmarried women should be sent to the Colonies. No—don't start so! Save your words! The editor, it turns out, knew what he was about. You see, a great deal of indignation was raised by that editorial, and there is a growing feeling that women *should* be better fitted for single life. Sometimes satire, even savage satire, will get the attention solemnity will not."

Caroline was silent a moment. Then she suddenly said: "I'm sorry I called you unprincipled."

"And I'm sorry I was cynical about your plans to improve your properties. What will you do now, Caroline? I understand your work is finished."

"I don't know," she answered forlornly. "Mr. Joachim thinks I should buy other properties and manage *them*. And of course what I already have will need keeping up. . . ."

"Then you have your life planned."

"Oh!" she said suddenly, "planned! What plans? I hate you! There you stand tormenting me, letting me suffer, crowing over my misery, I suppose!"

"Why, Caroline!"

But he could not stop her. When had he ever been able to stop her? "I wish you'd go away," she said, angrily, "and never come back again! Go to those foreign cities—Paris, Berlin—wherever you sprang from. Then I could forget you."

Tears glistened like diamonds in her eyes, shimmered and fell, making little rivulets on her cheeks and falling from her quivering chin which she could no longer hold firmly. She had begun again to wind back the black veiling, but a sob shook her as she groped for her reticule on the red and green surface of his Turkey carpet. He dropped down on his knees beside her chair, and he tried to raise her chin so that he could look into her obstinately down-drooping, tearful face. He said:

"I love you. You love me! You wouldn't be crying otherwise. You want to marry me!"

"I never said—"

"Oh, but you did! You just asked me to go away so that you could forget me. And even you would have to admit," he added with a grin, "that you couldn't forget me unless I *did* leave! You came here to marry me. Miss Hamilton, I accept your offer of marriage. No, not a word! Don't speak, you'll get us off the point! I love you, Caroline—let's not have any more confusion between us. We should get married at once. Then you can quarrel all you like with me. I'll be right on the premises."

A quick retort came to her, prompted by the last splutter of her too great pride, but before she could utter a word, before anything else could go wrong, he kissed her, and then to make everything perfectly plain and perfectly certain, he kissed her again.

She laughed through her tears. Her hair had come down in wisps as she unwound her veil, and now because she wanted him to know everything about her, everything that was wrong, or that presented her as she felt she was not, she pulled away from his arms and tore out the three great steel hairpins that secured most of her hair to her small head. Those horrible hair combings that Aunt Millie had taught her to save for "rats" to increase the bulk of her upswept coiffure now fell out and scattered on the Turkey carpet. She tossed back her curly, short black hair and faced him. He looked astonished, for a moment, at the "rats" on the floor, and the girl with the definantly short hair before him, and then he laughed.

"Now you look fifteen again," he told her, grinning, "undisciplined, like a tomboy but awfully direct. Little Caroline Hamilton who could never learn the art of dissembling, but always had to be herself." His heart knew a leap of joy and then they fell into each other's arms, laughing with youth and happiness.

She would never be easy to be married to. She was too independent for that. But marriage to her would never be dull. He could see a life before them full of contention, but full also of interest, and of moments of bliss. They clung together in a wild disorder of kissing—heads, eyelids, hands. Then he sat back on his heels and looked at her as she tried to gather her curly hair, her "rats", her black veiling, her scarf. Her face was so beautiful now, but so changed in these last weeks. Her expression now held dignity and purpose. Such a few months had passed, but the selfish and petulant and wayward girl had turned into a woman, lovely, poised, dignified, and immensely worth loving. Caroline had grown up. The growing up had cost her, and others, much, but she had done it beautifully. She was a real person—a person he could not only love, but respect.